Matty flushed, received in her bedroom.

Taking a quick sip of tea to clear her throat, she met the gentleman's eyes and smiled affably. "I suppose that no one has ever told you that it is highly improper for a gentleman to visit a lady in her bedchamber," she said sweetly.

"And I suppose that no one has ever told you that it is unladylike to talk with your mouth full," the gentleman replied, just as affably.

"Well, of all the rude—" she gasped, as he grinned and moved closer to the bed to dispose himself in the chair at her side.

"Ah, but my dear Miss Cresley," he continued smoothly, "we are already agreed that I am not a gentleman."

"I am not your dear Miss Cresley," Matty snapped, "and if you're expecting me to now say that I am not a lady you can wait all day, for—" she blushed hotly as she realized she had just said it, and was guiltily aware of the unholy amusement crinkling the corners of Pettigrew's eyes.

Taking another tack she reclined against the pillows at her back, saying "I pray, sir, that you will forgive me. I am not myself this morning. The fall... the sprain... indeed, I hardly know what I'm saying." She closed her eyes in what she congratulated herself was a faithful reproduction of her Fainting Aunt Francis....

THE MERRY CHASE

Judith Nelson

WARNER BOOKS

A Warner Communications Company

All the characters in this book are fictitious,
and any resemblance to actual persons
living or dead is purely coincidental.

WARNER BOOKS EDITION

Warner Books, Inc.
75 Rockefeller Plaza
New York, N.Y. 10019

W A Warner Communications Company

Printed in the United States of America

First Printing: August, 1985

10 9 8 7 6 5 4 3 2 1

Chapter I

To those unfamiliar with the inhabitants of Morningdale Manor, the scene in the morning room there was one of domestic tranquility.

The fire burning cheerily on the grate crackled and snapped from time to time as if in happy defiance of the grayness seen through the large French windows, which in good weather opened onto Morningdale's not-inconsiderable gardens. Those windows, so good at welcoming the sun on cloudless days, were now shut tight against the cold and showed unrelieved gray as the wind drove showers of rain onto the glass, providing constantly changing patterns for those who cared to look.

The three ladies seated in the airy room were not looking, however; indeed, they appeared deeply engrossed in their work. It is true one now laid aside her embroidery to receive the just-delivered letter handed her by the elderly butler; but the eyes of the other two remained determinedly on their flying needles. If the elder's color was raised, who would see? And if the younger lady's lips, more often drawn in a laughing smile, were now firmly compressed as if

1

to keep her from saying something she would rather not, who would notice?

Baxley noticed, of course, and guessing that Miss Dru and her Aunt Hester were again having one of their periodic turnups over Miss Dru's refusal to be driven into matrimonial bliss, he made his stately retreat. His bow concealed from everyone but himself how intent he was on being absent when it grew as stormy within as it was without.

Drucilla Wrothton at twenty-five was a handsome young woman whose gray eyes today matched the dove-colored gown she wore in mourning for her brother. She was—as her aunt was quick to point out—no longer in the first blush of youth, but neither—as she was quick to reply to her aunt—had she ever felt the ignominy of being left partnerless at a ball. Men of all ages were often content to pass up ingenues to dance with the laughing lady whose figure was trim, whose smile delightful, and whose conversation stimulating. But Dru's quick mind, which led to that stimulating conversation, could also lead to unwise speech when she was angry.

She was angry now, but just before Baxley's soft closing of the morning-room door prompted her into hot and hasty speech, her attention was drawn away from her aunt when a soft moan escaped her mother.

The Lady Jane Wrothton sat with a look of dismay writ large upon her face as the recently delivered letter fell from her suddenly nerveless grasp.

"Why, Mama," Dru said, alarmed. "Whatever is it?"

"The Hovingtons," Jane whispered as Dru took the letter from her hands. Her face showed that that was indeed something dreadful.

"The Hovingtons?" Hester demanded. "What do those worse-than-Cits, far-removed relations—although I admit, not far enough removed—but what do they have to do with our present conversation concerning Drucilla's marriage—or the deplorable lack of it?"

Dru shook her head impatiently, her soft brown curls bouncing gently against her cheek. "Nothing, of course," she snapped, rapidly perusing the letter which had had such a powerful effect on her mother. As she did, she wished for the thousandth time that her aunt did not exhibit quite as much of the famous English bulldog tenacity when she got a thought in her head.

"Or everything," Jane put in, looking sorrowfully at her daughter's now-surprised face.

"Everything?" Dru echoed, settling gracefully on the arm of her mother's chair and giving that good lady a gentle pat. "I don't understand. How could my not being married have anything to do with the Hovingtons coming here?"

"Coming here?" Hester's voice rose dramatically as she heard the end of her niece's speech. "The Hovingtons are coming here? No. They cannot." Her face filled with horror at the thought.

"You must send them word, Jane," she continued energetically. "Tell them we cannot receive them now. To drop in when we are in mourning—rag-mannered. Rag-mannered by far."

Hester considered this, the latest in a long series of lapses by the unwelcome branch of the family, and her brow darkened. "It grieves me deeply to think that somewhere in our ancestors there was one with the common blood which flows through George Hovington's veins," she pronounced, working herself into a performance her niece critically thought might compare well with those given by the great Keane. "I have often thought that the real George must have been stolen by gypsies at an early age and this changeling substituted—" She brightened considerably at that thought and looked hopefully at her sister-in-law for confirmation, but Lady Jane only smiled slightly and shook her head.

Hester shrugged. "You must write them, Jane," she ordered regally. "Write and tell them it is inconvenient for us to entertain them now. Say you will let them know a more convenient date."

But her sister-in-law made no move to carry out that order; instead she sighed unhappily. "I can't," she almost wailed, "they've already set out. This letter is to tell us we may expect them momentarily."

That news had a powerful effect on the Lady Hester, daughter of a marquis and widow of an earl. Sputtering angrily about encroaching mushrooms, bad breeding, and worse blood, her eyes fell on her niece who still sat with an arm around her mother, thinking deeply.

"It's all your fault, miss," she snapped, making Dru start.

"My fault?" her niece repeated doubtfully.

"Yes, yours. For if you were married they wouldn't be coming."

Dru started to protest, but Hester, rapidly working herself to an even higher pitch, rose dramatically. "They expect you to die a spinster, and they're already counting Morningdale as their inheritance." She shuddered. "It doesn't bear thinking."

Noting that Jane had nodded vigorously in agreement with her last statement, she felt herself gaining support and pointed a stabbing finger at Dru. "Let me tell you, miss, as much as I love this manor," (and here, for effect, she waved a sweeping arm to encompass the room), "I would set it to the torch before I would see George Hovington or his young bullock of a son become master of these sacred halls."

A moment's silence followed her impassioned performance as Jane stared open-mouthed and the twinkle grew in Dru's eyes. Then that young lady sprang from her seat clapping, shouting, "Bravo, Aunt Hester, bravo indeed. Mrs. Siddons herself could not have done better. 'These sacred halls'—a very nice touch."

Hester froze immediately, favoring her errant niece with one of the famous societal frowns which had been known to turn eager young matrons pale and send usually stalwart butlers cringing to the lower regions of the house. She turned on her heel and stalked back to her chair, where she seated herself and proceeded to arrange her skirts stiffly, wounded dignity apparent in every movement.

"Really, Dru," her mother reproved gently. "While I trust we will not have to employ such drastic measures as fire to ensure young Hovingtons will not grow up here, I do understand your aunt's strong feelings, and I share them. When your father was dying, I promised him I would see that the manor remains with direct Wrothton descendants for years to come."

She shook her head as if to brush away the lingering memories and gazed at her daughter sadly. "While your brother was alive, I was content to let you seek a man you might esteem, but after that—that unfortunate accident—you must marry, Dru. For the manor."

Eager to brighten her mother's thoughts and to avoid a prolonged discussion of her marriage—a topic she felt bitterly was much too important to too many people—Dru quickly changed the subject, saying as mildly as she could that that might be a way to keep the Hovingtons from the manor in the future, but keeping them out at present was their more-immediate problem.

Both her mother and aunt appeared to agree, and silence grew as three very intent ladies cudgeled their brains for ways to rid themselves of their as-yet-unarrived but very unwelcome guests.

"I see nothing for it," Lady Jane said regretfully at last. "They are family, and even though we know their sole purpose in coming is to look over the manor, I cannot think of anything we can do when we have all this room but to greet them with a show of graciousness and hope they do not linger long."

Hester snorted. "Not linger long, dear Jane? You know as well as I that George Hovington would rather eat anyone else's mutton than his own, and where there's a room to stay, he'll—" She broke off abruptly as Dru rose with great resolution and crossed to the bell pull, giving it an enormous tug.

"This is no time for tea, Drucilla," she said testily, but that young lady merely stood tapping a foot impatiently as Baxley's stately tread was heard approaching the door.

"Baxley," Dru said as soon as he appeared, "we shall need sheets draped throughout the main hall and over the furniture in the upstairs guest bedrooms."

"Sheets?" three voices echoed.

"And paint buckets, Baxley," she continued determinedly. "Paint buckets, and a ladder here and there would be nice."

"Paint buckets, Miss Dru?" the old butler questioned, his face showing that either he felt he had heard wrong or she was—as he would delicately put it—not quite right upstairs.

"Paint buckets, Baxley," Dru reiterated, then smiled. "The Hovingtons are coming to visit, Baxley."

"The Hovingtons?" he repeated, faint but pursuing.

"Such a shame," Dru murmured, lowering her eyes. "They've come all the way to see us and here we are painting the guest rooms. If only we'd known."

"Painting the—" Comprehension dawned on his face, and the correctness of his bow indicated he understood perfectly. "Of course, Miss Dru," he agreed as he bowed himself out. "A shame."

Dru watched in admiration as the door quietly latched behind him. "So dependable, Baxley," she murmured. Then, turning to her mother and aunt, she saw a look of mirth on the first's face and deep gloom on the second's.

"I suppose you think it's dishonest," Dru said defensively as she faced her aunt.

"Dishonest?" Hester echoed. "Distinctly. It makes me quite proud of you. For a moment I had hope. But you forget the Buxtells."

"The Buxtells?" Dru repeated, wrinkling her forehead.

Hester nodded gloomily. "At Collier's Corners. Mrs. Buxtell is Lavinia Hovington's sister. If they can't stay here they'll go there, and they'll still be close enough to poke their noses into our business.

"Oh, dear," Jane sighed, but Dru would not give up. "You may be right, Aunt Hester," she said as she moved to the door to see if Baxley and the other servants needed any supervision in the sheet and bucket arrangements, "and I'm sure if you are, we shall still see too much of them. But be that as it may, we shall not constantly see them here. And I for one am very grateful." With that she walked out of the room, slamming the door behind her and leaving her older relations to eye each other doubtfully.

Later that day as Dru straightened her dress for luncheon, she reflected that, much as she disliked the Hovingtons, their letter had proved provident in allowing her to escape the discussion of marriage Aunt Hester was so intent on pursuing. Uttering a prayer that the topic would be forgotten in the face of impending disaster, Dru went down to dinner.

Chapter II

She soon found her prayer was not to be answered. Between bites of cold sirloin and roast chicken, Hester paused to wave her fork at Dru and say, as if several hours had not passed, "Now, miss, about your marriage—"

Caught unaware, Dru choked on a crumb of muffin and had to be pounded on the back by an anxious Baxley.

"Aunt Hester—," she began angrily, but her mother's soft voice interrupted.

"Your aunt is right," Jane said sadly, "and I have been remiss in my duty for not arranging for you to marry sooner. The Hovington's letter has reminded me of the promise I made your father."

She eyed her stubborn daughter's face doubtfully, and her eyes were pleading as she continued. "Oh, Dru," she said, "you know that while your brother James was alive we saw no reason to push you into a marriage you could not like. Indeed, I do not wish to do so now.

"But couldn't you like one of the gentlemen of your acquaintance?" she coaxed after a short pause. "Your great-grandfather wisely handled his estate so it is not entailed to a male relative, but you know that if you die without an heir, Morningdale Manor will pass to the Hovingtons."

Hester shivered eloquently at the thought, and Jane's gentle face crumpled. "I can't bear to think of that loud, coarse man as master of these halls. You must make a match, Dru. Surely you see that?"

7

The stormy look in her daughter's eyes convinced Mrs. Wrothton that Dru did not see at all, but after a moment the anger seen there melted in concern for her mother's obvious distress.

"Oh, Mama," Dru said, her dinner forgotten, "you know I don't want the Hovingtons at Morningdale. But to marry just to prevent that—to be put upon the block—"

Hester sniffed audibly. "On the block. She heard that from her Cousin Mathilde, Jane, you can be sure of that. People marry for worse reasons than to preserve their family homes, my dear—"

"And surely for better ones, too, Aunt," Dru retorted warmly, but Hester was not finished.

"And marriage would be good for you," she continued complacently. "Your own husband, your own home, your own children. We wish only to see you happy, Drucilla. Surely you see that."

"No, Aunt," Dru replied, two red spots showing bright on her cheeks, "I do not see that. I see only that you want an heir, and my happiness has little to do with it."

Before Hester could respond, Jane intervened, assuring her daughter that they did indeed care about her happiness and asking if there wasn't at least one of her suitors she could learn to love.

Dru's answer was emphatic, drawing her aunt's attack immediately.

"Nonsense," Hester declared loudly, for she tended to raise her voice when upset. "You must simply make up your mind to love him. Any him. You could if you would."

Dru looked mulish, and Hester continued in exasperation.

"I have never understood why you do so little to encourage your beaus," she said roundly. "You've had so many of them, all eager to lead you to the altar. And all you did was laugh."

Her temper growing as she reviewed her niece's folly, she began to tick former suitors off on her fingers. "Why, there was Reginald Marsten. He dangled after you forever, and you wouldn't accord him a single glance. And Philip Richley said he'd die for love of you, and you just went your way—"

"He didn't die—," Dru murmured, but Hester ignored her.

"You would be a countess now if you'd married him, but did you care for that? Oh, no. And now that you're five-and-twenty, on the shelf, and when you should be grateful for any offer, you speak of marrying for love or not at all. It puts me completely out of patience, Drucilla. I do not understand you at all.''

But Dru would not let that pass quietly. ''You mention Reginald Marsten and Philip Richley as suitable suitors and say *you* do not understand *me*?'' she asked angrily. ''Would you really have had me marry one of them, Aunt Hester?

''Reggie Marsten dangled after very passable-looking girl who ever emerged from a schoolroom; and though he's married now, I understand he continues to do so.''

''Well, Philip Richley—''

''Philip Richley,'' Dru pronounced awfully, ''would have liked to have my hand almost as much as he would have liked to have my fortune. Having gambled away his father's estates, he was quite willing to start on mine.''

''Well, perhaps Reginald and Philip were not quite the thing,'' Hester conceded reluctantly. ''But beggars can't be choosers.''

Dru stiffened, and Jane closed her eyes resignedly, but Hester, unaware of how that last remark was fanning her niece's anger, continued her reverie. Unconsciously pushing one of her unlikely blonde curls back under her cap, she said, ''What about old Peckingham? Lord knows he's wanted you these past five years, and you can't say he's either a lady's man or a gambler.''

''Nor,'' Dru said dangerously, ''can you say he's a day under sixty. He has a granddaughter coming out this season; there is always snuff on his waistcoat, and his gout is so bad he can barely move. Hardly the man to beget the Wrothton heir you're so set on seeing.''

Her mother gasped at such unladylike talk; but Hester, too wrought to note in time what she said, countered quickly with, ''It's not gout that begets or don't beget a child, miss—'' Then she caught sight of her sister-in-law's shocked face, and the color rose in her own. ''That is—I mean—well—

''Peckingham would be an indulgent older husband who would let you go your own way,'' she continued belligerently as Dru tried to

9

hide her amusement. "I'm sure you're bound to do that anyway, so you might as well have a husband who won't fight it.

"Remember you're not eighteen any longer, Drucilla. You must make do."

"Make do," Dru spat. "You say it as if my life were a bonnet which could be refurbished and worn again. Bah!"

"Drucilla—," Jane began.

"I won't forget I'm no longer eighteen, Aunt Hester," Drucilla said frigidly. "Even if I wanted to I could not. But I will not have Peckingham."

"However," she paused, and a speculative gleam grew in her eye, "if you think he's such a good catch, dear Aunt, perhaps you would like—" She let the suggestion hang delicately in the air and was delighted when her aunt's gasp assured her she had received the hint.

Again Jane hurried to the rescue.

"Now Dru," she said comfortingly, "of course you don't have to marry Peckingham. And I wouldn't have been happy if you'd had either Reggie or Philip, although if I had thought you loved one of them I would have quieted my anxieties for your sake. But there are other men in the world. We must look about for one. That is all."

Dru smiled, but Hester gave her usual harumph. "Look about for a man, Jane?" she repeated scornfully. "Do you think they grow under cabbage leaves? Where are we going to find eligible gentlemen who—" She stopped abruptly as a rapt look stole into her eye.

"Of course," Hester murmurred. "Of course. Why didn't I think of it before?"

Lady Jane eyed her sister-in-law in puzzlement and Dru with a great deal of uneasiness. When the silence lengthened, Jane felt it best to prod Hester and asked her gently what it was that she hadn't thought of before.

"A ball!" Hester replied triumphantly, coming out of her reverie with surprising energy. "We must have a ball."

Ignoring Dru's loud groan, Hester's enthusiasm grew. "We have been sad too long, Jane, first with Henry's death and then James'. We must have a ball.

"We will have a ball. We will make lists of food and guests and things to do. The ballroom must be refurbished, and I think we should have new draperies in here," she said, eyeing the suddenly offending curtains distastefully. "These are becoming positively shabby."

"This is January," she said, growing quite animated as the project bloomed in her mind. "We'll plan the ball for late March. Before everyone returns to London for the season. Then after the ball we will go to London. Almacks. The theatre. Oh, it will be grand."

Jane demurred. "Our mourning, Hester—," she began, but Hester interrupted, frowned severely, and pointed out that the family's official mourning for James was over the end of the month. She added that one could not wear weeds forever.

Jane looked doubtful, Dru determined. "Aunt Hester, I do not want a ball," she announced. "I do not like balls. Next to afternoon visits I find them the most insipid events ever invented by the English nobility."

"Oh, no, dear," Jane interrupted, shocked. "Indeed they are not. Why, balls can be quite lovely. I met your father at a ball. We danced three times in one night. My mother scolded me for being quite abandoned."

"It's Mathilde who puts these ideas into Drucilla's head, Jane," Hester interrupted crossly. "That girl—although she certainly isn't a girl any longer—has the most outrageous opinions. Balls insipid. Ridiculous. A ball, Drucilla, is a very good way to let suitors know you are available."

"On the block."

"Why do you talk like that?" Hester demanded. "It is so vulgar. Quite unbecoming in a Wrothton lady. Especially a lady making her second coming out."

Dru, who had been sipping her tea, found some in her lap, and her voice rose as she repeated, "Her *what*?" but Hester was unwise enough to repeat the statement.

"No," Dru said, banging her cup down and causing her mother to wince for the saucer. "I will not make such a cake of myself as to have a second coming out. I am five-and-twenty, Aunt Hester—"

"No need to advertise it—," Hester hastily assured her.

11

"And I have no intention," Dru continued with finality, "*no* intention—of dressing up like some featherbrained ingenue, wearing white, and simpering at any man who might deign to smile my way."

Before Hester could tartly retort that had she done that at her first coming out, there might be no reason for a second, Jane's gentle voice was heard, calmly agreeing with Dru that a second coming out would not do at all.

"However," she said, "a ball for its own sake is a fine idea. It will open the season for us; and even though we have been retired much of the last three years, you can be assured that a ball at Morningdale Manor will be well attended."

"Hester is right," she continued, shaking her head. "It is time we got on with living in this house. A ball will bring music and laughter into the manor. I think it is a fine idea."

Dru appeared unconvinced, but before she could argue, further conversation was halted by a loud pounding on the manor's main door. The three ladies stared at each other, startled, and were even more so when Baxley returned and announced that a Mr. Crandon Pettigrew was outside, demanding to see Miss Wrothton.

Chapter III

"Demanding?" Hester's voice and eyebrows both rose. "Crandon Pettigrew? I don't know a Crandon Pettigrew. Do you know this Crandon Pettigrew, Dru?"

Suppressing a sigh, Dru explained that she did not know the

gentleman, but she did know of him, since during a recent visit to a neighbor a comfortable half hour of gossip had been devoted to the newcomer renting Green Corners from the Moores while that family took their eldest daughter to London for the season.

"The season hasn't started," Hester snapped.

"No," Dru agreed, "but they're visiting various relatives until the season begins."

"Sponging off them, more like," Hester snorted. "Just what you'd expect from a man who rents his ancestral home to perfect strangers."

"Joshua Moore is the cheapest man who ever lived," she continued indignantly. "Imagine renting your family home to a stranger. Joshua's father must tremble in his grave, for he was a free-spending gentleman if I ever saw one. Not," she said hastily as a new thought occurred to her, "that I would know personally, for of course Joshua is older than I am, and I was so young when his father died—" Her voice trailed off as she caught Dru's amused eye, and the color in her cheeks was not all due to the rouge so carefully applied by her dresser that morning.

"Now dear," Jane said farily, "perhaps the Moores need the money." Hester's loud "ha" did not prevent Jane's adding, "And perhaps Mr. Pettigrew is not a stranger to them."

But Hester was not convinced. "I don't care what you say, Jane," she replied, a statement her sister-in-law dryly agreed with. "I say it is in bad taste to rent your familial dwelling to anyone. And you and I both know Joshua Moore does not need money. How could he need what he never spends? I do not believe there is a more shabbily behaving man alive. The last Moore party I attended had watered wine, Jane. Watered wine!"

The look of horror on her aunt's face convinced Dru that that was indeed unforgivable, but Hester was not finished.

"And they served champagne ices instead of pure champagne," she remembered, the thought of that night still filling her with loathing. "My sainted Jonathan—God rest his soul—used to say Joshua Moore had the first shilling he was ever given. As a matter of fact—'' Her reminiscences ended abruptly as Dru rose and moved toward the door.

"And where are you going, miss?" she demanded.

Dru looked surprised. "To see Mr. Pettigrew, of course."

"Why?"

Dru was even more surprised. "Because he has called."

Hester harumphed. "I think you should deny yourself to him."

"She can hardly do that to a neighbor, Hester," Jane protested.

"Neighbors do not come *demanding* admittance, Jane," Hester countered. "But if you think she should see him, I suppose she should. Show him in here, Baxley," she decreed, but before the exasperation which leaped into Dru's eyes found its way out her tongue, Baxley coughed.

"Begging your pardon, Lady Martin," he began, fixing his gaze on a point just right of her shoulder, "but Mr. Pettigrew asked to be shown to the library, him not feeling he was dressed well enough to be received in anyone's parlor."

"Not dressed well enough?" Hester's voice and eyebrows rose again. "And pray why would he come making calls—especially calls on a house where the inhabitants are unknown to him and in mourning besides—if he is not dressed well enough to do so?"

Baxley's expression remained wooden. "I cannot be sure, my lady, but he appears to have taken a spill. His riding habit is—ah—rather muddy."

"Oh, poor man," Jane said, her sympathy easily aroused. "Is he injured?"

Baxley coughed again and his eyes appealed to Dru. "Ah, no madam," he answered. "He does not appear to be injured, except perhaps for his temper. That seems somewhat lacerated."

"Well!" Hester exploded. "It is just like Joshua Moore to rent his family home—which I'm sure he shouldn't do, and this is what comes of it—to a man who would appear on our doorstep with a lacerated temper." Pleased that no one had an answer to that statement, she proceeded in her most regal manner to ask Baxley if she might know why this Mr. Pettigrew had chosen them for his ill-tempered display.

14

But here Dru laughingly intervened, drawing her aunt's fire from the grateful butler. "No, dear Aunt, you can't know why. At least, you can't have an answer until I go find out.

"And by all accounts," she said, her eyes crinkling thoughtfully, "it does not sound as if Mr. Pettigrew is here to be angry with us, but with me. Although I can't imagine why he should be when I don't even know him."

By now Baxley's look of entreaty had grown so that Dru felt it would be cruel to keep him waiting any longer, and she slipped through the door he held for her just as Aunt Hester opened her mouth with another protest. With great presence of mind and an alacrity not usually seen in a man his age, Baxley closed the parlor door and followed Dru toward the library.

"I wonder what it is the mysterious Mr. Pettigrew wants," Dru murmured as they walked toward the library. But Baxley could give her no reply, noting that the gentleman had only demanded her and snapped at him when he inquired of the gentleman's business. The look on his face convinced Dru he had more to say, and as she stood with her hand on the door handle she smiled encouragingly at him.

"I'll be working here in the hallway, Miss Dru," he said with dignity, "so that if you should want me I will be close by."

Touched by Baxley's loyalty, Dru thanked him warmly as she chuckled inwardly at the picture presented by his offer. Nearly sixty, Baxley was smaller than Dru, and she wondered how he would begin to oust a gentleman her neighbor had described as tall, dark, and powerful. Assuring him that she would be all right, she added it comforted her to know he would be nearby.

Baxley bowed, and Dru opened the library door and stepped inside. One quick glance convinced her the neighborhood gossips were right. The gentleman was indeed tall. And dark. And right now he looked ferocious as well as powerful, for his riding habit was generously spattered with mud and a deep scowl creased his forehead.

Smiling politely, Dru stepped forward, her hand outstretched. "Mr. Pettigrew?" she questioned. "I am Drucilla Wroth—"

Few gentlemen approached by the lovely Miss Wrothton, clad in a simple gray gown which showed silver as she walked, would have

15

failed to greet her approach with a smile. Mr. Pettigrew appeared to have no trouble doing so. Indeed, he went so far as to interrupt her beginning speech and ignore her hand completely.

"Yes, yes," he said impatiently, "you are Drucilla Wrothton. I would assume you are Drucilla Wrothton because I came to see Drucilla Wrothton. Had I come inquiring for the Prince Regent, I would expect to see the Prince Regent."

"You would be disappointed," Dru murmured, and the gentleman's brows drew together.

"He is not here," she explained demurely, but Mr. Pettigrew was not amused.

"Do not try me too far, Miss Wrothton," he warned, "for you have already caused me considerable discomfort this day." At her surprised look, he pointed to the lane outside the library window and inquired in a voice of a man keeping a tight control on his temper if the horse being walked by a strange groom there was indeed hers.

"Why yes," Dru replied, surprised. "That is my lovely Jade. But what is she doing out on a day like this? And who is that with her?" She turned to face him, her large, gray eyes widening.

Ignoring her last two questions, Pettigrew uttered a short bark of laughter. "Jade, is it?" The look on his face was not one of amusement. "A most fitting name. That damn horse—" He realized what he had said as Dru stiffened, and he reddened slightly. "I beg your pardon, Miss Wrothton, but that infernal beast—that horse—your lovely Jade, as you call her—visited my paddock this morning and obligingly opened the gate for the horses I keep there. Now a friend, my groom, and I are careering across the countryside looking for them."

"Oh, dear," Dru said guiltily.

"Oh, dear," Pettigrew repeated. "We have spent four hours in the rain, and your only comment is 'oh, dear'? Miss Wrothton, you do realize this is not the best of English days?" She nodded, her eyes downcast. He continued. "It is raining. It has been raining all morning. At times it rains quite hard. I had planned to spend this day in my library, not far from a friendly fire. Instead I am in your library, thanks"—and although he did not grind his teeth, Dru had the distinct impression he would like to—"thanks to that da—infernal horse."

He then inquired testily if it was the custom in her part of the country to allow one's livestock to roam at will, disrupting others' lives.

Dru blushed rosily, a sight known to captivate many men. Mr. Pettigrew was not moved.

"I am so very sorry," she returned, raising her eyes to his angry face. "Jade has really been quite good lately. I don't know how she got out of her stall. What with the rains and all I haven't been riding lately, and I suppose she got lonesome—" Her voice trailed off as the gentleman's left eyebrow rose alarmingly. Dru wondered irreverently who would win should Mr. Pettigrew and her Aunt Hester ever indulge in a staredown.

"Lonesome"? His voice was silky, but it made her jump, and her color deepened. Her embarrassment at the gentleman's obvious anger was heightened by the fact that she knew him to be right. "Do you really expect me to believe that it was loneliness which made your accurst mare open my paddock gate and scatter my horses? Do you really—" He stopped as a new thought struck him. "Tell me, Miss Wrothton, how did that unnatural animal learn to open a paddock gate?"

Stung by his unfortunate references to her mare, Dru's color was not now all due to embarrassment. "Jade is not an accurst mare," she said, her voice rising as Pettigrew's had done and her chin jutting out in what her brother used to call her 'run for cover' stance. "Nor is she an unnatural animal. She is a sweet goer, a wonderful hunter, and an unusually intelligent mare."

The arrested gleam in Pettigrew's eyes was quickly hid as he sketched a bow, and Dru's anger increased as amusement colored his voice. "You are no doubt right," he said smoothly, "but never having seen her go so sweetly or hunt wonderfully, my view of your horse's accomplishments is no doubt colored.

"I acknowledge that it takes an intelligent animal to open a gate. I only question if it is an intelligent thing to do."

For a moment that appeared unanswerable, and the gentleman

watched as the lady before him unconsciously clasped and unclasped her hands, anger at his statement warring with her understanding of his view. Anger won.

"Well, you might think it an intelligent thing to do if you ever had to ride sidesaddle," she fired up, knowing she should apologize and most unwilling to do so. "It is such a nuisance always to have to open gates one cannot jump, so I taught Jade to take the gate thong between her beeth . . ."

"YOU taught her?" he thundered, all amusement now gone from his face. "You TAUGHT her? Well, Miss Wrothton," and here he ran his fingers through his already disordered hair, "your neighbors must love you."

Dru's eyes flashed, and she controlled her voice with an effort. "We always close the gates again," she said. "But Jade can't do that without me."

"Too bad, Miss Wrothton," he replied. "That is too bad. If she could, I might now be in front of my fireplace instead of in front of yours. I admit that your ingenuity and that of your horse intrigue me, and were this a social call I would inquire further into your horse-training methods. But I have horses to find, and I do not feel social."

"That's apparent," Dru said angrily, then wished she hadn't as the gentleman's cyes narrowed.

"In the future, Miss Wrothton, I would ask that you keep your horse at home," he said stiffly. "I would also ask that if any stray horses appear here, you will send me word. Thank you for your time. I will show myself out."

With that he sketched a short bow, strode across the library floor, and was gone before Dru could think of a suitable retort.

"Insufferable!" she sputtered at the now-closed door. "Absolutely insufferable!"

She stalked to the fireplace and poked angrily at the log burning there. When the door opened she turned, the light of battle still in her eyes, only to find it was her mother mildly inquiring if she was all right.

Before Dru could reply, Hester, standing behind Jane in the door, took command. "For goodness sakes, Jane," she said, "don't be such a goose. Of course she's all right. Do go into the room and quit blocking the door."

Jane moved obediently, and Hester sailed into the library, her eyes bright with curiosity. "Now Dru," she said, "who is he, and what did he want?"

"Who he is," Dru said darkly, the gentleman's recent sins fresh in her mind, "is the rudest, most odious man I have ever met. And what he wanted was to be mean and overbearing and insufferable."

Jane groaned gently, and Dru flushed.

"I'm sorry, Mother," she said contritely, her sense of fairness beginning to cool her anger. "He really wasn't *that* bad. And though it hurts me to admit it, he did have cause to be angry. Jade let herself out of her stall this morning and wandered over to Green Corners where she released several of Mr. Pettigrew's horses. He brought her back and came to request—quite strongly—that I keep her at home in the future."

"Oh, dear," Jane said worriedly. "She really shouldn't do that, you know, Dru."

Laughingly Dru assured her mother that she did indeed know that, and she promised that when she later went out to visit the errant mare she would pass along her mother's remonstrances.

Hester, disappointed that all the tempest had been for what she considered nothing, sighed, and her thoughts returned to her earlier—and favorite—topic.

"Well," she said, settling comfortably into one of the old leather chairs which offered refuge in the library, "at least we now know that we don't want to invite Mr. Pettigrew to our ball." Her eyes brightened. "And if the Moores are gone, we won't have to invite them, either. Oh, Jane, this is getting better and better."

A glance at Dru's exasperated face led Jane to believe that things were not getting better and better, and she surpressed a sigh.

"I don't want a ball, Aunt Hester," Dru stuck in, her sorely tried temper adding heat to her words. "I don't want a ball, and if you have one, I don't believe I'll attend it."

The agitated ladies quickly assured her that there was indeed to be a ball and that her presence there was crucial, Hester even going so far as to say the ball was all for dear Drucilla's sake, a statement her niece promptly—and hotly—contested.

"Well, I don't know how I'll survive it," Dru murmured mulishly, "it's so ridiculous." Disinterestedly she flicked through the letters Baxley had left for her on the library desk, and one of them made her eyes brighten. "Of course," she cried excitedly, causing both her mother and aunt to jump. "That's it!"

"It?" they echoed.

"Cousin Matty," she explained. "I'll invite Cousin Matty to come and see me through this ball ordeal."

"Matty?" her mother repeated slowly, but Hester's reaction was more intense. "Your Cousin Matty?" she gasped. "Oh, no, my dear. Not Matty."

Seeing the distinct challenge in Dru's eyes, she hurried on. "Oh, Drucilla, do consider. Your Cousin Matty is not the thing. A positive antidote. Not married at thirty, eccentric, and given to saying the most horrible things—oh, Drucilla, she is not at all the type person one cares to claim as a relation."

"Bah!" Dru snapped.

Hester turned beseechingly to Jane. "Oh, Jane, you remember. I presented Matty twelve years ago. Even at eighteen she was past praying for. I'll never forget the first day—she marched into my sitting room and said 'Aunt, I don't want to get married, and I see no reason for either of us to waste our time.'"

After all those years, the memory still made Hester pale. "I took to my bed for a week, Jane, but it did no good. She didn't want to get married and she didn't get married. I was never so ashamed in my life.

"Really, Drucilla," she assured her niece earnestly as she swerved in that young lady's direction, "your crazy Cousin Matty is not at all the person to have around if we're to find you a suitable husband."

"Now Hester," Jane interposed quietly. "Matty is not crazy. She's just—just"—two pairs of eyes watched as she searched for a word—"just—different."

"So is an Indian nabob different," Hester snapped, "But Drucilla doesn't want to invite one to her ball."

"Do you know any?" Dru inquired sweetly, causing her aunt to sink back in her chair with a loud groan. Dru fixed her with a stern stare and said firmly that if Matty did not come, she would not go to the ball.

Hester took refuge in her smelling salts, then rallied for one last effort. "Oh Drucilla, consider," she pleaded desperately, "if not for yourself, then for Matty. Think how she will feel appearing with you. You tall and slender, she short and plump, you dark and lovely, she pale and—well—surely you wouldn't subject your poor cousin to such a humiliating experience."

But Dru, sensing victory, stalked to the library door, said, "Ha!," and slammed out in a way her aunt—had she not been so afflicted— would have characterized as most unbecoming in a Wrothton lady. Jane's eyes met Hester's, and after a moment she smiled. "It will be nice to see Matty again," she said softly. "Very nice indeed."

Chapter IV

Upon leaving the library Dru stormed up to her room, the look on her face so ferocious that the newest housemaid, encountering her on the stairs, dropped the clean sheets she was carrying. Aghast at her own clumsiness, she looked fearfully at her young mistress, who, engaged in her own thoughts, did not see the mischief done; had she known that she had startled the girl so, she would have been heartily sorry.

But Dru, as was usual when she was in one of her tempers, did not notice what was not on her mind and so passed on to her room, leaving the housemaid to breathe a sigh of relief.

In the privacy of her own apartment Dru paced angrily, at one point picking up a vase she had never liked, intending to smash it against the wall. At the last moment she relented and threw a pillow instead, sighing sadly when it made only a soft thump instead of the satisfying smash which would have released her pent-up feelings.

"Not as young as you once were—," she repeated as she stalked. "Beggars can't be choosers—oh, I'll show them. Matty *will* come, and we'll turn the countryside upside down. It will be a ball Aunt Hester will not forget—"

Inspired by that thought, she settled herself at her desk to write her cousin, begging her support in the upcoming ordeal. But before she had gotten past "Dear Matty, The most ridiculous thing—," She heard the sound of carriage wheels clattering up the drive.

Moving to the window, she groaned aloud at the sight which met her eyes. "The most ridiculous thing—," she murmured, wondering how she could have thought only an hour ago that nothing worse could happen on this disastrous day. Now, coming up the drive at a tired pace, was an outmoded carriage drawn by a team of horses.

"The Hovingtons," Dru sighed ruefully. "And without enough style to drive four horses."

Bracing herself with a small shake, she moved to the mirror, straightened her hair and smoothed her gown, and, regretting the fact that she was no longer of an age where she could crawl under the bed when disliked visitors appeared, she left her room and stood for a moment, hand on the bannister, as she gazed down into the main hall.

There was already a great deal of commotion below as George Hovington, ignoring Baxley, surged toward Lady Jane, talking loudly all the time. He was followed closely by his angular wife and ponderous son, the sight of whom made Dru's lips twitch. How *could* Cousin Percival ape the dandy set so? His tight pantaloons, white-topped boots, and many-caped coat with nearly saucer-sized buttons were simply appalling.

Meanwhile, George had reached Jane and was wringing her hand vigorously, assuring her that she was looking well and that it was a pleasure to see her again. Dru wondered critically how he could discern her mother's looks when his gaze seemed to rove more over the tables, vases, and mirrors which stood in the main hall. Her lips wrinked distastefully as she noted that Cousin Lavinia did not even make a pretense of greeting her would-be hostess before moving to one of the hall paintings so she could better inspect the artist's signature. Aunt Hester's bristling was clearly visible as Dru slowly descended the stairs.

"Cousins Hovington," she said midway down, drawing three pairs of eyes toward her. "How good to see you again. And how sorry we are that we cannot receive you now."

George, who had started forward to clasp her hand—and, Dru thought, her waist too, if he could manage it—stopped suddenly. "Uh?" he said, and Dru now knew what her favorite authors meant when they wrote that someone's eyes "started from his head." Noting with satisfaction that three pairs of Hovington eyes were fixed incredulously on her face, her smile widened.

"Oh, so sorry," she cooed, avoiding her mother's and aunt's eyes, "but you can see we are in disrepair." She paused for a moment and gently waved a hand toward the sheets and ladders decorating the stairway. "We're painting the stairs and our spare bechambers. I'm sure you understand."

"Now see here—," George blustered, then quickly changed his tone to hearty good will as out of the corner of his eye he saw Hester fire up. "Surely not all your bedchambers, my dear."

Dru, portraying her vague Aunt Margaret admirably, turned to a wooden-faced Baxley and asked if any of the bedchambers were done being painted. Relieved that he could reply truthfully, his "No, Miss Dru," was prompt and forceful.

George started to sputter, and Hester could no longer refrain herself. "Had you informed us of your plans to visit earlier, we might have sent you word that you had nowhere to visit," she said maliciously. "Unfortunately, George, you were never well versed in the customs of polite company."

Hovington's face reddened alarmingly as his wife gasped and his son gaped. Lady Jane rushed into the breech, quelling her sister-in-law with a glance.

"We are sure that you are surprised to find us in such a turmoil," she said smoothly, gently laying her hand on George's arm. "And we are indeed sorry for it. But we would not for the world inconvenience you, and to be sleeping in a room with ladders and sheets and paint buckets must always be counted an inconvenience. Thus when we received your letter this morning we were sure you would be happier staying with your in-laws, the Buxtells."

Smiling sweetly at the three bemused faces turned toward her, Jane invited her guests to join them all for tea in the sitting room before they journeyed on.

George, who had stood as if rooted to one spot during her last speech, now glared at her. "See here, Jane—," he began belligerently, but when she turned and looked at him enquiringly her quiet dignity confused him further, and he began to sputter. "It's a fine thing when a man's own relatives don't have a place to spare—"

"But we could not ask you to share the turmoil of our household now, Cousin George," Dru interrupted demurely. "It wouldn't be polite."

And before he could assure her that he would not consider it impolite at all, Hester struck in, saying "The Wrothtons, George, are always polite. Not like some families..." When she let the sentence hang meaningfully his color rose again, but Jane forestalled the expected explosion.

"Actually," she said gently, her warm smile emcompassing the three impartially, "I imagine you would really rather stay with the Buxtells. We are so quiet here with our mourning, and there would be nothing to amuse you." George was heard to say that he did not wish to be amused, but Jane continued, smiling at Mrs. Hovington who was regarding her as if she had just grown an extra head. "Dear Lavinia will have a chance for many comfy cozes with her sister at Collier Corners, and you, George, can ride out with your brother-in-law. It will be delightful for you."

George looked anything but delighted, and Dru, who knew how

well he and his brother-in-law got on, hurriedly turned a laugh into a cough.

"Unless you think you won't be welcome there, George?" Hester challenged, and George, who thought just that, demurred instantly, casting her a look of great dislike. Lavinia, however, was heard to say doubtfully that the last time they visited the Buxtells, dear Edmund had suggested that short visits should be followed by long absences. George irritatedly begged her to hush and glowered at one and all. Never of a very even temperament, he was inclined to turn surly when his plans were overset.

"Tea, George?" Jane repeated her offer softly, but he shook his head angrily and, after reassuring himself that the ladies were not going to change their minds, he said that if his family was to travel on to Collier Corners, they had best leave at once, since Edmund was a nasty man when kept waiting for his dinner.

"Although what he's going to say when we arrive—," he thought aloud; then, aware that Hester was watching him gloatingly, he pulled himself together and turned to Jane. He looked appraisingly at the hall walls and at the sheets and ladders draped artistically throughout the area and asked when she thought the painting would be done.

Hester audibly ground her teeth, but before her suddenly flustered mother could reply, Dru intervened.

"It's really hard to say, Cousin George," she said, bestowing a dazzling smile upon him as she captured his arm and moved him toward the door. "But when we are ready to receive you we will send you word. Until then, we know the Buxtells will be as happy to have you as we would." And taking Hovington's hat from the helpful Baxley, she settled it on George's head and opened the door for him.

He looked at her suspiciously but took the mischief in her eyes for delight in seeing him, and with his wife and son trailing after, he went reluctantly down the steps. Halfway down he turned, promising to "ride over from time to time to see how the manor—I mean, how you and your mother—do."

"Of course," Dru answered composedly.

"And you'll send us word when we can move in," he repeated.

"We'll send you word when we're ready to receive you," Dru corrected.

With that George had to be content, and he unhappily followed his wife and son into their carriage. Engaged in berating the coachman, he gave the orders to drive on and did not hear Hester's low "And that will be when Bonaparte rules the world, George Hovington." Had he looked up he might have wondered what it was that was causing his cousin to dissolve in laughter on the manor's front steps.

Chapter V

With the Hovington threat momentarily averted, the ladies of Morningdale Manor ate a quiet supper and retired early, each to recruit her strength for the days ahead. The last sound Dru heard as she drifted off to sleep was the gentle pattering of rain on the shutters, and she thought dolefully that continued cold and the Hovingtons were all of one piece—tiresome bordering on unbearable.

Thus it was with no real expectation that she opened her eyes the next morning, yet the moment she did so she was pleasantly surprised, for as Constance drew back the curtains shielding the east windows, sunlight poured through.

"It's bright as spring out, Miss Dru," the maid announced with satisfaction. "I've brought you your morning hot chocolate; and if you sit here in the sun while you drink it, perhaps it will warm you awake."

Dru agreed readily to that scheme, sipping the chocolate as she marveled at the change a bright day could make in the world. Below her, the gardens which had appeared sodden and miserable for the last week seemed almost to stretch in relief. Although blooms were sparse this time of year, the garden again appeared an inviting walk and one Dru thought she would take before the rains once more descended.

"The sun has come not a moment too soon," she said to the maid who was moving busily about the room. "I was beginning to think it had deserted England completely. You may say it's only January, but I swear it has been a terribly long winter already."

Constance, noting her mistress's wistful voice, suggested that when Miss Matty arrived the days would seem shorter. Beyond that she forebore comment, although she suspected that it was actually the happenings of the past few days which made the winter seem so long for Dru. Reflecting darkly on Lady Hester's propensity for stirring bumblebaths and even more darkly on the audacity of family relations who were born Quality but didn't act like it, Constance reached briskly into the wardrobe and pulled out Dru's riding habit.

Her automatic "Will you be riding today, miss?" was only polite form, for she knew the answer before Dru nodded and was already adding a warm cloak to the pile of garments her mistress would soon be donning.

"Tom says the horses are quite restless after the week's rain," she continued, consciously avoiding Dru's eyes. "He thought you'd like to take Jade out while he exercises Tristan."

Normally Constance's volunteering of such information would bring a quick grin to Dru's lips and a gentle teasing about her maid's source of information. Today, however, her thoughts were elsewhere, and she merely nodded in agreement. After a moment, though, she suggested that Constance tell Tom to take Tristan out without her, for she wanted to ride by herself this day.

"Thomas doesn't believe ladies should jaunter across the countryside by themselves," Constance argued primly, her devotion to her employer raging with her devotion to the head groom, whose opinion she valued highly.

"Nor does he think a lady should ride at faster than a slow trot,"

Dru returned dryly, watching with amusement as the color rose in Constance's cheeks. "Both his opinions are heartily shared by my Aunt Hester, who goes even further and does not think a lady should ride at all. Nevertheless, I will ride, I will ride alone, and I shall gallop—yes, gallop—whenever and wherever I please."

And with that she drained the last of her chocolate and slipped into the habit her maid held patiently. Her tying her hair back with a ribbon drew an audible sniff from Constance, who agreed with Aunt Hester that that was no way for a lady to appear in public. Or even in private, Hester said, unless she had been ill with influenza and still was feeling not quite the thing. When Dru thought of the wigs her aunt never appeared without she was thankful she preferred the ribbon.

Out of the corner of her eye she saw Constance reach into the wardrobe again and stopped her by saying, "No, Constance, I shall forego the bonnet." In the mirror she saw her maid's disapproving face and laughed. "Yes, I know. Neither Tom nor Aunt Hester approve of a lady riding without a hat." She bit her lower lip as she studied her reflection in the mirror, her gray eyes staring seriously back at her. "Well, maybe I am not a lady."

"Miss Dru!" Constance breathed, scandalized.

Dru sighed and her face was rueful as she turned back to her longtime servant and friend. "You're right," she agreed. "I think my real problem is that I am too much a lady. But," she added, moving to the door and forestalling Constance's eager movement, "I still will not wear a bonnet."

Picking up her cloak from the chair near the now-opened door, she smiled winningly and coaxed her maid not to be cross. Then, with a twinkle in her eye, she asked that Constance tell Tom she would be riding alone after breakfast, suggesting that such information might not displease him so much if he heard it from the right source. Delighted that that sally had drawn one of Constance's ready blushes, Dru left the room and with a quick step descended the stairs to find her mother and aunt already at breakfast.

"Good morning," she said, dropping a light kiss on her mother's forehead and smiling at her aunt.

"Good morning, dear," Jane returned, watching fondly as Dru moved to the sideboard to select eggs and ham, toast, and a cup of tea. "You have a lovely day for a ride. You're wise to catch the sun while it lasts."

Hester, who was never at her best in the morning, took up one of her continuing dissertations on riding in general and on Dru's riding in particular, saying querulously that she had never understood how anyone could care to career across the country on the back of a nasty beast which would probably do one great bodily harm if possible.

Jane protested mildly that she hoped Dru knew better than to career, and Dru added that Jade was not a nasty beast, but Hester was not finished.

"I shall instruct Mrs. Waddington to prepare a poultice for you, Drucilla, since I am sure that if you insist on riding this morning, you will certainly have influenza by nightfall." Dru, who hadn't been ill a day since she contracted measles from her brother James at age five, began to speak, but Hester swept on majestically. Glancing with disfavor at the cloak Dru had draped across the back of an empty chair, she pointed out that her niece had forgotten a bonnet. That young woman's continued silence suggested that she did not intend to wear a bonnet, a fact her aunt found disgraceful.

"Really, Jane," she said, seeking aid from her sister-in-law, "I do not know what the world is coming to when young ladies ride about the countryside—which they shouldn't—bareheaded, in the dead of winter. Or any other time, for that matter. Why in my day—," but her sister-in-law forestalled that reminiscence by pointing out mildly that Dru did have her cloak and would pull the hood up if she were cold.

"I might have known you would uphold her," Hester sputtered, incensed.

"Yes, I think you might," Jane answered tranquilly, her eyes twinkling as they met her daughter's.

Dru laughed and thanked her aunt for her concern over her health, but Hester informed her tartly that it was not only her health which concerned her. She pointed her fork at her niece and said sternly that if Dru had forgotten that the Hovingtons were coming to supper that night, she had not, "and I would rather you were in the drawing room supporting us than in your chamber supporting a cold."

Dru appeared much struck by that, but her Mother interposed mildly, saying that Hester made a family dinner sound like a battle.

Chewing on a piece of ham she had just popped into her mouth, Hester was unable to answer for a moment. When she did, she waved her fork for effect as she said grimly, "There are three Hovingtons, and there are three of us. Even odds. Although we must make up in tact what they want in manner." Remembering her aunt's recent exhibition of tact where the Hovington's were concerned, Dru hastily turned a laugh into a cough, meeting her mother's eyes as Jane murmured, "Just so."

Hester, oblivious to the understanding glance exchanged between her relations, continued. "I rather think that given the choice between driving into a battle and spending the evening with the Hovingtons that I am much inclined toward the battle."

Dru nodded in understanding. "I had for the moment forgotten they were coming," she said. "One does tend to put unpleasant thoughts out of one's head."

"Sometimes unpleasant tasks are one's duty," Jane pronounced gently, "and since they did come to see us, it would be very bad form to snub them completely. Which reminds me," she continued as she delicately buttered a biscuit, "I've decided to redo the hall and some of the guest rooms. It will be good to freshen them before the ball, and I will feel better knowing we are not lying to George and Lavinia."

She bit into the biscuit and looked up to find two pairs of startled eyes fixed upon her. "Deception has never suited the Wrothtons," she explained.

"Of course," Mama, Dru answered mechanically, exchanging a guilty glance with her aunt. This particular deception had bothered neither of them.

Hester sipped her tea, gazing at her sister-in-law reflectively. Finally she lowered her cup and granted that while they had practiced deception, it was at times necessary, "for if we hadn't done it, we'd now have the Hovingtons constantly under our feet, poking into every nook in the manor, and constantly appraising the worth of every vase, painting, and piece of silverware they could get their hands on.''

Jane, much struck by Hester's words, paused as she reached for the teapot. ''You're right,'' she said. ''And thank goodness we avoided that.''

Breakfast over, Dru told her mother she was off for a canter across Foster's Mead, smiled gaily at her aunt's loud harumph, and, tying on her cloak as she went, walked briskly down to the stables. There Thomas had Jade saddled and waiting for her. Ignoring his pointed offer to ride with her and his even more pointed grumblings when she declined to let him, Dru set happily off, she and Jade both tossing their heads in enjoyment of the sunny day. Seeming to hope that spring might be imminent, Jade danced playfully against the bit, breathing deeply as if she might catch the scent of awakening grasses.

Relieved she was at last alone, and lost in her own thoughts, Dru let the mare make her own way. Once Jade's initial playfulness passed, she let the reins slacken, and her thoughts turned again to the breakfast conversation which had dampened her spirits. ''The Hovingtons,'' she said distastefully, causing Jade to prick her ears.

Dru knew her mother and aunt were right. The Hovingtons did come to Morningdale to inspect the estate. Their tasteless actions made it clear they considered the manor theirs. ''Living on the expectations,'' she thought angrily, and the idea of Percy's children in the Wrothton nursery made her clench her hands, involuntarily pulling on the reins and causing a surprised Jade to stop.

''I'm only twenty-five,'' she said aloud as she gave Jade the office to start again. ''If I were a man I'd be quite a catch. It's not fair.'' But unfair or not, Dru knew that she could not bear to see the Hovingtons ensconced at the manor. Even marriage to Peckingham would be better than that.

Deep in such dismal thoughts, the short distance to Foster's Mead passed quickly. When they reached the gate Jade obligingly undid the latch; and, feeling slightly guilty, Dru made certain it was securely fastened behind them. She looked with satisfaction at the brown, open meadow now before her. Unencumbered by sheep or cattle or anything else which would interrupt a gallop, it sloped gently to a stone fence at the far end. Beyond the fence was a seldom-traveled road, and Dru, smiling at Jade's impatient dancing, did not see the two riders rounding the far curve there.

As if to outrun all the thoughts which had so recently plagued her, she shouted, "Now, Jade," and the two were off across the meadow, Dru easily adapting herself to the horse's graceful stride. The ribbon she had tied in her hair was not proof against the morning breeze, and her cloak billowed out behind her as she rode.

Down on the road two companionable riders were startled by the sight they saw plunging down the slope toward them and drew in their horses to watch.

"My word!" exclaimed the first gentleman, admiring the fine black mare glinting in the sun and trying to recognize the gray figure which, from a distance, seemed to have great black wings spreading out behind it. "What is it?"

His taller companion languidly raised his quizzing glass. "It strongly reminds me of the mythical figure of death," he drawled. "Most unusual."

The golden spaniel accompanying the two men obviously found nothing as forbidding as death in the figure, however; for once he spied it, his tail began to wag vigorously and, slipping through a nearby gate, he sped off across the meadow in pursuit, barking madly as he ran.

The tall man, noting the dog's movement too late, called, "Hamlet, heel," but the spaniel was out of hearing. "Oh, damn the dog," he said disgustedly. "I shall never have him trained."

His companion laughed, his eyes on the spaniel and it's fast-approaching target. "I am disappointed, Crandon," he said pleasantly. "Your figure of death is only a cloaked lady out for a gallop. I thought we were to have a fight on our hands for sure."

Pettigrew, now peering closely at the approaching lady, shook his head ruefully. "You may yet be right," he sighed, drawing a quizzical glance from his friend. But before the latter could inquire further, Hamlet reached Jade, and the horse, who majestically ignored all the yapping dogs at the manor, instantly took exception to this one. As she kicked out dangerously, she missed the wily spaniel but broke stride and caused her mistress to lose her balance. The ground loomed close before Dru regained her seat and pulled Jade to a halt, glancing around for the cause of the near-accident. She saw the dog now happily returning to its owner and, when she recognized that owner, her brow darkened. Moving forward, she ignored one gentleman as her eyes met those of the other.

"Mr. Pettigrew," she said, her voice icy, her back rigid. "How delightful to see you again." Noting with satisfaction that her tone made his jaw tighten, she eyed his panting dog disdainfully. "I wonder, sir, if you would care to say a few edifying words concerning people who cannot control their animals?"

"Hamlet," he returned tightly, "is young and very indiscriminate as to those he would make his friends." Watching his shot go home, he continued smoothly that he had not, however, yet been able to teach the dog to unlatch gateposts.

Before the fight could escalate, the smaller gentleman, who had quietly been appraising the young lady as his friend fueled her anger, judged it time to intervene. "May I compliment you on your riding, miss?" he asked gently, reminding Dru that she and the detestable Mr. Pettigrew were not alone. "You have a beautiful mare. The two of you go well together."

Slightly mollified, Dru smiled at Mr. Pettigrew's companion. Shorter than that odious man, he was yet taller than average, with an open, friendly face, sandy hair sweeping back from a forehead which capped humorous brown eyes, and Dru noticed with approval that he was dressed in the first style of elegance.

Noting with amusement that the two seemed inclined to continue staring at each other, Pettigrew intervened smoothly. "I beg your pardon, Miss Wrothton," he said, receiving a darkling look for his pains, "but may I make you known to my companion? This is Sebastian, Duke of Ratchford, recently come to this charming neighborhood." Then he turned to the gentleman who was smiling at the young lady and said informatively, "Sebastian, this is Miss

Drucilla Wrothton, whose fine mare Ruby led us such a merry chase only yesterday."

Dru inclined her head toward the Duke, seemingly ignoring the last part of Pettigrew's introduction. "A pleasure, Your Grace," she said. "And I am sorry for any inconvenience my horse might have caused you yesterday." Her stress of the word *you* was not lost on either of her companions, making the Duke grin broadly and Pettigrew's lips tighten. Then she turned to the latter and, between clenched teeth, said, "My mount's name, sir, is Jade."

"Quite, quite fitting," he murmured provocatively, but before she could reply, the Duke hurried into speech.

"I enjoyed the ride yesterday," he assured her, moving his horse forward slightly. "I don't think I've enjoyed anything half so much in months."

This kindness earned him a quick smile which was just as quickly erased when Pettigrew dryly commented that London must have indeed grown dull.

Assuming her best Aunt Hester manner, Dru regally ignored Pettigrew and turned Jade toward the gate. Ratchford moved forward to open it for her and then stopped, fascinated, as Jade took the latch in her teeth and the gate swung open.

"A remarkably talented mare," Pettigrew said at his most dry, noting with satisfaction the color which rose in Dru's cheeks as she self-consciously closed the gate again. With difficulty she preserved her Aunt Hester composure and bit back the angry retort she dearly wanted to make. Instead she gave her hand to the Duke, bestowed a pleasant smile upon him, and said, "If you will excuse me, I must return home."

Ratchford bowed and said he looked forward to seeing her again. She murmured that that would be nice, nodded stiffly at Pettigrew, who grinned back in a way which made her long to slap his face, and nudged Jade into a fast trot. Had she turned, she would have seen one man's eyes following her thoughtfully while the second eyed his companion in speculation.

Thomas was waiting for Dru when she arrived back at Morningdale, and a look of relief crossed his face as she rode in. He helped her dismount, then led Jade away to be groomed, crooning softly to the mare and promising her an extra ration of grain if she stood quietly while he rubbed her down.

Walking slowly up to the manor, Dru tried unsuccessfully to recapture her hair with the ribbon. She patted her cheeks in a vain effort to cool the color there and devoutly hoped she would not encounter anyone before attaining the privacy of her chamber. When she walked into the hall and saw her aunt descending the stairs, Dru sighed ruefully and wondered what she had done to incur so many unfortunate encounters.

One sharp glance at her niece's face convinced Hester something was amiss. She surged forward, declaring that it was not riding which had raised such color in Dru's cheeks and demanding to know what had made her angry.

"Really, Aunt Hester," Dru began, then gave up, knowing that nothing but the truth would appease that curious lady. "Well, if you must know, it was that odious Crandon Pettigrew and his equally odious dog, a spaniel with the unlikely name of Hamlet."

"Pettigrew and his dog?" Hester demanded. "What have they to do with you?"

"The dog surprised Jade this morning and almost caused her to throw me," Dru replied pettishly. "You would think he would learn to control his own animals."

With that she moved to the stairs and began ascending. "I do not understand why the Duke of Ratchford would have such an insufferable and boorish man for a friend, for the Duke himself seems to be a man of breeding."

"Most dukes are men of breeding," Hester replied absently, watching Dru go. "But what of the Duke of Ratchford? We were speaking of that man Pettigrew."

"The Duke was with Pettigrew," Dru said as she disappeared.

Hester's mouth dropped open as she realized the full implications of those words. "But Dru—," she protested to the empty staircase; then her voice rose almost to a wail. "And you without a bonnet!"

Shaking her head sadly, she tottered to one of the chairs which lined the open hall and fell into it, there to sit for a full five minutes bemoaning the ways of the younger generation in general and one member of it in particular.

Chapter VI

The expressions on the faces of the ladies who gathered in Morningdale Manor's drawing room that evening did not suggest three eager hostesses ready to welcome friends for a convivial dinner party. Indeed, a casual observer might have suspected each was to have a tooth drawn shortly. That suspicion would have strengthened when Baxley, his face calm, opened the drawing-room doors to announce sonorously, "The Hovingtons."

"Thank you, Baxley," Jane said as she moved forward to greet her guests. Hester and Dru, who had been seated, rose slowly, each with a marked lack of enthusiasm. Dru twitched with distaste the brown silk gown she had chosen for the evening and wished wistfully that she had fulfilled her aunt's dark prophecies and contracted influenza. She disliked excessively the dress she wore and had chosen it in the devout hope it would make her appear so unattractive that even Percival Hovington's roving eyes would be diverted elsewhere.

With a small smile she wondered if Aunt Hester had had similar thoughts, for that good lady wore a gown which made her complexion appear sallow even beneath her heavily rouged cheeks. Only Jane Wrothton in her quietly elegant mourning clothes appeared herself.

Lavinia Hovington entered the drawing room first, and her eyes, which reminded Dru forcibly of a blackbird's, darted quickly over and into everything in the room. Dru felt her temper rising.

As Lavinia limply kissed the cheek of each of the ladies in turn, her son followed her awkwardly into the room. Dru wondered if his valet had sewn the yellow pantaloons onto his fleshy legs; she could imagine no other way to make them fit so tightly. Pointed shirt collars tickled his cheekbones, and his neckcloth, which emphasized his extremely short neck, fell from beneath the points like a runaway waterfall. Dru wondered in astonishment if her cousin's valet was settling an old score with his master in sending him out looking so; had she known the truth, the gentleman's gentleman was often moved to tears by the knowledge that his master's appearance reflected on him. Master Percy stubbornly refused his valet's advice and wore only those styles most unbecoming to him, in the happy delusion that he was indeed a Tulip of the Ton.

Reading Dru's amazement as approval, Percy approached her ponderously and, carrying her hand to his lips in a way which made her stiffen, said condescendingly, "Cousin Drucilla, you look lovely tonight. Brown becomes you."

Choking on an unconvincing cough—Dru wondered if her cousins might think she had a bad cold, for she coughed a lot in their presence—Dru thanked him and removed her hand from his damp grasp, wiping it surreptitiously on her skirt as she did so. I may blacken his eye, she thought dispassionately, and at that idea she brightened, a sign mistaken by her cousin to mean that she approved of his fulsome manner. His smugness increased.

Dru looked from Percy to his father, who had just entered, and sighed. Perhaps one could not blame Percival for his bad manners, she thought, as George, after a cursory bow to each of the ladies, began to wander about the room, inspecting the furniture, the paintings, and all other items he could find.

Ignoring this crudity, and with a glance quelling the acidic comments rising on Hester's lips, Jane apparently forgot her earlier concern about deception being unbecoming in the Wrothtons as she said, "How pleasant it is to see you all again. Won't you be seated?"

Her guests showed no disposition to do so, appearing happier to continue with their inspections of the room. Jane invited them to sit again, and this time her sweet voice held a note of command as she instructed Lavinia to come sit beside her and George and Percival to take the chairs by the fire. Reluctantly the three did as they were bid, and Dru bit her lip at the looks of consternation which appeared upon their faces.

"I trust you are comfortable with the Buxtells?" Jane inquired politely when no one else seemed likely to break the growing silence.

"Oh, indeed yes," Lavinia replied, "although the chimneys do smoke, and Edmund is being quite rude—that is, we are of course disappointed that we cannot stay here at Morningdale. We quite look upon it as home, you know."

Hester's color rose alarmingly but before she could speak, Jane continued. "Yes," she said comfortably, "it is a pity we are redecorating the guest rooms." Lavinia regarded her with suspicion, wondering if the word "guest" had been as emphasized as she thought. "Of course, we had no idea you were coming. Had you let us know—" Jane's voice trailed off delicately, and Dru marveled at her mother's ability to maintain dignity while administering a gentle setdown.

Lavinia had the grace to blush, and George thought it time to change the subject. Let Hester get a word in about his manners, he thought, and he'd be in for a very uncomfortable evening. Aloud he said, "Yes, well, of course, although a man feels he always has a place in what is his—" He encountered the fire in Hester's eyes and coughed hastily. "That is—meant to say—" He rose and stood by the fireplace, mopping his brow. "We do find it very gratifying that you're keeping the place up so well."

That was too much for Hester, who told him roundly that they weren't about to let their home fall down about their ears. "After all," she said, and there was a distinct challenge in her eyes, "there have been Wrothtons at Morningdale Manor for generations, and there will be Wrothtons here for generations to come."

George could not meet her eyes, but Lavinia gave her humorless titter, then turned to Jane. "You know, Jane," she said reflectively, "I do not believe I have ever visited Morningdale's dower house. Where is it located?"

Hester gasped audibly, but Jane's calm was unruffled as she replied. "There is no dower house, Lavinia. We have no need for one." At Mrs. Hovington's incredulous lifting of her eyebrows, Jane explained that generations had always lived amicably together in the manor. "Why, my husband's dear Mama lived with us for years, and we were delighted to have her. We are a very close family."

Lavinia gave a shrug eloquent of her disbelief, then turned to Dru with a smile which put that young lady strongly in mind of a reptile she had encountered in the garden last summer as it lay on a rock sunning itself. "I do hope you'll give us a tour of the manor after dinner," Lavinia said. "It seems so long since we've seen it, and one likes to keep acquainted, you know. I am particularly interested in seeing the schoolroom and nursery—both are quite large as I recall."

She ignored the amazement in Dru's face as she continued. "This is a marvelous house in which to raise children. I have often said so. Percival," she added pointedly, smiling proudly at her son, "plans to have many sons."

Dru looked at her cousin, who nodded his agreement. "Many," he said on a note of self-congratulation.

"You will astound medical science," Dru murmured politely, and as the color rose in Percy's face, Baxley, whose timing was always excellent, entered to announce dinner.

All rose, the Hovingtons glowering and Jane and Hester barely able to restrain their laughter. George offered his arm to Lady Jane, and Percival, huffy over his cousin's last remark, approached Aunt Hester. Eyeing him disgustedly, she gingerly placed her hand on his arm and allowed him to lead her off. Lavinia fell in beside Dru as they left the drawing room.

"Dear Drucilla," Mrs. Hovington said, the lack of warmth in her voice making it apparent she considered Dru anything but dear, 'you've become such an outspoken young woman. Although not as young . . ." She eyed Dru speculatively to see if the shaft went home, then continued.

"I do think it very good of you to have renounced the married state to remain at the manor and care for your dear mother and aunt, although I have often thought you might all be happier in smaller quarters—perhaps a suite of rooms in town. Yours is a selfless sacrifice for which I applaud you."

"I pray, Lavinia, that you will not applaud too loudly," Dru replied, her eyes bright, "for in truth I do not know what you mean. We enjoy the spaciousness of the manor, and my mother is far from her dotage and quite able to run it without me. As for the thought of Aunt Hester needing my care—I hope you will not suggest that to her, for I am sure she will speedily disabuse your mind of that absurd notion. And," she added with satisfaction as she noted the growing look of disapproval on the older woman's face, "I certainly have not renounced marriage. Far from it."

She nodded to herself when she saw how that had penetrated Lavinia's smugness. But the older woman would not concede, saying sharply that her niece seemed to be letting her embarrassment at her spinsterhood run away with her tongue. "I know you had offers in your youth, and I know you turned them down," she continued, watching closely as Dru's eyes flashed. "Surely you realize that you are now quite beyond marriageable age."

"I am not *quite* without hope," Dru said, making a strong effort to keep her voice low and soft and hoping that Lavinia would take her downcast eyes as a sign of maidenly confusion.

"You mean there actually is someone?" Lavinia questioned sharply, and Dru was satisfied she had pierced the Hovington smugness. "Is it a widower, perhaps? Old Peckingham?"

Dru's lips closed tightly at that, and she was grateful she did not carry a fan, for she certainly would have broken it.

"Drucilla, are you engaged?"

At that her mother's words on the Wrothton's view of deception ran guiltily through Dru's mind, and she shook her head no. The look which instantly brightened Lavinia's face was enough to overcome her recent scruples as she immediately added, "But I do have expectations."

"Oh?" Lavinia said speculatively, and then, since they had reached the dinner table, raised her voice so all could hear as she inquired who the gentleman was who was soon to receive their felicitations. As she did so, she glanced quickly at Hester and Jane, but she could not read the looks on their faces. All eyes turned toward Dru, who squirmed uncomfortably.

Hester rallied to her aid. "Really, Lavinia," she said, annoyed, "you should not tease Drucilla so, for it would be highly improper for us to be talking of engagements now, while we are still in mourning."

Then she drew herself to her full height and, in her grandest manner, favored Mrs. Hovington with an unwavering stare as she said, "You may be sure you will be among the first to be informed when the gentleman has made his offer. Until then you need not concern yourself, for what the Wrothtons of Morningdale judge to be correct must always be acceptable to the Hovingtons of Delham."

George sputtered, and Lavinia's color heightened, but no more was said about Dru's engagement as the six sat down to dinner. In truth, little was said throughout the meal, for every topic introduced with the happy thought of aiding conversation seemed to trail off to an uncomfortable end.

Dru, sorry she had let her tongue run away with her so completely, tried to atone by making conversation with George, seated at her right. He, however, had a poor opinion of any woman's ability to discuss politics, and since he was intent on his dinner and found it hard to keep his mind on more than one thing at a time, that conversation languished.

Hester, guiltily aware of her sister-in-law's reproving glances, tried to initiate conversation by explaining that the painting now being done was in preparation for a forthcoming ball, but as soon as the words were out of her mouth she realized that it was not a felicitous topic. Jane and Dru turned astonished and reproachful eyes upon her, and Percival brightened perceptibly at the thought.

"We shall certainly want to stay in the neighborhood until the

41

ball,'' he assured Dru. "The Buxtells tell me there are many charming young ladies in this area.''

Repressing a sigh of annoyance, she nodded and countered with, "And many charming young men, as well.''

"A ball,'' George muttered deeply, between bites. He looked at Dru speculatively. "Is this ball for any—er—interesting announcements?''

It was Jane who answered, forestalling the quick retort which sprang to her daughter's lips. She calmly explained that the ball was to reacquaint them with the world since they had been in mourning so long.

"I suppose you'll have many guests staying here for the ball?'' he grumbled discontentedly, still angry that there was no room for him.

"We hardly know yet, George,'' Jane replied, "though we do expect Dru's Cousin Matty any day now to help us with the preparations.''

"Mathilde?'' Lavinia's voice held obvious disapproval. "Why have Mathilde come when you already have us at your disposal?'' Before Dru could tell her, another thought occurred to Lavinia, and her voice rose as she demanded to know where Mathilde was to stay if all the guest rooms were being painted.

"She will stay with me, of course,'' Dru answered civilly, wondering how any dinner could be so long. "Matty and I are quite like sisters.''

Lavinia sniffed. "I suppose one cannot choose one's relations.''

"I suppose not,'' Dru agreed sweetly.

Impervious to that shot, Percival joined the conversation. "I remember Matty,'' he said. "She blackened my eye once.''

"An impertinent child,'' his mother pronounced disdainfully.

"I never knew Matty to have such sense—,'' Hester began hotly, but she was interrupted by Dru, who fixed Percival with a minatory eye.

"As I recall the incident, Percy, she blackened your eye after you threw my kitten into the pond. And, if I remember correctly, the poor thing would have drowned if Matty hadn't pulled it out again.''

Percival looked embarrassed. "It was a childish prank," he excused himself with what Dru indignantly thought was a chuckle.

"And childish pranks are no reason for a young lady to behave like a brawling street urchin," his mother said haughtily.

It was fortunate that at that moment Baxley served dessert.

Tea was served early that night, and once served, the Hovingtons were not encouraged to linger. After they took their leave, Hester remarked crossly that they were the only ones who could push her into taking Matty's side in anything. Complaining of a headache, she made her way up to bed, muttering darkly about slow tops, encroaching windsuckers, and prosy bores.

Dru and her mother exchanged wry glances and agreed that they, too, had spent more pleasant evenings. Each went to bed early, Jane to deep slumber and Dru to dream fitfully of herself as Lady Peckingham, nursing her ancient husband through interminable cases of gout. As such, she was pleased to awake in the morning.

Chapter VII

The following days passed quickly for Dru, for they were filled with continued skirmishes with the Hovingtons, visits to ailing tenants, and, on days which were not too cold, brisk morning rides. She received a brief note from her Cousin Matty saying that lady would be along as soon as she got herself out of the tangle she was presently in, and Dru was content. Aunt Hester snorted, prophesying that someday Matty would find herself in a knot even she could not untie.

Dru smiled at that comment, for she could not imagine a situation which would have her droll cousin at a stand for long. Knowing that she had won a battle in getting Matty to come bear her company through her husband-hunting (how she detested the thought), she wisely ignored her aunt's provocation. Aunt Hester might not like Matty, but she disliked the thought of a spinster Dru even more.

As days turned into weeks, Dru lived in hourly expectation of her cousin's arrival, but no Matty appeared. The sheets in her room were aired daily, the holly Dru placed there was thrown out and replaced, thrown out and replaced again; Hester was looking decidedly hopeful, and Jane worried that perhaps Matty had fallen victim to the virulent bouts of influenza said to be traveling through many country estates. Deciding that speculation was hopeless, Dru shrugged, said that Matty would be along when she arrived and went about her business.

Dru was out on that business the day her cousin finally did come, thus missing a performance which would have pleased her mightily. She had ridden out to visit an old retainer who lived on the far-eastern edge of her estate and missed Matty's arrival, but the account she heard of it left nothing in the telling. Hester, who had been lying in wait for over an hour, spied Dru the minute she entered the house and proceeded to enlighten her with a highly colored version of what she termed Matty's Latest Madness.

The longer Dru listened, the more pronounced grew the gleam in her eye and the more she wished she had chosen that day to stay home, for the cause of Hester's repeated headshakes and declarations that "I've never seen anything like it, Drucilla, the girl is mad; that I should ever live to see the day—" readily appealed to her sense of humor. She knew Matty would certainly enliven the days ahead.

"Now, Aunt Hester," she soothed, gently pushing that lady into a chair, "you are talking in circles and I can't understand what has upset you so. I understand Matty has arrived and that her method of arrival has put you sadly out of countenance. Why don't you just sit here and tell me the whole story from the beginning?" Then she settled herself in a nearby chair to enjoy the show.

Hester eyed her severely, and her tone was ominous as she began.

"First," she said, "your cousin—for you must take full responsibility, Drucilla, you're the one who invited her here—your cousin—that is—your cousin's coach, arrived.

"Well, not her coach, either," she corrected herself. "It was her brother's coach. Dear Cecil, being such a dutiful brother, did not want his sister jauntering around the country in a hired vehicle so he made her the loan of his excessively nice one. That man is kindness itself to her and—well, that is another topic entirely." She lapsed into silence as she thought of it.

Dru, impatient to hear the story, prompted her with a gentle, "The coach arrived?" and was rewarded with a glare as Hester remembered.

"Yes," she said, "the coach arrived, and your mother and I—and that horrid Percival Hovington, who had ridden over for tea—went down the stairs to greet her. And what did we find?"

Hester turned red with the memory, a sign she had been affected mightily.

"What did we find?" she repeated rhetorically, indignation apparent in very line of her body.

"What *did* you find, Aunt?" Dru asked sweetly, knowing that whatever had upset Hester so would delight her immensely.

"A monkey!"

"A monkey?" Dru echoed. "Whyever a monkey?"

"The very question I asked," Hester replied earnestly, shaking her head at her niece. "The very question. When Matty finally did appear, I asked why a monkey arrived in solitary splendor in her brother's lovely coach while she appeared in hurly-burly fashion, not looking anything like a lady, and she said—she said"—Hester choked and waved her fan several times to refresh herself—"she said—as if it made any sense at all—that she had told Cecil she'd be a monkey's aunt before she rode in his coach, when she was quite able to hire one of her own and much preferred to do so."

Dru's shout of laughter betrayed her, and her aunt's tone was censorious. "Cecil is a very good brother to look after Matty so," she declared, "and she flouts him at every turn. The woman is mad, Drucilla. Quite mad."

Dru's lips twitched, and she decided not to contest her aunt's pronouncement, for she was eager to hear the rest of the story.

"Are you saying Matty was not in the carriage, Aunt Hester?" she asked solicitously, sending her aunt off again.

"That's exactly what I'm saying," Hester nodded vigorously. "Her brother's carriage arrives bearing a monkey and a mountain of luggage and no Matty.

"I can tell you, my dear, your mother and I were stunned. Completely stunned. I hope the shock has not been too much for dear Jane, for you know she has neither my constitution nor strength of mind."

Dru agreed readily with that, not telling her aunt that Lady Jane's strength of mind probably saw her through the unusual arrival quite well; indeed, knowing her mother, Dru was quite sure she had enjoyed it immensely.

"So there we were," Hester began again, Matty's transgressions too great to be forgotten quickly, "standing by that coach, peering in at that dratted monkey—a half-wild beast, probably with a disease, and it chattered at us nastily—and the wind was blowing, Drucilla, a very cold wind, and it's to be hoped we didn't catch our deaths—and along came another carriage. Naturally we again hastened to make your cousin welcome, Percival even going so far as to open the carriage door ahead of the footman."

Her eyes grew bright at the memory, and her voice trembled slightly as she fixed Dru with a dramatic stare. "And what do you think we found in that carriage?" she demanded in a tone which left no doubt that it had not been something she considered proper.

"Matty?" Dru asked sweetly, sure that it had not been.

"No," Hester answered sharply, and the snap of her fan showed she had been profoundly moved. "Not Matty. Just her dresser and her groom. Her *groom*, Drucilla! Riding in her carriage like a grand gentleman while Matty was out careening across the country like a—like a—there are no words to describe your cousin's behavior."

"Careening?" Dru asked, puzzled.

"Yes, careening," Hester snapped with a nod which sent her cap down over her left eye. She righted the offending article and continued. "You can imagine my feelings on not finding Matty in that coach, either." Dru smiled. She could indeed.

"So I asked those two—Matty's groom and dresser—where their mistress was, and the groom looked at me and said, 'She's gone off with Caesar, ma'am. She'll be along directly.'"

Hester paused, and her hands flew to her heart. "It brought on my palpitations, Drucilla. Had I died then, my death would have lain at Matty's door.

"'Who is Caesar?' I demanded, for it would be just like your cousin to run off with some unknown heathen, and my first thought was to apprise dear Cecil of the information that she had gone so that he could go after her—although why he would want to, when I think about it—but then the dresser spoke up and said that Caesar is Matty's dog, 'And she is quite safe with him,' she said. Oh Dru!"

Noting that Hester was losing herself in her sentence, something she was always prone to do but which grew more pronounced when she was agitated, Dru bit her lip to refrain from laughing. Her aunt was almost tearful as she continued. "A dog, Drucilla. My niece—however much I hate to admit it, she is my niece—riding across the countryside with only a dog for a companion. It is not seemly. It is not *done*!

"And when I told her groom how sadly lacking I found him in feelings of duty—for he should have ridden with her, he really should—even though she shouldn't have ridden, she really shouldn't—but when I took it upon myself to instruct him he looked at me—he looked me straight in the eye, Drucilla, I don't know what the world is coming to—and he said, 'Ma'am'—yes, he said 'ma'am', not 'my lady', and it's just like Matty to employ a groom who calls me 'ma'am'—he said, 'Ma'am, Miss Matty does what she wants to do. And when she tells me to get in the coach and ride, I get in the coach and ride. Nobody can follow Miss Matty if she don't want to be followed. And nobody can drive her, neither. It would take a fool to try. And I am no fool.'"

Hester dabbed at her eyes and breathed heavily of the pungent aroma of her vinegrette. "I nearly swooned, Drucilla. Baxley had to help me into the house. When I told Matty she should turn the man off immediately, she replied that he possessed an uncommon amount of good sense and that if I stay out of his way he will not offend me. As if I would have anything to do with a groom—oh, the woman is mad. I believe your mother was hysterical, for when I looked up from Baxley's arm she was laughing and laughing. It was a mistake of you to ask Matty here, Dru. A very big mistake.''

Dru ignored that comment, for she felt they had not yet reached the end of the story. "Aunt Hester," she asked curiously, "if Matty was not in Cecil's coach and she was not in her carriage, where was she?"

"I have told you," Hester answered reproachfully. "Off with that dog—that Julius—Emperor—whatever she calls him. Riding, Drucilla, Riding. Last night they stopped at a small inn along the way and what must your monstrous cousin do this morning but ride the last twenty miles. On horseback. Along the public roads, to be ogled by any commoner passing by—although who would ogle Matty—well, that is beside the point. It is too bad of her, Drucilla, it really is. And when I taxed her with it, she opened her eyes at me and said only, 'But it is a beautiful day for February, Aunt. A lovely day for a ride.' ''

"Matty did arrive, then," Dru said, knowing she should not prolong her aunt's agitation but reaping such enjoyment from the tale that she could not resist.

"Oh yes," Hester said, leaning back against the chair and again refreshing herself with her smelling salts. "Matty arrived, her hair in a tangle, her habit muddied, one glove lost—her hands are actually reddened, Drucilla, and her skin is rather brown, for she will not wear a hat—and accompanied by that—that—that dog, who is the size of a small horse and who you will, I am sure, confine to the stables."

It was perhaps unfortunate that at that moment said dog chose to enter the room where the ladies were sitting, using his nose to push open a door he found invitingly ajar. Caesar was losing no time accustoming himself to his new abode.

Inside he found two ladies, one of whom he had seen before. He advanced toward her slowly, inviting a pat, but the lady sat frozen on her chair, staring at him horrified. He nosed her hand in invitation.

"He's going to bite me, Drucilla," Hester shrieked, pulling back. "He'll eat me alive."

Dru laughed. "He only wants to be patted, Aunt Hester. Give him a pat."

Caesar glanced at the young lady who had just spoken. She might be an easier mark, for she was smiling at him, and he guessed her to be a human who understood a dog's needs. Yet manners prevented him from leaving the lady in front of him before she had been given her chance.

When the lady remained in her frozen position he nuzzled her hand again, and when he received no response he sighed. Humans could be so dense. He began to rise on his back legs, intent on putting his front paws on the lady's shoulders so that he could give her a friendly lick to give her the idea. His plan was never executed, for Hester, seeing him rise, rose faster, leaping to the edge of the chair on which she had been sitting and shouting, "Go away, you beast. Go away."

Caesar was surprised at such odd behavior. He barked. She screamed. He barked more, and Hester beseeched Dru to rescue her. Dru tried to rise, collapsed with laughter, and fell back into her chair. She called, "Here, Caesar," several times but could not get the words out clearly since they were garbled by the laughter in her voice and the tears running down her cheeks.

In desperation Hester threw her smelling salts at the dog; they missed him and landed several feet away. He obligingly retrieved them for her and brought them back to place them on the cushion at her feet. Fetch had always been one of his favorite games.

Hester screamed again, and Caesar barked invitingly. He didn't understand the rules of this game, but he would certainly try to play.

Dru at last managed to rise and laughing, had just gotten her arms around the dog's neck when a voice spoke from the doorway.

"Tell me, Aunt," Dru heard, "Is it now considered ladylike to stand on the furniture?"

Both Dru and Caesar turned at the sound of that voice, and the dog, delighted at seeing the human he adored most in the world, bounded toward her, throwing Dru off balance and leaving her in a laughing heap at her aunt's feet.

Matty smiled quizzingly at her, a twinkle in her eye. "No, I beg of you, Dru, don't get up," she said. "It's only me."

Giggling, Dru rose and advanced to throw her arms around her cousin. "Matty, Matty," she said as she hugged her. "I feel better already. I don't know when I've laughed so. Certainly not in the last two years."

Matty hugged her affectionately. "I see you've already made Caesar's acquaintance," she said; then a naughty gleam grew in her eye. "And I'm glad to see Aunt Hester has taken so readily to him."

Hester, realizing the figure she cut standing on the chair, descended with all the majesty she could muster, declining her nieces' offered arms with freezing civility.

"Your dog attacked me, Mathilde," she said haughtily. "I see he has no manners, either."

But Dru protested. "He didn't attack you, Aunt Hester. He merely wanted to be friends. He thought you were playing."

Hester favored her with a disapproving stare. "Already your cousin is affecting you, Drucilla," she said. "You know I never play. He attacked me. I suggest you send him to the stables immediately."

Since at that moment the "attacker" chose to sit at her feet and thump his tail invitingly, Hester felt the ground being cut away beneath her and decided to withdraw, saying grandly that her nerves had suffered a great shock at the beast's expense. The "beast" rolled onto his back with his paws waving in the air.

"I would say it is Caesar who has suffered the shock," Matty said consideringly, gazing at her faithful hound and with difficulty keeping the laughter from her voice. "I believe you frightened him, Aunt."

"Well!" Hester said, her hand on the doorknob. "Well!" Then, as she saw the smiles on both faces before her, the color rose in her own and she swept from the room in search of more sympathetic listeners.

Left to themselves the cousins embraced again, and Matty asked if her "ferocious beast"—who was now curled comfortably by the fire—was indeed to be banished to the stables.

Dru laughed and said she did not think such extreme measures would be needed if he could just be kept away from Hester.

"That's something both Caesar and I should try to do," Matty returned dryly, and the cousins began to laugh. Caesar opened one eye, grinned affably at them, and sighed himself to sleep again, leaving them to their conversation.

Chapter VIII

Percival Hovington's first visit to Morningdale Manor that day was instigated by his mother, who sped him on his way adjuring him to seek out his Cousin Drucilla, make himself pleasant to her, and extract from her all confidences concerning her possible marriage plans.

Convinced that he was a lady's man—and moreover, one who had an inside track because he had known the young lady in question from childhood—Percy assured his momma that this would not be the least bit difficult. Lavinia eyed him and sniffed, but he was not dismayed. He did not tell his mother, but privately he thought it would not be surprising to find his cousin harboring a secret, burning passion for him. That he aroused quite different emotions in Drucilla did not occur to him. Surely any woman he came in contact with would be affected.

(His Cousin Drucilla would have murmured, "How true," to

that, and would have been happy to tell Percival just how he affected her. Luckily for his self-esteem, she was not present to do so.)

Assuring his mother that he would have his cousin confiding in him immediately—and that he would inquire about the Morningdale painters' progress while he was about it—he hoisted himself into the smart curricle so begrudgingly lent him by his Uncle Edmund and was off. He was disappointed to find Drucilla out when he arrived and was debating whether he should await her return in the hopes his aunts would invite him for luncheon—a prospect which, from the look on his Aunt Hester's face, was extremely unlikely—or whether he should return to his Uncle Edmund's and try his hand at Drucilla later when the sound of an approaching carriage broke his concentration. He hurried out of the house with Aunt Jane and Aunt Hester and watched in growing amazement the arrival of his Cousin Matty.

The monkey in the first carriage startled him; the groom and maid in the second carriage shocked him; but when his cousin at last rode up on a lovely chestnut mare, which she appeared to handle with no trouble at all, he found himself entranced by a young woman who, years earlier, had threatened to push him down a well.

Ignoring his Aunt Hester's half-hysterics, he moved forward, enthusiastically exclaiming, "By jove, Cousin, you are complete to a shade—top drawer!" Matty, in the process of dismounting, turned at the sound of his voice, and a look of distaste crossed her face. She looked him up and down before murmuring, "And you are the bottom, dear Percy, the definite bottom," but if she hoped to put him off with that she was disappointed. He took no umbrage at her remark, knowing himself to be such a Tulip of Fashion that he realized at once that she was quizzing him, and he laughed heartily at her "droll remarks."

Matty quirked an eyebrow and smiled as if she would say more, but she was interrupted by her Aunt Jane's welcome as, with many happy hugs, that lady invited her to come into the house at once. Percy wasn't quite sure how it happened, for he was right behind the ladies as he started up the steps, but when the door closed he found himself on the wrong side of it. He raised his hand to knock to gain admittance, for he wanted to pursue his acquaintance with this cousin whom he felt he was seeing for the first time, but just as his knuckles touched the door he again pictured Hester's hysterics.

He paused a moment, thought deeply, and decided to return later in the day in the hopes of finding Dru—and her newly arrived cousin—at home. He was so impressed with that idea and his imagined plans of what he would say to each lady when he returned that he was able to deal with unruffled calm with his uncle's rude remarks about coming back to eat and wanting the horses put to again immediately after. Indeed, he smiled a superior smile which made his uncle wish to slap his face and said grandly that when he ruled at the manor, his uncle must drop in on him whenever he wished.

Muttering that he'd like to drop many things in on his nephew, the ill-tempered Edmund retired to his study, there to wonder why he hadn't had anything about visiting relatives written into the marriage settlements when he wed his wife.

Meanwhile, said nephew drove jauntily back to Morningdale, pictures of the ladies hanging on his every word as he delighted them with his rapier wit dancing through his mind. So engrossed was he in such thoughts that for several moments he did not notice the rider approaching him as he neared the manor drive. When he did see the horseman, it was with a stab of envy, for Percy could never see a man able to fill out a riding coat without shoulder padding without reflecting on the unfairness of nature. Unconsciously he touched his own shoulders, which sloped sadly, then bent a critical eye to the oncoming man's attire. His closer inspection of the rider convinced him that the gentleman's simple dress could not compare with his own fashionable clothing. Deciding that the rider must be one of the area gentry, Percival sat up straighter so that the man could better see—and perhaps count—the many capes on his greatcoat. Thinking that the gentry must be impressed by such a man about town as himself, he swiftly became convinced that if anyone on the road were to be envied that day, it was he. Believing that, he saw it as his clear duty to impress the horseman not only with his apparel but also with his ability to drive to an inch.

Were his Cousin Matty present, she would have said candidly that

Percy wasn't able to drive to a yard. Since she was not present to quash his actions, he fixed his hat at what he believed was a rakish angle (but which really managed to impair the vision of his left eye) and proceeded to whip up his horses just as he should have been slowing them for the turn. The grays, who had more sense than their driver, managed to swerve into the Morningdale lane while allowing only one wheel to momentarily wobble perilously close to the ditch. Percy, who felt he had proven himself at home to a peg, smiled and turned with a flick of his whip to catch the look of admiration on the horseman's face.

The horseman, who noticed how close that little whip flick came to knocking the driver's hat off, was not lost in admiration. In fact, if Crandon Pettigrew weren't such a good rider, he might not have avoided the near collision caused by "that dolt's" driving. Swearing savagely under his breath, he held his mount safe and thought blackly of persons who should never be allowed to take to the roadways except on foot.

It was only as he rode on that the comedy of the situation began to strike him, and he chuckled at the thought that the young popinjay just encountered must be making a romantic visit to Miss Wrothton. At that he laughed aloud. "I must say they deserve each other," he murmured, grinning at the picture of the impertinent young lady with the fiery temper matched to the plump, young dandy who couldn't drive horses any better than he could pick great coats. That thought sent him happily on his way.

Inside Morningdale Manor, Matty and Dru were delighting each other with stories of their adventures since they had last been together. Their delight was arrested at Baxley's announcement of Percy's arrival, but finding no way they could refrain from seeing him, the two exchanged looks of mutual chagrin before composing their faces for their cousin's grand entrance.

It was just as well that both young women were bent on composure, for otherwise the advent of Percival Hovington in all his glory might have betrayed them into most unladylike gasps. To see the hefty Hovington bursting through the doors with his legs encased in pale blue pantaloons and a yellow waistcoast struggling to stay closed across his chest—a waistcoat whose gaudily embroidered dragons vied for attention with the huge brass buttons on his topcoat—was enough to make even the most composed lady blink.

His collar points jabbed his cheeks relentlessly, and Matty rather feared one might put out his eye as he bent (with difficulty) to kiss her hand.

"My dear, dear Cousin," he intoned, oblivious to her efforts to remove her hand from his wet grasp. "How happy I am to see you again. Would that I might see more of you."

Dru choked as Matty told him practically that there was no more of her. "What you see is what I am, Percy," she began, which so amused him that he burst into laughter, asking Dru if she didn't think their cousin was the most droll person alive.

Matty rolled her eyes at Dru, who agreed that their cousin was surely the most consciously droll person, a remark which went by Percy but which made Matty hastily smother a laugh.

At last releasing Matty's hand with obvious reluctance, Percival was recalled to his true mission for visiting the manor by Dru's civil inquiry as to whether he would like a cup of tea. He assured her he would, then rather astonished her, when she handed him a cup, by seating himself on the sofa beside her instead of moving to the chair she had expected him to occupy.

With an arch smile he turned heavily to Dru and astonished her by asking if the bloom he saw in her cheeks might be attributed to an expected visit from her mysterious suitor.

"Mysterious—," Matty repeated, puzzled, but a quick glance from Drucilla made her subside.

"I'm expecting no mysterious suitor today, Percy," Dru returned tranquilly, passing him a biscuit in the hopes of moving his thoughts into a less dangerous train of thought. Unfortunately, he was not distracted.

"Now, Drucilla," he said playfully, waving the biscuit at her, "you can't fool me—"

"Nature already did that," Matty murmured, but Percy didn't hear her.

"You can tell me who this gentleman is," he cajoled Dru, putting one fat hand on her knee in a manner which made her long to box his ears. "I'm the perfect confidant for your little secrets."

"Really, Percy," Dru returned lightly, moving his hand from her knee to his own as Matty grinned in delight, "you let your imagination run away with you. There is no mysterious suitor coming. I've no secrets to share—"

"Which is a shame, when one has the perfect confidant at hand—," Matty murmured, causing Dru to choke and Percy to regard her doubtfully.

"You must know who it is, Matty," he suggested, but she shook her head vigorously, denying any knowledge of mysterious suitors.

Percy stared from one lady to the other, his raised eyebrows and pursed lips eloquently expressing his disbelief.

"I see I will have to guess," he said and proceeded to do so, sending Dru and Matty into peals of laughter with each name he suggested. Regarding the two with growing disfavor, he hit at last upon the gentleman he had seen on horseback that morning, "a tall, dark stranger, rather haughty appearing for country gentry—"

Matty was inclined to be amused at the thought of a tall, dark stranger, but the laughter in Dru's eyes was quenched by this last guess.

"Now you *are* being foolish beyond permission," she sniffed, glaring at her cousin in a way which took him aback and made Matty regard her with interest.

"Tall, dark stranger indeed! You must mean the abominable Crandon Pettigrew."

"Crandon Pettigrew?" Matty repeated, mystified. Percy crowed happily. "Me thinks the lady does protest too much," he quoted, delighted to have stumbled onto the truth. "You're going to marry Crandon Pettigrew." He paused. "Who is Crandon Pettigrew?"

Dru was only too happy to tell him. "Crandon Pettigrew is the most odious—the rudest—the least likely man I would ever marry. Do you understand that, Percy?"

He did indeed. Touching her hand in comfort, he consoled her for what he now saw as her unrequited love for a man who did not return her affection. "Poor Drucilla," he mourned. "No wonder you say such hateful things about him, trying as you are to hide your broken heart. I am so glad you have confided in me."

Matty, watching the scene with intense enjoyment, moved from her seat to the window where her stifled gasps of amusement might be more easily hid. Dru regarded her cousin in growing amazement as she begged him to use what little sense God gave him.

"Don't be such a dolt, Percy," she said. "I am telling you that I have no love for Mr. Pettigrew—unrequited or otherwise—"

"Of course you don't," he soothed in a tone which showed how much he disbelieved her.

"I wouldn't have Crandon Pettigrew if he begged me on both knees!" Dru cried, stamping her foot.

"Not very likely if he's already rejected you," Percy said, unwisely thinking aloud. Dru regarded him dangerously.

"Percival Hovington," she said slowly, speaking between gritted teeth, "watch my mouth. Listen to my words. Crandon Pettigrew has never rejected me. He does not like me. I do not like him. We detest each other. In fact—"

Percy regarded her doubtfully for a moment before asking why she had then led him to believe Pettigrew was her mysterious suitor. Matty dissolved into laughter, and Dru refrained with difficulty from hurling the tea tray at her dim-witted cousin.

"I never—," she began, but Matty was before her.

"I believe she was playing a May game with you, Percy," she said blandly, which so incensed the young gentleman that he rose at once to take his leave, bowing stiffly to each of the ladies and pausing at the door to say he knew when his presence was not welcome. Since that last statement sent both ladies into laughter, he left in a great huff, merely assuring Dru and Matty that he would return when they could be counted on "to behave as ladies."

"Well, I hope that means never," Matty remarked mildly as she wiped her eyes of the laugh tears which had appeared there. "I don't know *when* he'll be able to count on *me* to be a lady!"

Dru agreed but chided her cousin for telling Percy that she had been making a May game of him. Matty remained unrepentent, merely asking if she had wished to enjoy Percival's company any longer.

"Endure, more like," Dru returned, deciding that anything said to rid them of Percy was not such a bad thing after all. She would have changed the subject then, only Matty was keen to know more about Percy's belief in a mysterious suitor and more about the insufferable Mr. Pettigrew. Dru thus found herself confiding somewhat guiltily her earlier dinner conversation with the Hovingtons and telling her cousin about her disastrous meetings with Mr. Pettigrew. She ended by mentioning that she had also met the Duke of Ratchford with Mr. Pettigrew, and she wondered aloud how the personable Duke could be a friend of such an odious creature. Matty regarded her quizzically and professed herself interested in meeting "said creature."

Chapter IX

Matty got her hoped-for acquaintance with Crandon Pettigrew much sooner than she expected and under circumstances she felt left her at a most regrettable disadvantage.

Dru had ridden out to visit an ailing tenant, and Matty, with the laudable notion of removing herself and Caesar from Aunt Hester's vicinity, set off for a brisk walk in the woods. She, Dru, James, and her brother Cecil—before Cecil grew up to be so stuffy and long before James died—had often played there as children, and she had no fears of getting lost while the sun shone as brightly as it was that afternoon. Huddling her cloak more closely around her as proof against the February breeze, she spoke lightly to Caesar and set off for what had been her favorite trail when she was ten.

Once in the woods, the sun did not shine as brightly due to the thickness of the trees, and Matty found that the paths the four had traversed as children had long grown over with disuse. Matty couldn't decide if branches really did hang lower than they once had, ready to catch at a careless tendril of hair, but she was quite certain that at ten she had never been troubled by gnarled roots rising to catch an unsuspecting ankle. She was saddened by the sight of her childhood playground and thought fleetingly that what the woods really needed to put them to rights again was children. She remembered how enchanted and special the trees had seemed when the Fearsome Foursome, as they had christened themselves, slew dragons there.

Caesar, as if sensing her mood, nuzzled her hand, and as she stroked his head she smiled down at the big brown eyes raised to her. "Nothing ever stays the same, does it, old fellow?"

She gave herself a shake and laughed as Caesar did likewise, feeling as if they had now removed the mists of melancholy under which Matty so seldom labored, then set off briskly, for as she was ever wont to tell Aunt Hester, who thought her niece strode like a savage, Matty could not abide dawdling women.

"You know, Caesar," she said conversationally as they moved deeper into the woods, "you might not know it by looking at me, but I used to be able to climb any tree in this forest.

"Oh, it's not a forest, you say?" she continued as the dog cocked his head at her questioningly. "Well la, sir, you have fine notions indeed. Perhaps you are right, but people cannot be the Fearsome Foursome of the Forest without a forest, can they? Of course not," she said, giving his head a pat. "You're perfectly right."

The dog wagged his tail gently.

"There was one tree especially," she mused, looking up at the tall branches above her. "Down by the brook. We must definitely visit that tree. James couldn't climb it so he forbade me to do so. I had no intention of doing so until his order." Cacsar brushed against her, and she absently stroked his back. "I cannot stand to be ordered, Caesar."

At the sound of his name the dog looked up, then moved ahead of her down the path they were taking, seeking the promising scent of a rabbit or a covey of quail.

Matty looked after him and laughed. "Yes, sir, I am glad you find my story so fascinating. And this predilection you have for my company—you can hardly bear to be parted from me, can you?" By then the dog had disappeared around a bend in the path, and she hurried after him.

"Caesar," she called when she turned the bend and found him gone. "Caesar, you great hound, come here this instant. Cousin Dru will not take kindly to your disturbing her rabbits and birds. Caesar. Come sir. Come now."

But although an angry squirrel chattered busily at her from above as if to scold her disturbing his rest, no Caesar appeared. Matty looked up at the squirrel and laughed, dropping him a mock curtsy. "Pray excuse me, Sir Fuzzy Coat," she said, "but I seem to have lost my royal companion. Have you seen him?" As she moved away, the squirrel continued his angry chattering, reminding her forcibly of Aunt Hester.

Walking on down the path, she made her destination the brook and the infamous tree from which she had fallen and broken her shoulder after James had commanded her straitly to stay away from it. She knew that if she did not find her dog, he would eventually find her.

"What a fuss there was," she remembered aloud as she walked along. "James shouting it was my own fault when I fell and Cecil ringing such a peal over me while Dru danced around crying, 'Does it hurt, Does it hurt?' "

"We were so young," she murmured, smiling. "So very young."

Such musings were unlike her, Matty decided as she moved along, for she was not given to fanciful flights or dwelling on the past. Perhaps the forest really is enchanted, as we said so long ago, she thought with a smile, looking up to watch the sun as it threw patterns through the moving branches. As she did so her foot caught in one of the errant roots now dotting the path, and she fell hard.

"Damnation," Matty swore, reaching for the offending foot which lay awkwardly in a swirl of petticoat and root. Her frustration increased as she heard a chuckle nearby.

Looking up quickly, she saw a tall man standing on the other side of the brook, regarding her with cool eyes and a glinting smile.

"A quite fitting expression under the circumstances, I'm sure," he said mockingly, "but hardly one fitting a lady."

"A proper thought, sir," she replied quickly, anger at her situation taking control of her tongue. "But hardly a proper thing for a gentleman to say aloud." She allowed her gaze to travel over him slowly, then added, "If, of course, one is a gentleman."

An arrested gleam appeared in his eye, and he said smoothly, "Or if one is speaking to a lady."

Matty blushed, knowing she deserved that and sorry that the temper which so completely matched her hair had led her to speak unwisely. "I beg pardon, sir," she said stiffly, her hand reaching to feel the damage done her ankle. "I spoke out of turn."

"But not without provocation," the gentleman murmured, an understanding light in his eye.

That was too much for Matty. If he wouldn't accept her apology politely, she had at least tried. "Certainly not without provocation," she agreed, glaring at him.

The gentleman gave a shout of laughter and jumped the brook. Matty could not help noticing as he approached her that he moved with grace and that his clothes proclaimed him not only a gentleman, but a sporting gentleman.

"Are you hurt?" he inquired as he stood looking down at her.

Feeling at a great disadvantage because of her position on the ground, Matty glared up at him crossly. "Of course I'm hurt. I never say 'damnation' unless I'm hurt." She considered that for a moment, then added conscientiously, "Hurt or angry."

The gentleman grinned at this bit of incurable honesty and bent to examine the wounded ankle. Matty hastily pulled her skirts down over her foot. He looked into her eyes, and she saw furiously that his were laughing.

"I can hardly examine your foot if I cannot see it, now can I?" the gentleman inquired soothingly, and Matty felt a strong inclination to box his ears.

"I did not ask you to examine my foot, did I?" she challenged, then blushed at her angry words as his eyebrows rose.

"But could a gentleman do less?" he asked, and Matty noted with indignation that his mocking voice stressed the word "gentleman." "Our conversation only moments past led me to believe that I must in all things here act the part of the gentleman."

"Well, I'm sure it will be a great act," Matty retorted, then bit her tongue as the laughter grew more pronounced in his deep gray eyes.

"Nevertheless, I shall endeavor to play the role," he replied, reaching firmly for the wrist which held her skirt just as firmly over her ankle and, unable to resist, added, "After all, one of us should remember the position to which we were born."

He was pleased to see the color rise alarmingly in the lady's face at that shot, and his gaze was so fixed on her blushing countenance that he did not see danger approaching from behind. At that moment Caesar, triumphant from flushing a covey of quail, turned the last bend in the path, his tail wagging. At the sight of his mistress on the ground with a strange man bending over her, he paused but only for a second. His was a long and proud heritage, and he knew where his duty lay. Gathering himself together, he launched snarling, and the gentleman had only a moment to half turn before the black streak descending upon him had hit him full force, pushing him to the ground and settling threateningly on his chest, a deep growl rumbling in its throat.

"What the devil—," the gentleman began, thunderstruck, trying in vain to push the beast off. But the dog remained firm, its great paws resting threateningly on his shoulders. It was then that he indignantly heard the delighted laughter of the lady he had so recently been trying to assist.

"And what, may I ask, do you find so hysterical?" he inquired, pardonably annoyed as he turned his face toward her.

"You sir," she replied sweetly. "You."

The gentleman's face was a study of anger, exasperation, and confusion. Gradually enlightenment dawned, and in a frosty voice he ventured, "I take it, miss, that since you have no fear of this beast, he must belong to you."

"Very perceptive," she murmured.

"Then you will call him off immediately."

The lady shook her head sadly. "Not so perceptive."

There was a long silence before the gentleman tried again. "Tell me," he said, striving to make his tone conversational and wishing he could get his hands around the female's neck, "does this animal have a name?"

She nodded, grinning widely at him.

"Would you mind telling me that name?"

Matty lowered her eyes demurely to hide the lights which were dancing there. "I call him Killer, sir."

There was a pause. "Killer?"

"Yes sir. Because—" She let the explanation dwindle delicately.

There was another short silence as Matty considered the face of the gentleman in front of her and as the gentleman considered the face of the dog on top of him. A tentative try to shift the animal's weight off him brought another deep rumbling, and he quickly subsided.

"Tell me," he said at last, "do you ever intend to call him off, or are the three of us to spend the rest of our lives here? It is a charming spot, of course, and not for the world would I have you think I find the company less than delightful, but I cannot help but wonder if in time it might get a little tiresome."

Matty's gurgle of laughter bubbled again in her throat, and the gentleman glanced at her consideringly. "You have a lovely laugh," he said.

"For my part, sir, I find you merely absurd," she countered, and at his puzzled look continued, "I cannot see what it is which makes my cousin call you insufferable."

"Your cousin?"

"Unless it is your sharp tongue—"

"Your cousin?"

"Your ungracious manners—"

"Your cousin?"

"Or the fact that no matter how hard you act, you continually forget that your part is that of the gentleman."

"You must be related to Drucilla Wrothton," he said, his tone one of disgusted resignation.

Matty looked pleased. "No doubt it is our close resemblance which makes you say so," she replied dulcetly. "Everyone remarks upon it."

"No, madam, it is not," the gentleman retorted, stung into losing his temper again. "It is your hurly-burly gypsy ways and the lack of control you have over that runaway tongue, and let me tell you—" Here he so far forgot himself as to try to sit up, but the warning in Caesar's throat and the baring of that dog's excellent teeth made him hastily resume his reclining position.

"Yes?" Matty encouraged him brightly, thinking that if it were not for the increasing pain in her ankle, she would be enjoying herself immensely.

"Let me tell you—," the gentleman exploded, incensed, turning toward her so quickly that he surprised the gleam in her eye. He paused, and an answering gleam stole into his own.

"Let me tell you," he finished mildly, "that I am very glad your cousin is not here to enjoy this also."

Matty laughed delightedly. "How kind of you, sir, but be assured—it will lose nothing in the telling."

He glanced at her again, and his arrested look grew. "I accept your assurance. Indeed, I am sure you are right."

There was another short silence, after which the gentleman heaved an exasperated sigh and said, "Do you possibly suppose you could get this great beast off me? While I appreciate his heroic efforts to keep me warm, I rather think I prefer my fireplace for that."

Matty grinned. "Tell me, Mr. Pettigrew, do you intend to keep a civil tongue in your head?"

"Of course," he promised promptly. "One of us should."

Matty blushed and wished for the thousandth time that she didn't color so easily. "And will you go away and leave me alone?"

"Gladly."

"All right," she conceded and clapped her hands together. "Here, Caesar."

Relieved of the weight on his chest, Pettigrew rose hurriedly. "Caesar?"

"After the Roman emperor," she said as if to a child, the twinkle in her eye belying her kind explanation.

"Not Killer?"

Matty opened her eyes wide. "Why Mr. Pettigrew," she said, "whatever gave you that idea?"

His lips twitched. "A hearing problem, no doubt."

"No doubt."

He grinned, then quickly wiped the expression from his face. "I suggest that we quit sparring and turn our attention to your ankle, Miss—Miss—as my own sojourn there convinced me the ground is rather damp for prolonged sitting."

Matty ignored his obvious fishing for her name and, also ignoring the fact that she could not rise, reminded him that her ankle was quite fine and that he had promised to go away and leave her alone.

"I believe your ankle to be sprained," he said gravely, kneeling beside her and saying that it was foolish beyond permission to refuse aid when one so obviously needed it. Matty glared, and Caesar moved forward threateningly, but the man merely reached out to scratch his ears, commanding "Down, Caesar."

The dog was confused and turned to Matty for direction, but she was looking at Pettigrew.

"I did not make you free with my dog's name, sir," she said haughtily, then colored brightly as his short bark of laughter exploded on the air.

"Down, Caesar," he said again, and the dog, recognizing the voice of authority, settled himself comfortably on his haunches and grinned at the new human as if to explain that what had just passed had all been a silly mistake.

"Now, my dear, let us have no more of your nonsense," Pettigrew commanded as he might speak to one of his five-year-old nieces. "I am going to examine your ankle."

Matty gasped angrily and informed him that she was not his dear and that she did not speak nonsense. At his amused smile she bit her lip and amended the last comment by adding "not much."

But Pettigrew was ignoring her and had already extracted the foot from its tangle of skirt and tree root. "Your ankle is sprained," he announced as he saw the swelling all ready visible above her walking boot. "Just as I thought."

"Well of all the odious—," Matty snapped. "Sounding so satisfied—oh!"

He glanced at her questioningly, and she informed him roundly that she had no time for a sprained ankle.

His amusement at the angry look on her face was genuine. "Do you always plan sprained ankles for when you have time for them?" he asked.

"Don't be foolish," she snapped. "I never have time for them. I am never unwell. I am never injured. And I am perfectly capable of caring for myself." To prove that, she started to rise, and when she found she could not she fell back, furious.

"Perhaps you are, Cleopatra," he returned, a certain sympathy mingling with the laughter already dancing in his eyes. "Unhappily, your ankle is unaware of that fact. Therefore, this time I believe you need some help," and so saying he bent and lifted her easily.

"Oh!" Matty stormed. "You uncivilized—put me down. Put me down this instant."

The gentleman paid her no heed, starting back across the brook along the path from which he had come, an anxious Caesar whining at his heels. Where was this man taking his struggling mistress? To bite or not to bite, that was the question. As he had almost made up his mind to do so, the gentleman looked down and murmured sympathetically, "There, there Caesar, I shan't hurt your Cleopatra. Come along, old man, come along." Recognizing the tone of authority, Caesar subsided.

"And you, Cleopatra, stop squirming," he commanded to the indignant lady in his arms. "You're upsetting the dog."

The lady did indeed cease her movements but more in astonishment than in concession to his command. "WHAT did you call me?" she asked in amazement.

Pettigrew's lips twitched. "Cleopatra."

She opened and shut her mouth several times, then looked at him wryly. "My great beauty, no doubt."

Again his lips twitched, "That," he agreed, "and the fact that I can think of no one else who might come with Caesar."

"Brutus would," she snapped, but the gentleman quickly countered that it would be most ungallant of him to call her that.

Matty looked up into his face as if she would like to murder him, then gazed off across the meadow to the large house they were fast approaching.

"You know," she said conversationally, "I do believe my cousin was right."

"Your cousin?" Pettigrew repeated abstractly, the better part of his mind absorbed in wondering what he would do with this tiresome woman once he got her foot bandaged.

"Yes," Matty said, looking at him sharply to see what effect her words would have. "You *are* insufferable."

But if she hoped her words would cut she was disappointed, for the gentleman merely gave his explosive bark of laughter and carried her into the house.

Once inside he ignored the gaping footman, but Matty was much aware of the underling's startled appearance, and her discomfort increased as Pettigrew carried her swiftly to the library and deposited her unceremoniously on the couch. Matty was so busy glaring at him that she did not notice that the room was already occupied until a mild, "I say, Cran, that's no way to treat a lady," was heard from the occupant of a chair by the fire. Swerving toward that voice, Matty saw a puzzled face regarding her through his quizzing glass. She felt her ready blush rising, well aware of the picture she must present, and turned again to glare balefully at Pettigrew, who ignored her displeasure completely.

"You here, Sebastian?" he said carelessly to the chair's occupant.

The second man coughed apologetically. "I was invited, old boy."

"Of course," Pettigrew agreed absently, frowning down at Matty, who frowned back at him. "Shulton," he said to the very superior person who had just glided noiselessly into the room. "Bring me a basin of warm water and some bandages. And you'd better send for the doctor too, just to be sure."

"Very good, sir," Shulton replied and, ignoring Matty's protest, retired. Looking at his face, no one could tell that his master did not bring injured young women home every day of the week.

"Oh, I say," the second gentleman murmured sympathetically, rising from his chair to make his bow to Matty. "Hurt yourself, have you?"

"Twisted her ankle," Pettigrew answered briefly before Matty could reply, earning himself another fiery look from that lady. "The boot will have to come off. Have you got a knife about you?"

The second gentleman looked startled and patted his coat pocket ineffectually. "Well, no, Cran, I don't seem to—that is, it's not an article I usually carry on my person." His face fell. "I'd have brought one if I'd have known you'd be wanting it."

"Never mind," Pettigrew said, feeling his own pockets. "I believe I've got one after all."

Matty threw a searing look at the back of Pettigrew's head, which was all she could see as he bent over her offending ankle. Then she turned her attention to the second gentleman, who was looking downcast because he had not been able to help. "There's no reason you should have a knife," she informed him kindly. "It is not something a gentleman would be expected to carry."

Her emphasis on the word "gentleman" was not lost on Pettigrew, who grinned unseen as he finished cutting off her boot. "Sprained all right," he said with satisfaction. "Badly, too."

"Well, you needn't sound so happy about it," Matty snapped, her temper as shredded as the discarded boot now lying on the floor.

"Oh, no, miss," the second gentleman interrupted hurriedly. "I'm sure you misunderstand. Cran would not be glad you've hurt yourself. Really good sort of fellow, old Cran. That is, Miss—

Miss—'' He looked at her inquiringly as he became lost in his periods.

"Cleopatra," Pettigrew supplied smoothly.

"My name," Matty said through gritted teeth, ignoring Pettigrew's interruption and smiling engagingly at the second gentleman as she raised her hand to his, "is Mathilde Cresley. I am in the neighborhood visiting my cousin, Drucilla Wrothton."

"Of course," the gentleman said, brushing his lips to the extended hand, a courtesy which rather startled Matty and amused Pettigrew. "Miss Wrothton's cousin."

"You will note their close resemblance," Pettigrew interposed, straight-faced. "Everyone remarks upon it."

The second gentleman was plainly startled and didn't know what to say, and Pettigrew grinned openly at the violent look Matty threw him. Turning to address the second gentleman exclusively, she inquired sweetly, "And you, sir, are—''

"Forgive me, Miss Cresley. I have been remiss. I am Sebastian Weston."

"The Duke of Ratchford," Pettigrew added helpfully.

Again Matty ignored him. "But I should have known," she said, smiling brilliantly at the Duke, who sensed that all here was not as it first seemed. "My cousin has told me what a pleasant person you are. I should have guessed."

"She has?" Ratchford echoed, pardonably pleased.

"Of course," Matty smiled. "A *true* gentleman." As she said that she glanced at Pettigrew and was chagrined to see he took no umbrage at the pointed comparison. Indeed, he seemed to enjoy it.

"Miss Wrothton is too kind," Ratchford answered automatically, bowing again and wondering mightily what was going on. An inquiring glance in Pettigrew's direction was met by a most unhelpful grin.

Further conversation was ended when Shulton entered with the required water basin and bandages, which in his usual efficient manner he placed on a small table at the foot of the sofa. Pettigrew reached purposefully for the rolls of lint and gave further instructions. "Shulton, dispatch a man to the Wrothtons' with a message that Miss Cresley has met with a trifling accident and has taken shelter here.''

''Been kidnapped, more like,'' Matty snapped, for she had not appreciated Pettigrew's description of her accident as trifling. Shulton, blank-faced, ignored her and withdrew with a prim, ''Very good, sir.''

Matty sat up angrily and reached for the bandage Pettigrew held in his hand. ''I can bandage my own foot, thank you,'' she said hotly. ''It is such a trifling hurt.''

He hid a quick smile. So that had rankled, had it? Retaining his hold on the bandage, he reached for her foot. ''But my dear Cleopatra,'' he said, ''it is you who have assured me that you are never hurt, so if you are now hurt, surely you cannot be hurt badly.''

''No, of course I am not,'' she agreed irritatedly, wondering how this man always seemed to be one step ahead of her and vowing that one way or the other, she would yet get the best of him. ''And don't call me Cleopatra. And furthermore—'' She stopped abruptly and tried to rise. ''Caesar!'' she cried.

Ratchford gazed at her with great concern. ''I believe her injury is more than trifling, Cran,'' he said. ''I think she's in shock. Perhaps some tea—'' He moved to ring for Shulton.

But Matty was shaking her head impatiently, her face flushed. ''I am not out of my mind, my lord,'' she said. ''Caesar is my dog—in fact, he is the reason this abominable man calls me that abominable name—and he is out there somewhere. He followed us, but now he isn't here, and he doesn't know this country. I wonder—''

''Will you sit still?'' Pettigrew inquired in exasperation. ''How can I bandage your ankle if you don't hold still?''

''Did I ask you to bandage my ankle?'' Matty countered angrily.

''No, you asked me to leave you there. That was singularly foolish, too.''

''Well!'' she gasped and sank back against the cushions. Pettigrew glanced at the two bright spots glowing in her cheeks and at her overly bright eyes and sighed in resignation. ''Sebastian,'' he said, ''be a good fellow, and go see if you can locate a big black beast which answers to the name of Caesar. And be careful that he doesn't sit on you.''

Ratchford, obedient to his friend's request, had moved toward the library door, but at the last sentence he paused. ''Doesn't sit on me?'' he repeated, his brow wrinkled as if he could not have heard right.

''Don't worry, my lord,'' Matty replied brightly. ''He never bothers gentlemen.''

Looking at the spirited lady and his grinning friend, who had murmured ''touche'' at her remark, the Duke said, ''Quite,'' and went in search of the dog. He hadn't far to go, for he found the faithful hound waiting impatiently by the front door. Caesar had seen Matty carried in, and he was waiting for her to come out again. Since she had not come out, he was quite willing to go in search of her and did so enthusiastically, gamboling into the library and frisking joyfully at sight of his mistress; so joyfully, in fact, that he managed to knock over the basin of water in which her ankle had soaked.

''Uh, dear,'' Matty said guiltily. ''Caesar, come.'' She looked up into the amused face of Crandon Pettigrew and knew her face was as red as her hair. ''I am so very sorry.''

''Ah, no, Cleopatra,'' he returned with utmost affability, making her again yearn to box his ears. ''It is quite all right. Indeed, it is what I expect from you and your cousin. She and that Jade of hers sent us scouring the countryside, and your delightful dog assaults my person and soaks my carpet. Such well-trained animals.''

Ratchford looked at the young lady's face as she bit her lip in consternation and was moved to expostulate, ''I say, Cran, it's not that bad. Shulton will know what to do for the rug, and I rather enjoyed searching for the horses. It gave me a chance to see a great deal more of the countryside than I've experienced in years.''

Matty smiled at him with real gratitude, and he politely changed the topic by again suggesting tea. Matty agreed that would be nice, for she found she was feeling tired and sore and rather cold from her long sojourn on the ground.

''Such a true gentleman,'' she murmured loudly as Ratchford

moved to ring for tea. She avoided looking in his direction, but had she seen Mr. Pettigrew's face, she would have been most disappointed to find an even bigger grin there.

Silence lengthened in the library as the three waited for refreshments. It was broken unsuccessfully again and again by Ratchford, who struggled heroically to keep polite conversation flowing. He had little aid, for the lady was apt to answer only in monosyllables and Pettigrew not at all. Had it not been for his good breeding, he might well have lapsed into the sulks himself. As it was, he continued to chat with himself, vowing silently that his friend would soon have to explain himself for this strange start and thinking that it had better be a very good explanation.

It was a grateful Duke who saw the tea tray rolled in. Matty had just received a cup of the restoring brew from Shulton's hand when the doorbell pealed, followed by a sharp tattoo on the door. Acting as if such disturbances of Green Corner's tranquility were normal, the butler moved with measured tread out of the library and to the front hall.

As he opened the door, a loud and agitated female voice was heard. The voice was unknown to the two gentlemen, who gazed inquiringly at each other, but it was well known to Matty, who looked rueful and tried in vain to straighten her hair and smooth her gown.

Pettigrew gave her a quizzing glance as Shulton returned to the library with his most measured pace followed closely by Matty's Aunt Hester.

Chapter X

"Aunt Hester," Matty said faintly. "What a pleasant surprise."

"Surprise?" that good lady sputtered. "Why should you be

surprised?'' She moved into the room like an aged and agitated butterfly, coming to rest beside her niece and, hand over her heart, announced dramatically, ''I have come to rescue you.''

Matty was puzzled. ''Rescue me, Aunt Hester? It's very kind of you, but I have already been rescued. And I believe once is enough for any day.'' She glared at Mr. Pettigrew, who was now placing a chair for her aunt, the two gentlemen having risen when the older lady entered the room.

But Hester, this latest escapade of Matty's added to her long list of shocking behavior, was not to be put off. Giving her famous snort, she fixed Pettigrew with an icy stare and sputtered, ''Rescued indeed. A gentleman finds an unaccompanied lady lying injured in the woods—at least, that is what I gather happened from talking with that terribly dense young man who brought us word of your accident—and why you must go out unaccompanied, Matty, when you know it is not ladylike—although that has never weighed with you—''

''Aunt Hester, Caesar was with me,'' Matty protested, acutely aware of the scene her aunt was making. ''And I was walking on Wrothton land, after all.''

''Ah ha!'' her aunt said, pouncing on that. ''If you were on Wrothton land, what are you doing here? Answer me that, miss. Answer me that!''

Matty groaned in exasperation, and Pettigrew came unexpectedly to her aid, saying that although he had found Miss Cresley on Wrothton land, she had been closer to Green Corners than to Morningdale, and he thought it best to carry her to the nearest shelter.

''You thought,'' Hester repeated bitterly, rounding on him. ''You thought. HA.'' Matty winced at that ''ha,'' and Pettigrew appeared rather taken back. ''It is apparent to me that you never thought at all, young man,'' Hester said crossly, ''for it you had, you would realize how it looks for an unmarried young woman to be in a bachelor's establishment—although Martty is not so young, after all, and I acquit you from having any improper designs upon her, for after all, it *is* Matty—but be that as it may, the situation is still highly improper and appears quite compromising, and I will not have it. So I have come for my niece. Come Matty," she said regally and turned to sweep out of the room. Matty remained where she was.

"Well?" Hester demanded.

"You're forgetting one thing, dear Aunt," Matty said as that good lady paused at the doorway.

"And what might that be?"

"I cannot walk."

Hester was chagrined, for despite their differences she was genuinely fond of her niece. "You mean you really are badly injured?" she asked, hurrying back to the sofa where Matty reclined. "My dear, you do look pale—" She reached. out to touch Matty's forehead but hastily withdrew her hand as Caesar's head appeared next to his mistress. He had been catching a dog nap behind the sofa, but this new arrival had wakened him.

"That beast!" Hester gasped, turning rather pale herself. Said beast thumped his tail at her.

"He won't hurt you," Matty assured her wearily, and dubiously Hester inched her way forward until she could seat herself by her niece. Suddenly a thought occurred to her.

"Mathilde," she demanded, "you didn't fall out of a tree again, did you?"

Pettigrew choked, and Matty wished disgustedly that her aunt's memory were not so good.

"Do you fall out of trees often?" he inquired politely.

"Of course not," Matty said. "It has been several years since I've even climbed a tree and considerably longer since I fell out of one. I don't know why one's childhood must follow one forever."

"Probably because one never outgrows it," Pettigrew murmured, but the lady could only dart daggers at him with her eyes, for her aunt had again demanded her attention by repeating her question.

"No, Aunt Hester, I did not fall out of a tree. I merely tripped on the root of one, injuring my ankle, which I must say hurts like the devil."

"Matty!" Hester gasped. "Such talk in mixed company! She is probably feverish," she said hastily to the gentlemen, one of whom nodded understandingly and the other of whom looked exceedingly skeptical. Turning to the more agreeable gentleman, she inclined her head graciously and acknowledged him as the Duke of Ratchford, "For," she said, smiling at him in a way which astonished her niece, "you've got quite a family resemblance to your father, my lord."

Then she turned back to Matty, and her smile vanished. "Well, you've done it this time, miss, for how we're to get you home—of course. Mr. Pettigrew, you carried her here, you must carry her to the coach immediately."

But Mr. Pettigrew had no intention of doing so. Instead he informed her that Miss Cresley had suffered what he believed to be a severe sprain and he thought it better that she remain where she was at least for a night. Hester colored alarmingly at that idea and her chest swelled. Matty, knowing the signs, sighed and waited for the impending storm to break, but the Duke of Ratchford hastily stepped into the breech, saying that he had seen the doctor's gig approaching as he stood gazing out the window and he rather thought that gentleman would be the one to decide if Miss Cresley could be moved at the moment. Pettigrew and Hester glared at each other, then agreed that that was indeed the most sensible course to follow. Matty thought gratefully that the Duke really was a most conciliating man.

The doctor, an old family acquaintance who had set Matty's shoulder, was shown into the room just then and, upon seeing his patient, considerably incensed that lady by asking, as Aunt Hester had, if she had been falling out of trees again. Pettigrew burst into laughter, Matty frowned darkly at him, and the doctor suggested that everyone but Miss Cresley leave the room for a few moments. When they were all admitted again he informed them that he thought it best that Matty not be moved for the evening, "Although I'm sure that by tomorrow she'll be able to travel in your coach," he said to Hester, forestalling her impatient outburst.

"But it will not *do*!" Hester almost wailed. "It is highly improper that she should stay here. Every tongue in the district will be wagging."

Matty sighed, for the throbbing pain in her ankle was moving up her leg and she felt unequal in sparring with her aunt.

"My dear Aunt Hester," she said, "you've often told me that the gossips of the district long ago gave me up so I don't see what this latest indiscretion—as you choose to call it—will matter. I certainly don't wish to impose on Mr. Pettigrew's kindness"—here she refrained from looking at that gentleman—"but I really do not feel up to jouncing across the February ruts in the road tonight. I am sure I will feel much better tomorrow."

"But Matty," Hester remonstrated, for she was sincerely shocked, "how can you even think of such a thing? To spend the night in a strange man's house—"

Matty regarded her would-be host from under her lashes. "Well, he certainly is that," she agreed, causing Pettigrew to grin, but Aunt Hester had not been listening.

"You young people are too loose by half," Hester pronounced, "although you always have been the most hurly-burly girl—not that you're a girl any longer—"

Matty shut her eyes resignedly, knowing that her aunt could go on like this forever, but it was the doctor who, casting a quick glance at her from under his bushy eyebrows, settled the matter by saying his patient was looking quite fagged and by suggesting that she be carried to a bedchamber immediately. He added that he was sure Miss Cresley had a maid who could come and share her room, protecting her reputation and bearing her company at the same time. Pettigrew added that his housekeeper had the highest moral character and would have him out of the building in a trice if she thought he had any evil designs on a young woman of Miss Cresley's quality, and with that Hester had to be content. Far from reconciled to the situation, she did realize that Matty was looking quite pale and understood why the idea of several jolting miles in a carriage might be even more than her usually indomitable niece was up to.

"Well—," she clucked uncertainly as Pettigrew ignored her and bent to pick Matty up, "if you think so, doctor—" By now her niece was out of the room, being borne upstairs in Pettigrew's arms, and she hurried after them. Standing at the bottom of the stairs, she assured the fast-vanishing Matty that she would send Polly over with her things. Considerably agitated, she allowed the Duke to escort her out of the mansion and into her waiting carriage. Ordering Ben Coachman to spring the horses—an order so unusual from her that he did not believe he had heard right—she settled back onto the cushions and fretted impatiently until she arrived at Morningdale.

Once home Hester found Jane looking anxious and Dru pacing the floor. Glad to have such an attentive audience, she told them of Matty's recent accident, making it clear that she thought it just like her niece to sprain her ankle in such an unladylike fashion.

She finished her tale with, "And we must hurry and send Polly to her immediately, for while the Duke of Ratchford is a perfect gentleman, I cannot vouch for that Pettigrew, who, I can assure you, dear Jane, is just as insufferable as Drucilla has said. You would not credit the high tone he took with me when he said Matty could not come home. Why," she said irrelevantly, "I was reminded of my sainted Jonathan—God rest his soul—"

She paused as Dru rose from her seat and inquired where her niece was going. Upon learning that that young woman planned to change into her riding dress and accompany Matty's maid, Hester was quite appalled and said so. Since she often appalled her aunt, Dru was not impressed and hurried off. She believed that Matty must indeed be in pain to agree to spend the night in the abominable Mr. Pettigrew's home. Not that she believed he had designs upon her cousin's person, for even she could not believe him guilty of that, but she did think her presence might save her cousin from an evening spent in his odious company. Flinging on her cloak, she followed Polly down the stairs, there to be met by her aunt and mother.

Hester tried again to dissuade her from accompanying the maid, pointing out that she would have to ride home alone and noting with a sniff that *ladies* should never ride alone, especially at night. Dru pooh-poohed such advice, and her aunt promptly threatened to retire to her room with a headache, declaring that she could not believe how short a time it had taken Matty to turn her proper cousin into a regular ragshag. She was incensed when Dru seemed rather pleased with that description and took herself off without a backward look. Jane smiled understandingly at her daughter, bade her tell her cousin they were all thinking of her, and reminded her to be careful.

In a short time Shulton was opening the main door of Green Corner's to them, and, showing no surprise at seeing two ladies where he had expected to see one, bowed slightly and led them to the library where the Duke and Pettigrew sat amiably discussing the world over a bottle of the latter's best port.

Upon Dru's breathless entrance they both rose, one gazing in admiration at the young lady before him, the other raising an eyebrow at her windblown appearance. Dru had kept up with Polly, whom Matty had selected as a maid because she was more at home on horseback than in a lady's chamber; and the ride to Green Corner's had been fast and furious, Aunt Hester having taken the greatest pains to impress upon the maid's mind the need to arrive at that decadent den as quickly as possible to save her mistress.

"But where is Matty?" Dru questioned, for it was apparent she was not in the room.

"Upstairs, resting comfortably," the Duke assured her quickly, moving forward with a warm smile and drawing her toward the fire. "May I suggest that you warm yourself here for a moment while her maid steps upstairs to see if she is sleeping?" He smiled pleasantly at Polly as he spoke and placed a chair for Dru. The maid dropped a curtsy and departed, anxious to see her mistress.

Meanwhile, Pettigrew lazily observed Drucilla's dishevelled appearance and inquired if she too labored under her aunt's misapprehension that he had evil designs upon her cousin's virtue.

Ratchford started and turned amazed eyes upon his friend, and Dru fired up quickly. "Certainly not," she said coldly, casting him a look of great dislike. "My cousin is more than capable of taking care of herself, and it would take a better man than you to compromise her virtue if she were to choose that it shouldn't be compromised—" She broke off, aghast at her unruly tongue, and her discomfort was heightened by Pettigrew's burst of laughter. She did not find the situation at all humorous and stiffened.

"Sir," she said frigidly, "I shall not remain in this room to hear my cousin laughed at. She is the finest, most capable, kindest person imaginable, and if you, like so many others, find her odd, that is your loss, sir, not hers.''

"Ah, Miss Wrothton, believe I was not laughing at your cousin," Pettigrew replied amusedly.

"You weren't?" she asked suspiciously.

"Assuredly not. I was laughing at you."

"Oh!" Her gasp made him grin more widely and brought a look of shocked reproof from his friend. Before she could reply, Polly appeared in the doorway, saying that Miss Matty was anxious to see her cousin, and Matty's cousin, just as anxious to be gone from the room, swept out, head high. Her anger was not decreased when, her foot on the first stair, she heard Pettigrew laugh again.

"That man is insufferable!" she said, storming into the pleasant room where Matty lay propped among the pillows of a four-poster bed. "Insufferable!"

"The Duke?" Matty inquired innocently, to which Dru replied that of course she did not mean the Duke—for a finer, more thoughtful gentleman she had yet to meet—but that odious, loathsome, despicable Pettigrew.

"He laughed at me, Matty," she said, the wrongs she had just suffered burning grievously in her mind. "He LAUGHED at me! Oh!"

Matty informed her mildly that he had laughed at her, too, but rather than appeasing Drucilla, this seemed to fuel that young lady's anger.

"How dare he!" Dru sputtered. "Who does he think he is?"

"An actor," Matty replied promptly, causing Dru to pause in her mutterings.

"An actor?"

"He acts the gentleman," Matty explained.

"Not well he doesn't!"

Matty agreed, schooling her lips not to smile. "I am afraid Kean need not worry about competition from that quarter," she agreed sadly.

Reluctantly Dru grinned. "Matty, I don't know how you do it," she said. "You are the only one I ever knew who could laugh me out of my bad humors." She hugged her cousin affectionately, and her conscience smote her as she realized her mind had been so preoccupied that she had not even inquired after Matty's ankle.

Her cousin assured her cheerfully that it was still there and asked what it was which had fueled her temper so. Dru explained darkly about Pettigrew's unfortunate remark about evil intentions, then ventured on a little joke as she asked if her cousin's virtue was still intact.

"Ah yes," Matty sighed, "and likely to remain so. Aunt Hester made it clear to all of us that she considered it impossible that anyone—even Mr. Pettigrew—could have any interest in compromising my virtue."

Puzzled that her cousin seemed distressed at that assertion, Dru patted her hand consolingly and changed the subject. She changed it many times in the next half-hour, and Matty soon realized in amusement that no matter what they meandered into talking about, Dru always brought the topic back to the admirable qualities of the duke of Ratchford.

"Such a gentleman," Dru enthused. "How he and Pettigrew can be such friends—"

"But look at us," Matty protested, "We are such good friends, besides being cousins, and Aunt Hester will tell you that we are even more different from each other than Pettigrew and the Duke."

But that Dru would not allow, even after Matty told her that sometimes when they walked into a room together she could mentally hear Aunt Hester looking at Dru and murmuring, "Silk purse," and at Matty and muttering, "Sow's ear." That did make Dru laugh delightedly, though, and so they spent a happy hour, interrupted at last when Mr. Pettigrew's upright housekeeper scratched at the door with a tray of supper for Matty.

"Mr. Pettigrew requests the honor of your presence for dinner," she said to Dru, dropping her a respectful curtsy. "He and my lord Duke are waiting for you below."

Dru demurred but Matty would not hear of her missing her dinner, so at last she reluctantly followed the housekeeper from the room, sped on her way by her cousin's wicked reminder to keep a civil tongue in her head, and if the conversation should lead to blows, to lead with her right.

Chapter XI

Later that night, after Dru passed the evening under review, she would be satisfied that she had followed Matty's orders well—at least, as well as could be expected with Mr. Pettigrew nearby. As she drifted off to sleep, she felt content that she had kept her temper in check admirably, even though her odious host had done little to help her do so.

Upon leaving Matty's room, she had followed the housekeeper back to the library, where both men stood before the cheerful fire. The Duke again held a chair for her, bestowing upon her his most attractive smile, which Dru found more warming than the fire. She smiled back, just as Pettigrew, a growing glint in his eye, asked if she had found her cousin in good spirits.

"As good as can be expected, thank you," she replied stiffly, quite able to refrain from smiling at him.

"I hope she will be recovered quickly," the duke said, concern apparent in his face. "A sprain can be quite painful and so tiresome. Especially if one is an active person, and I am sure your cousin is active."

Again Dru smiled at him, appreciating his concern. "Indeed, Matty is not used to being off her feet," she agreed. "I am sure it will be most trying for her."

"Oh, I am sure you and your cousin are both quite used to being trying—or I should say, to trying times," Pettigrew interrupted smoothly, causing her to glare at him again. Thereafter the conversation lagged, for Pettigrew was disposed to staring into the fire, and Dru was quite content to remain quietly glaring at him. For the second time that day, the duke's good breeding saw him through a trying time, all efforts of conversation directed toward Pettigrew meeting with monosyllabic answers, with those directed to Dru doing little better. Finally the lady, after directing another darkling glance at her host for his rude behavior, rattled gamely to the Duke's aid, earning her a look of gratitude from Ratchford who was growing quite tired of talking to himself. They continued to converse politely but languidly, for Pettigrew's lengthening silence did nothing to improve their moods. It would not be an exaggeration to say that both brightened considerably when dinner was announced, although each was too polite to admit it.

Shulton's welcome announcement moved the party to a small but elegantly appointed dining room where a fire glowed cheerily, casting warm shadows upon the wainscoted walls. Candelabras on the table and the sideboard held an abundance of candles which added light to the setting, and as the first course arrived Dru realized that she was indeed famished. As such, her mind fastened on the excellent dinner now being set before her, and her part in any conversation languished, leaving the Duke again wondering if he sounded as foolish to the others as he did to himself.

Halfway through the second course, Dru almost failed to keep Matty's warning in mind, for it was then, as she was eating heartily, that Pettigrew's smooth voice interrupted the Duke's manful attempts at conversation by saying, "I am glad to see that your concern for your cousin has not in any way diminished your appetite, Miss Wrothton."

Dru choked, visions of Aunt Hester warning her always to eat like a bird in company rose in her mind, and she looked hastily into the laughing eyes regarding her well-filled plate. She felt her cheeks growing red, but before she could reply, a shocked "I say, Cran!" issued from the Duke, who was regarding his friend in amazement.

"What a devilish—I beg your pardon, Miss Wrothton—thing to say, Cran," the Duke said rebukingly. "I don't know what's gotten into you." Then he smiled at Dru. "I enjoy seeing a woman wise enough not to think she has to pick at her food for appearances' sake if she is indeed hungry. And I am sure that with all you have endured today, you must be exceedingly hungry."

Dru's look of thanks was eloquent, and the Duke felt himself amply rewarded. The look she threw Pettigrew was also eloquent but of an emotion in no way resembling thanks. That seemed to increase his amusement a great deal, and Drucilla's annoyance grew accordingly.

"I believe, sir, that you take great joy in baiting me," Drucilla said stiffly, setting down her fork and preparing for battle. Matty's advice to lead with her right floated through her mind, bringing a twitch to her lips which was promptly and sternly banished.

But before Pettigrew could reply, the Duke once again hurled himself into the breech.

"Oh, no, Miss Wrothton, I assure you. The best of good fellows, old Cran. Sometimes he says things that do seem a trifle odd, perhaps, but that's just the way he is." Then, realizing that he had just described his best friend as odd, the Duke hastened to set that straight. "That is—well—at any rate, I don't think one can accuse him of baiting females.

"I tell you what it is," he said confidentially as inspiration struck. He lowered his voice and spoke directly to Dru, as if his host were not in the room. "It's the smoked oysters." He regarded those items which were among the delicacies on his plate.

"Smoked oysters?" Dru repeated incredulously.

"Yes," Ratchford continued in his confidential tone, nodding vigorously. "I've known Cran for a long time, and I've noticed they always seem to put him a trifle out of curl." He paused, and, in the tone of a man making a great confession, added, "Myself, I should never eat cabbage."

For an instant Dru stared at him amazed, but her attention was distracted by the strangling sounds issuing from her host. Presently he gave up all attempts to maintain his composure and burst out laughing, shaking his fork at his grinning friend.

"The oysters, Ratchford?" Dru had never seen him laugh so before, and she thought critically that it did much to improve his figure. "The *oysters*?"

Dru turned from one gentleman to the other in puzzlement, for now the Duke was grinning widely as Pettigrew continued to laugh. Finally the latter turned to her and, holding up his hands in mock defeat, said, "I beg of you, Miss Wrothton, that you will never again accuse me of baiting you, for you can see to what extremes my friend will go to excuse my behavior. I shudder to think what my cook would do if Sebastian's hasty words ever came to his ears, for the poor man prides himself on his oysters. I would hate to have him leave my establishment for that ill-chosen slur on his competence." Then he started to grin widely, and with an "Oh, Lord, the *oysters*!" was off into laughter again, this time joined by his two companions. Dru thought him much nicer when he was not mocking her.

Finally he regained his composure and stretched his hand out to her, saying with a smile, "Come, let us cry friends, or at least declare a truce for the rest of the evening, for I cringe to think what dish on my menu might next come under Sebastian's censure if his imagination is further tried."

Dru agreed to the truce, for she preferred to eat her dinner in peace. She held her own counsel on whether they could be able to cry friends, for she had many doubts on that subject.

Not quite sure of all the undercurrents which had just been at play, Dru was quite certain of one thing, and that was that the Duke had again come to her rescue, for which she was quite grateful. Bestowing upon him her most dazzling smile, she assured herself that she had not really needed to be rescued, for she believed she could handle Mr. Pettigrew herself. Yet somewhere in the back of her mind a small voice decided it was rather nice not to have had to.

Supper proceeded pleasantly after that, with Dru more than a bit surprised that her host could converse so knowledgeably on so many subjects. She was also pleased to find that neither gentleman seemed shocked that she had a number of opinions of her own—indeed, they seemed to encourage her to share them. She spared a bitter thought for those gentlemen of her acquaintance who were appalled to find a lady of quality could take an interest in both government and foreign affairs.

Thus she was particularly warmed when the Duke nodded in affirmation as she spoke of the need for better conditions for children left on the parish, saying, "It is a pleasure to meet a woman as well versed as yourself, Miss Wrothton. So few women seem concerned with such matters."

Before Dru could reply, she was interrupted by Pettigrew, who said, "It is my guess your cousin might be one of the few, however."

Dru nodded, pleased and rather surprised that such a boorish man should recognize Matty's intelligence after their short acquaintance.

"Yes, indeed," Dru agreed warmly. "In fact, it was Matty who first interested me in these sorts of things. She does a great deal for orphans in her neighborhood—much to her brother's annoyance, for he considers that most unladylike. And speaking of Matty, I really should take my leave of her and be on my way. I thank you for the dinner and for your assistance to my cousin Mr. Pettigrew." With that she rose, and the gentlemen rose with her.

"I will have your carriage sent around, Miss Wrothton," her host said, but she only laughed, saying that if he could do that he was a magician, since she had come on horseback and intended to return the same way. He bowed and said he would have her horse saddled, but the Duke interrupted to ask, "Do you mean you are riding, Miss Wrothton?"

As she assented, he looked surprised and asked, "Alone?" Dru laughed and said he was a man after her Aunt Hester's heart; then she blushed as she realized that at present almost any man Dru came in contact with was after her Aunt Hester's heart.

The Duke did not know the reason for the blush, but he was enchanted by it and asked to be allowed to escort her home. "I would not like to think of you riding alone at night."

Dru smiled in amusement. "I am quite used to riding alone, my lord," she assured him.

But the Duke was insistent, and after Dru had made her farewells to Matty and seen her settled for the night, the lady and the gentleman rode off together, accompanied by Caesar, Matty having felt that Pettigrew's hospitality should not be tried further by her large dog. In truth, Dru realized, she was quite happy to have his company.

The February evening was the type which Morningdale's old gardener, once a sailor for His Majesty the king, said sped ships at sea, and Dru loved the brisk though cold breeze blowing the clouds across the half-moon, making it appear and disappear again as if the heavens were an old man with one winking eye.

"I always think such nights like this are made for adventure," she said to the Duke, tying her bonnet more closely against the wind. "A night for highwaymen or smugglers or headless horsemen. Don't you?"

The Duke nodded solemnly, saying that if they didn't see at least one headless horseman on the ride home, he would feel deprived indeed. Dru smiled at his willingness to enter into her play, then asked him rather wistfully if he had had many adventures in his travels to America and the Continent.

The Duke, who had bivouacked in filthy cottages and holey tents, privately thought that adventure is not all it is proclaimed to be, but he decided not to say so, knowing one never realizes that until one tries it. Instead, he suggested that everyone has adventures, "especially on nights like these."

"Have you ever met a highwayman?" Dru asked hopefully, and the Duke had to admit that he had not, adding that perhaps tonight would be the night.

"Well," Dru said, happy with this flight of fancy, "then perhaps we should ride fast to avoid being kidnapped by dashing highwaymen. Don't you think so?"

The Duke agreed that he had no desire to be kidnapped by a highwayman, dashing or otherwise. Dru asked if he had his small sword beside him, just in case, and the Duke replied regretfully that he must have left it with the knife her cousin had stood in need of earlier. Then he had to explain about the knife Pettigrew had wanted to cut off Matty's boot, and that naturally led to Matty's comment that a gentleman couldn't be expected to carry a knife, a comment which made her cousin cry, "Well done!" and laugh heartily. So they rode conversing amiably for a while, until at last an owl hooted nearby, causing Jade to shy momentarily. Dru quickly brought her under control, said, "Ah, the sound of a highwayman for sure. Let us be off," and gave Jade her head. "To the bridge," she shouted to the Duke as both horses broke into a full gallop with the dog in hot pursuit.

Dru felt her bonnet fall back onto her shoulders as she rode, and her hair was soon blowing in the wind. She thought happily of how she enjoyed the feeling of the wind in her hair and the steady rhythm of Jade's hooves flying below her, the briskness of the February night, and the muted light thrown by the old moon. Her blood quickened as she urged Jade on after the Duke's stallion. She might be on the shelf, as Aunt Hester was so fond of saying, but she vowed she would never be too old for adventure. Ahead of her the bridge loomed, appearing ghostly in the dim moonlight, and the Duke was already slowing his horse as he approached it.

He was laughing and breathless as Dru rode up; a lock of hair hung across his forehead, the moon's sudden emergence from behind a gust-driven cloud shone upon the reckless sparkle in his eye. As if seeing him for the first time, Dru noted with approval the high forehead and fine facial structure which framed his friendly eyes. She found herself thinking that his quiet confidence made him quite superior to his friend Pettigrew's arrogant manners.

Sebastian for his part noted a similar sparkle in his companion's eye, as well as the way her windblown hair framed her face in the moonlight. Suddenly he felt shy and commented, "What a lovely spot," to fill the awkward silence as they rode across the bridge.

"It is," Dru agreed. "My brother James and I used to play here often. Though of course we didn't come here at night. I don't think I've ever seen it more beautiful."

"I don't believe I've ever met your brother," the Duke said, wondering if the young man had come up to town while he was on his travels. "I would like to do so."

"I wish you could meet him," Drucilla said softly, "for I'm sure he would have liked you so much. But he died nearly a year ago in a curricle accident. My brother was a splendid whip but inclined to be reckless.''

The Duke murmured his condolences, and they rode in silence for a time. At last Dru shook off her sadness and asked her companion if he planned to make a long stay in the neighborhood. He replied readily that he planned to stay long enough to put Maplehurst into the shape it was intended to be, for he felt it had been allowed to fall into disrepair. Dru found herself hoping it would take an extended time to complete his task.

''I like the country,'' the Duke continued conversationally. ''London grows tedious so quickly, especially when one is considered a most eligible match.'' Dru couldn't be sure, but she thought he shuddered in the faint light. ''You've no idea, Miss Wrothton, what it is to have some matchmaker on the catch for a title and fortune for her little girl. I grow so tired of balls and routs. But perhaps you enjoy them?''

''Oh, no,'' Dru chuckled. ''My views on balls are the bane of my aunt, although for all that she is at present turning Morningdale inside out for just such an event. You will no doubt be invited, but I will understand if you are called away on urgent business at the appointed time. I would not for the world subject you to what you left London to escape, for I know that there will be a number of anxious mamas with their eyes open for eligible bachelors at my ball. Indeed,'' she added feelingly, ''my aunt will be one of them.''

The Duke started. ''Does your aunt have an eligible daughter?'' he asked warily, wondering if he should stay out of that lady's way in days to come.

''Not at all,'' Dru laughed. ''She has something much worse, an overly eligible niece who is quite on the shelf.''

''Oh, I would not describe Miss Cresley so,'' the Duke protested.

''Neither would I,'' Dru agreed, laughing again. ''I am talking about myself. Quite on the shelf. Beggars can't be choosers. Past praying for. Do you know any other descriptions? I am sure they must apply.''

''You?'' the Duke asked incredulously. ''Why, you are teasing me, Miss Wrothton. You must be the belle of every ball you attend.''

Then, surprised at his own gallantry, he stuttered and said that he wouldn't miss the pending event at Morningdale, for he was quite sure he would enjoy it beyond anything. Dru doubted that very much but appreciated his saying so, and they rode on in companionable silence until in no time the welcoming lights of Morningdale appeared before them. Dru was startled to find the distance had passed so quickly and thanked the duke rather shyly for seeing her home.

Aunt Hester was standing in the hall when the Duke saw Dru to the door, readying her speech on the impropriety of staying so late at a strange gentleman's house and then riding home unaccompanied in the dark. She quickly had to revise that lecture, however, when the Duke bowed smilingly to her. Attempting an alternate scold on the impropriety of riding alone with only a gentleman after dark, the Duke explained that impropriety away so charmingly that she actually found herself thanking him for taking such good care of her niece. After he took his leave, Hester stood staring at the door, murmuring, "A most remarkable young man."

For once, Drucilla found herself in total agreement with her aunt.

Chapter XII

The sun was shining brightly as Matty sat propped in bed the next morning, and it cast a deceptively warm appearance over the small bit of garden she could see from her reclining position. She smiled at the trilling bird perched on a twig just beyond the window, then turned her full attention to the excellent breakfast provided by Mr. Pettigrew's equally excellent housekeeper.

"I suppose that a delicate lady who sustained such a grave injury to her person should barely be able to sip tea today," she said aloud as she lavishly buttered a biscuit. As she bit into it, she reflected wryly that this was not the first time she had proved she was not a delicate lady.

She took a second appreciative bite just as a soft knock was heard at the door, and, expecting Polly, she mumbled a mouthful "Come in."

A swift glance informed her that the figure coming through the door was not Polly, for that fine woman never filled a pair of riding breeches quite like Crandon Pettigrew. Matty flushed, for she had never before received a gentleman in her bedroom—actually his bedroom, she thought in confusion—or in such a state of deshabille. Both her Aunt Hester's and her brother Cecil's shocked faces rose before her eyes, and she choked on the last biscuit crumb she was hastily swallowing.

Taking a quick sip of tea to clear her throat, she met the gentleman's eyes and smiled affably. "I suppose that no one has ever told you that it is highly improper for a gentleman to visit a lady in her bedchamber," she said sweetly, her tone that of a kindly governess instructing a wayward and not too bright ward.

"And I suppose that no one has ever told you that it is unladylike to talk with your mouth full," the gentleman replied, just as affably, "or are you going to try to persuade me that your muffled 'come in' was not hampered by a mouthful of biscuit?" Matty, who had been absently sipping her tea as she regarded him over the rim of the cup, found herself choking again and glared balefully at him.

"Well, of all the rude—," she gasped as he grinned and moved closer to the bed to dispose himself in the chair at her side.

"Ah, but my dear Miss Cresley," he continued smoothly, "we are already agreed that I am not a gentleman."

"I am not your dear Miss Cresley," Matty snapped, "and if you're expecting me to now say that I am not a lady you can wait all day, for—" She blushed hotly as she realized she had just said it and was guiltily aware of the unholy amusement crinkling the corners of Pettigrew's eyes.

Taking another tack, she pulled herself up with dignity and reclined against the pillows at her back, saying, "I pray, sir, that you will forgive my hasty words. I am not myself this morning. The fall . . . the sprain . . . indeed, I hardly know what I'm saying." Then she leaned further back and closed her eyes in what she congratulated herself was a faithful reproduction of her Fainting Aunt Francis.

Pettigrew's tone was sympathetic but his eyes amused as he gazed at her empty breakfast tray. "Indeed, Miss Cresley, I do sympathize," he said. "I see that your injury also affected your appetite so that you could hardly eat a bite this morning."

Matty opened her eyes to glower at him and silence descended on the room. Finally she sighed and fingered the bedsheets as she stared out the window, a look of pained resignation on her face. "I fear you are right, sir," she said, her voice so low Pettigrew had to lean forward to hear her.

"About your breakfast?" he asked, puzzled, wondering if the lady had actually dined only on tea and toast before he entered.

"No," she said regretfully, her lips quivering as she avoided his eyes.

"About yourself."

"Myself—" he began.

"You really are not a gentleman." Ignoring the choking sound Pettigrew tried unsuccessfully to turn into a cough as he realized that he had walked into her trap, Matty continued. "It must be a constant tribulation to your relations."

"None of them have yet changed their names," he replied, to which the lady answered, "The English are always brave." But before that promising bait could be swallowed, an indignant Polly bustled into the room, scolding as she came.

"Begging your pardon, I'm sure, sir," she said in a haughty tone which did everything but beg his pardon, "but you shouldn't be in my lady's bedchamber. It's not gentlemanly."

"So I've heard," he began dryly, well aware of Matty's open grin at the entrance of her champion.

"Then you'll be leaving now," Polly said pointedly as he showed every inclination to stay. "I'm sure you have a great deal to do."

Plainly startled by such a forward attack, the likes of which he hadn't seen since his last visit to his dragon Aunt Agatha, Pettigrew rose uncertainly to his feet, his eyes on the wickedly smiling Matty. "Of course," he said, moving toward the door Polly held so purposely. "Of course. Much to do. I just wanted to make sure that Cleopatra—I mean Matty—I mean Miss Cresley—was feeling better and had everything she needs."

"She is and she does"' was the maid's austere reply.

Feeling more and more like a grubby schoolboy caught snitching pastries from the kitchen, Pettigrew turned to Matty and said, "I've promised to ride with the steward today and was afraid you might be gone before I returned. I know your cousin comes for you this morning, and I wanted to see if you are better and if you have everything you need . . ." His voice trailed off as he realized he was repeating himself, and he wondered savagely where his much vaunted sangfroid had gone when he most needed it.

"I am and I do," Matty replied primly, echoing her maid, her eyes dancing in evident amusement at his discomfort. "I want to thank you for your kind hospitality and to assure you that as soon as my cousin arrives, we shall trouble you no further."

"No trouble—," Pettigrew began, but at that the scandalized Polly could allow him no more time, and he found himself outmaneuvered, for with a "Thank you, sir, she does fine," that good lady had him out the door, which she shut with a decided click. Even after he found himself on the other side, he wasn't quite sure how she'd done it, and he rubbed his chin thoughtfully as he slowly walked away.

Inside, Matty was receiving a sound scolding from her faithful maid, and she heartily wished that she was free to get out of the bed and walk away.

"Now Miss Matty," Polly said sternly as she removed the breakfast tray and pulled the blankets up firmly around Matty's chin, "what were you thinking of, entertaining a gentleman and you in your nightshift and all? It's not proper."

"Well, you could hardly call it entertaining," Matty protested mildly, then grinned as she added, "besides, he's not a gentleman—" She chose not to finish her thought as she caught sight of Polly's firmly compressed lips, and set herself instead to cajoling the maid into a happier frame of mind.

"There was no harm done, Polly," she coaxed meekly. "Please don't scold. I told him he shouldn't be here. And I was so covered by blankets he would have seem more of me in Aunt Jane's morning room. I don't know what you think I could do—I was in no position to remove him bodily from the room."

Polly's lips relaxed slightly at the picture of her small mistress trying to push the large Mr. Pettigrew from the room, but she was not yet ready to resume her natural good humor.

"Don't you be thinking you're getting around me with that meek and mild manner, Miss Matty," she said austerely, "for you've been trying it for years and I'm well used to it now. It would be an uncommon day when I didn't recognize your trying to turn me up sweet." Then she bent to redeem the breakfast tray and smiled slightly as she straightened with it and headed for the door. "It would be an uncommon day it didn't work, too."

Matty smiled at the closed door and once again thanked heaven that it had blessed her with as understanding a companion as Polly. "Life with an eccentric is not easy," she said ruefully.

Leaning back in bed unaccustomed to such idleness, Matty glanced critically about the room and decided that she liked it in the morning light. The large windows opened onto a balcony, and the whole room appeared cheerful and relaxed.

"I could stay here," she thought lazily, then quickly banished the thought from her mind. Although her family might not credit it, Matty was well aware of the impropriety attached to spending the night in a bachelor's establishment, even with staunch Polly to defend her. The thought of her protectoress made her smile as she again pictured the easy way that determined woman had put Mr. Pettigrew to flight. It was evident he wasn't accustomed to being ordered about, and Matty thought with satisfaction that it would no doubt be good for him. It was her firm belief that men too used to having their own ways grew to be great bores quite quickly, and for some reason she disliked the thought of Mr. Pettigrew as boring.

Her thoughts continued in that direction until Polly once more came bustling through the bedroom door, this time her face alight with importance.

"Miss Matty!" Polly began on a note of congratulations as she busily drew the bedsheets up around her mistress' neck. "There's a gentleman here to see you."

"A gentleman?" Matty repeated, puzzled.

"A *real* one!" Polly assured her, delighted, and Matty smiled at the emphasis given the word "real." She also wished Mr. Pettigrew was there to hear it.

Perplexed, she wondered if she should remind her maid that she was still in her bedchamber but decided that would be to tease when she wanted to know who had excited Polly so. "But who knows I'm here, Polly?" she asked. "Who is it?"

Polly's meager chest swelled triumphantly, and awe touched her voice as she breathed, "The Duke."

"The Duke?" Matty echoed.

"Yes, miss," Polly assured her happily, "and don't I wish that brother of yours was here to see it."

Matty laughed, certain that her brother would not bear with equanimity the idea of her entertaining anyone—even a duke—while she lay abed and decided she was delighted by Cecil's absence. But she smiled kindly at her maid and suggested that she show the gentleman in.

Polly was only too happy to do so, and in a manner markedly different from that used to usher Mr. Pettigrew out, she was soon ushering Ratchford in, even going so far as to set a chair for him near the head of Matty's bed. Her mistress, aware of the high distinction this mark of favor conferred, was hard put not to laugh as she smiled up at the gentleman standing above her.

But the gentleman was not staring back. Indeed, his eyes were searching around the room as, oblivious to the lovely bouquet of violets he held in his hand, he murmured, "Ah, Miss Cresley. Alone I see."

Puzzled for a moment, the laughter grew in Matty's eyes as she realized who he had really come to see. "How kind of you to call," she said smoothly, motioning him to the chair as Polly moved to a corner where she felt she could be an unobtrusive chaperone.

The Duke took the chair and sat rather abstractly gazing at the ceiling. "I'm really much better, thank you," Matty said dulcetly, but he seemed not to notice the amusement in her voice.

"Oh!" he said, remembering his manners with a start. "Oh! Of course. Better are you? I'm glad. So glad. I was afraid you might have suffered a severe jolt—the fall and the sprain and all—but you're better?" Matty nodded and he nodded after her. "That's good. Very good."

That topic exhausted, he fell again into silence, and Matty, after watching him for a moment, decided to try again. "What lovely flowers," she said.

He looked down at the bouquet in his hands as if he had just discovered it. "The flowers," he said blankly. "Oh yes. The flowers." He was discomfitted for only a moment before rising and, with a very creditable bow, presented them to her.

Matty was touched by his kindness, for she knew only good manners made him give up what he had so obviously intended for her cousin. "Thank you, Your Grace," she said gently. "They're lovely. And I expect my cousin shortly."

Polly looked disgusted, the Duke embarrassed. "I apologize, Miss Cresley," he said, smiling ruefully. "I'm not usually such a clodpole."

"No need to apologize," she said warmly, approving his sincerity and kindness. "I admire my cousin myself." She motioned him back to his chair and suggested that until Drucilla's arrival he entertain her with the tales of his travels and his plans for Maplehurst, and so they spent a comfortable half-hour together, each listening for another person's voice and both too polite to let it show.

Chapter XIII

The sound of an approaching carriage was happily heard by both the Duke and Matty as they sat conversing, and in a short time Dru's step sounded in the hallway. Her cheery "How are you today, my dear?" as she opened the door caused two pairs of eyes to light, one in anticipation, one in amused relief. Polly merely sniffed, her growing disgust with the Duke apparent. Miss Dru was well enough, but Polly could not see how anyone could prefer that young lady to her beloved mistress.

Dru had arrived at Green Corners with a light heart, the knowledge that having met Pettigrew and the steward on the road, she would not meet him in his house. His deliberate bow and the sarcastic smile which played at his lips had tried her sorely in that brief encounter before her carriage swept on, and she wondered again how the Duke could be content with such an abominable friend.

Admitted by the butler, she hurried up to her cousin's room with a smile on her face, for the thought of having Matty back at Morningdale was all that had kept her from running away from home earlier that morning. Hester had flown into a pet over an unfortunate delivery of the wrong draperies for the dining room, and Dru, unhappy with the thought of the ball in the first place, thought it grossly unfair that she should now be called upon to sooth her aunt when preparations for that event went astray. But Dru expected things to be better when Matty was back among them, for her cousin's presence seemed to turn would-be catastrophes into jokes, and Matty could always be counted on to draw Aunt Hester's fire when Dru had been driven to the end of her rope.

The smile she had for her cousin grew as her eyes fell on the Duke sitting beside Matty, then wavered briefly as she saw the small bouquet Matty held in her hands. Banishing the quick stab she felt when it occurred to her the Duke had formed a tendre for her eccentric cousin, she sternly told herself that Matty deserved such a man and moved forward, her hand oustretched.

"Your Grace," she said, giving her hand to the Duke. "How nice to see you again. And Matty—I hope you are better this morning. Were you able to sleep last night? Does your ankle still pain you? I daresay you're as eager to return to Morningdale as I am to have you, for Aunt Hester is driving me to distraction and I need my reinforcements to come quickly."

Matty, who had seen the quick waver on her cousin's face, interrupted her hurrying chatter to present her with the violets. "The Duke brought these for you," she said gently. "I was admiring them when you arrived."

The Duke and Drucilla both cast Matty a look of gratitude, and Dru accepted the bouquet graciously, rewarding Ratchford with a sparkling smile. They chatted easily for a few moments before he rose to go, saying that he had already been away from Maplehurst too long, for it never failed that as soon as he left, the carpenters had a question that only he could answer, and all work stopped until he could be found. With a bow to both ladies and a special smile for one he was gone, leaving a momentary silence behind.

Matty, noting the sparkle in her cousin's eyes, chose to break the silence as she remarked teasingly, "A charming man, the Duke. I trust you had a pleasant ride home last night."

Dru blushed rosily, promising to tell her all about it later. "But now let us hurry and spirit you away before Mr. Pettigrew returns, for I've no wish to meet him again—I met him on the road, Matty, and he was most discourteous—well, not discourteous, precisely, but so, so,—oh, he's abominable. I cannot wait to be out of his house, and I am sure you will be glad to leave his oafish presence."

But Matty, to Dru's surprise, showed no disposition to hurry, remarking crossly that her foot hurt like the devil, and they'd have to move slowly so that she wouldn't injure it further.

Dru was instantly sympathetic and forebore to hurry her cousin further, merely picking up what few items of Matty's she could find scattered about the room as Polly helped her cousin into the morning dress the efficient maid had brought with her the night before. If Dru thought Matty's movements unusually languid and clumsy, she attributed it to her cousin's swollen ankle, although she did wonder why Matty was taking such pains in arranging her hair and why her eyes kept sliding to the window from which one could see the stables below.

Finally everything was packed, and Matty said with a sigh that she was ready, giving herself into her cousin's and maid's gentle hands as they helped her slowly out the door and down the ornate stairway of Mr. Pettigrew's leased mansion. The butler and house-keeper offered their assistance, but Polly jealously waved them away, saying she and Miss Dru knew just what her lady liked and were doing quite well without them. Matty shot her a look of exasperation but kept her thoughts on that subject to herself.

They were halfway down the stairs when the front door opened and Pettigrew strode in. Frowning at the sight of Matty's pained face, he moved quickly forward, sweeping the lady out of Dru's and Polly's astonished grasps and lifting her in his arms as he said, "Miss Cresley, you should not be putting weight on that foot. Allow me to carry you to your carriage."

"But—" Matty's weak protest was all Dru heard before Pettigrew bore that lady off. "Well I never!" she exploded as she and Polly exchanged glances. "To pick Matty up without even a by-your-leave, as if she were a common sack of flour. What an ungentlemanly thing to do!"

"Miss Matty says Mr. Pettigrew isn't a gentleman," Polly informed her earnestly. "She said so just this morning."

"Oh, dear!" Dru and Polly hurried after Matty and reached the door just in time to see her gently deposited in the carriage. Dru thought her cousin's face uncommonly flushed, and it grew even redder as Pettigrew quickly lifted her hand to his lips.

"Well!" Dru exclaimed, and the gentleman, hearing the indigna-tion in her tone, turned and bowed smoothly in her direction, offering his hand to help her into the carriage, an offer which she declined to his evident amusement. "Good day, Miss Wrothton," he said coolly as the carriage pulled away, and was rewarded with another indignant "Well!" Smiling, he turned and walked back up the stairs to his home.

The drive back to Morningdale Manor was a quiet one, all three ladies seeming disinclined to talk. Polly, anxiously watching her mistress's face for signs of fatigue, moved a pillow there and a blanket here in continuous efforts to relieve Matty's suffering. The fact that Matty did whatever her maid said so meekly and with such an abstracted air quite alarmed that good woman, who vowed she would send for the doctor the minute they arrived home. Dru appeared intent on the scene passing before her eyes, but in truth her thoughts centered on the donor of the hothouse violets she clutched in her hand, and she fingered them absently from time to time.

When they arrived at the manor, Baxley and two footmen hurried out to carry the invalid into the house, and Polly would have had them carry her right to bed, but Matty turned fractious and insisted instead that she be carried to the library, where a fire burned cheerily on the hearth. Not all of Polly's "tsk, tsks" or Lady Jane's anxious murmurings could move her, and although she was at first inclined to be snappish—which, Polly informed Lady Jane in a loud aside, her mistress never was, which must prove the pain the poor lamb was suffering—she was soon saved by her ready sense of humor, and she burst out laughing at the anxious faces around her.

"I really am not going to die of a sprained ankle," she smiled at them. "And I would so much rather sit here in the library with Drucilla than lie abed upstairs, out of sorts and out of place. I'll promise to keep my foot propped up on this comfortable little stool, and you can feed me tea and toast to your heart's contents if you'll just quit fussing so."

At the looks on their crestfallen faces, Matty's voice gentled, and she reached out a hand to both Lady Jane and Polly. "I am sure no one ever cared for me as you two do," she said, "and indeed I thank you. But I would like to sit here quietly for a while, and later I will retire to my bedchamber."

"When the doctor comes?" Polly pressed hopefully.

Uttering up a silent prayer that the doctor had been called to a distant place and wouldn't return until the morrow, Matty agreed. Lady Jane and Polly withdrew, and the cousins were left gazing at each other in perfect understanding. Dru promptly burst out laughing.

"Well, I'm glad you enjoyed that," Matty said mildly.

"Oh, I did," Dru gasped. "And I am sorry, Matty. Indeed I am. But if you could have seen your face when Polly offered to fetch smelling salts—" Dru was off again, holding her sides in a most unladylike way as her peals of laughter filled the room.

"Do be quiet," Matty begged, "or you'll have them in on us again demanding to know what's so funny."

Dru obediently clapped her hand over her mouth, but her shoulders still shook. "And then, when Mother offered to burn f-f-feathers—," she snickered through her fingers and was off again.

At that Matty grinned too. "I wanted to suggest the feathers from Aunt Hester's purple turban but thought it not the thing for such a tenderly cared-for invalid to say."

Dru wiped her eyes. "You looked as if you wished them both to the devil."

"Oh no," Matty protested. "I didn't."

Dru assured her that she had, but before the conversation could continue, a knock at the door was followed by Baxley's entrance. In his hands he carried a large tray.

"Yes, Baxley?" Dru questioned as he placed his burden on a small table beside Matty.

"Tea, Miss Dru. And toast." The butler's face was expressionless. He bowed, and as he left the room, stifled laughter burst from each cousin.

"Oh, dear," Matty moaned. "Oh, dear; oh, dear; oh, dear."

"Well," Dru said fair-mindedly, "you did tell them they could feed you as much tea and toast as they wanted."

"Unnatural girl," Matty scolded, surveying the pile of toast and large pot of tea at her side. "You're going to have to help me eat this for if I don't it will bring more reproaches down upon my head."

"But I'm not hungry, Matty," Dru protested, accepting one piece of toast but declining three others her cousin would have given her.

"Then pitch it in the fire," Matty ordered. "Bury it under the rug. Or call Caesar."

That idea appealing to both ladies, the dog was immediately sent for and the pile of toast safely disposed of.

"Now," Dru said briskly, "what about the tea?" She looked hopefully at the dog but Matty shook her head.

"He won't touch it. He much prefers ale." She patted his head gently as he nuzzled her hand. "Did you miss me last night, old fellow? You really should have left him with me, Dru," she said as her cousin solved the problem of the extra tea by pouring it out a window.

"How could I?" her cousin protested. "A dog of his tender years; who knows what he might pick up after a night spent in the odious Mr. Pettigrew's company?" Puzzled by the odd look on her cousin's face, Dru was about to question it when Matty changed the subject.

"Tell me about your moonlight ride," she invited with a smile. "The violets at your waist tell me it was not a total loss."

Under her cousin's teasing gaze, Dru blushed hotly and self-consciously fingered the violets. But her mind seemed to be elsewhere, only recalled by Matty's doubtful, "Well, I suppose I *could* ask Caesar..."

Dru laughed but avoided her cousin's eyes. "It wasn't anything, really," she disclaimed. "It was a lovely night and the Duke—don't you think he's a wonderful man, Matty? and so gentlemanly—well, the Duke offered to escort me home. Of course I told him there was no reason to do so, but he insisted—"

"And you arrived home in royal company," Matty finished lightly, "finding Aunt Hester quite appalled at the fact that you were riding at night with a gentleman—"

"But a duke—," Dru interrupted, her eyes alight like her cousin's.

"But a duke," Matty agreed, "which doubtless makes a great difference in Aunt Hester's mind. Although," she said, shaking a finger firmly at her cousin in a remarkable imitation of their illustrious aunt, "it is still not the thing to do, my dear. Dukes, like everyone else, should do their wooing in the parlor and the morning room—"

"Not wooing, Matty," Dru protested, blushing.

"Wooing," Matty continued inexorably, "—and not on horseback. Why in my day—"

Her homily was interrupted by another knock on the library door, and Polly entered to annouce the doctor's arrival. Her maid's lips were firmly set, and Matty knew Polly intended to hold her to her promise. A militant gleam grew in her eye as she said, "Now Polly, I am not feeling the least bit pulled about by sitting here talking to Drucilla, and I see no reason not to continue doing so. You may tell the doctor—" But her speech was interrupted by Baxley, who entered the room to inform the ladies that the Hovingtons had come to call.

At that Matty's eyes lost their militant gleam, and her face folded in lines of painful suffering. "It's about time the doctor came, Polly," she said faintly. "I am so glad you have come for me. I will go to my bedchamber immediately."

Ignoring Dru's indignant protest, she hobbled out of the room with the aid of a cane, Baxley, and Polly. Gracefully declining Percival's offer to carry her up to her room, she rolled her eyes at her cousin in such a way that that lady was hard put to turn her laughter into a cough as three pairs of Hovington eyes turned inquiringly toward her.

Chapter XIV

Three pairs of staring Hovington eyes and one indignant pair belonging to her cousin followed Matty as that lady made her slow progress from the library and up the Morningdale stairs. When she could no longer be seen, the Hovingtons turned toward Drucilla again, Lavinia moving to the recently vacated sofa and demanding pettishly to be told what "that impossible creature has done now."

Dru's lips tightened. "You speak of my cousin, Lavinia," she said shortly, but with great meaning. "She is very dear to me, and always welcome in my home." The growing color in Mrs. Hovington's cheeks made it clear that she understood Dru's meaning, and she muttered that she had not meant any harm, it was just that Matty was so odd. . . . The further tightening of Drucilla's mouth showed her that that tack found no favor either, and she shrugged her shoulders. Not meeting Dru's eyes, she said, "Aren't you going to tell us what has happened to your cousin?"

Unwillingly, Dru resumed her seat by the fire and waved the gentlemen into nearby chairs. Thinking that even with her sprained ankle Matty had the best bargain, she explained shortly that her cousin had been injured in a fall. Lavinia's eyebrows rose, but it was Percival who hurried into speech, appearing quite agitated by Dru's statement.

"Injured? In a fall?" he repeated. "But how can that be? I saw her only two days ago and she was quite all right then."

Dru regarded him with some amusement. "It hardly takes two days to fall, Percival."

Her wry wit was lost on him as he rose from his chair, saying, "I must go to her at once."

An explosive "no" from the ladies in the room stopped him, and he turned inquiringly toward them as each stared at the other in amazement.

His mother recovered first, and, patting the place beside her, she said in the voice she reserved for him alone, "That is, my dear, if your cousin Matty is in pain she will not want you to see her so. And besides," she continued waving her fan at him as if he were a naughty little boy, "—your cousin has retired to her bedchamber, and you know you are far too great a gentleman to venture into a lady's bedchamber."

Dru was as unconvinced of that as Percival appeared to be, but she kept such thoughts to herself, merely adding, "The doctor is with Matty now, Percy, and I imagine he will be there for some time. They cannot be disturbed."

Unwillingly, Percival sat down again, glowering at the fire and reminding Dru of the sulky boy he had always been. She sighed inwardly, wondering how she and Matty had managed to grow up while Percy only grew older. Deep in such thoughts, she missed the first part of Lavinia's next speech, but her attention focused quickly when she heard her aunt say, "And that is why we have come to take our leave of you."

"Take your leave?" Dru blurted, and Lavinia, annoyed, said, "Really, Drucilla, I do not believe you have heard a word I said."

Acknowledging that to be true, Dru explained that her mind had been on other things and begged her aunt to repeat her speech.

"Well, really, Drucilla," Lavinia said, eyeing her frostily. "It saddens me to see how quickly your cousin's influence erodes your own behavior." At the mulish jutting of Dru's chin, Lavinia thought it wise to hurry on, saying, "I was telling you that we must end our visit here—although we haven't really been staying here, have we? Brother Buxtell has had a great deal to say about that—" At her husband's impatient grunt, she realized she had run off track and closed her lips tightly. She began again with a smile that barely curved her lips and came nowhere near her eyes.

"Well. What I am saying is that your cousin Maude—sweet Maude, my elder child and only daughter—had sent us urgent word that all three of her children have contracted measles, and she is run distracted with worrying for them. Then what must that inconsiderate man she married do but contract them from the children, so she has four invalids on her hands and lives in daily fear of taking the disease herself—although she won't, of course, she had them as a child, and such a good child she was—but we will go to her at once. And I shall have a few words to say about grown men who run about contracting childish diseases."

Dru, well aware of her aunt's dislike for Cousin Maude's husband, was quite sure she would have and bit her lip to keep from smiling.

"Besides—," Lavinia began mysteriously, then stopped as she looked fondly at her son, who still sat with his hands thrust into his pockets, completely indifferent to the tale of Poor Maude's Sufferings.

"George, dear," Lavinia said brightly to her husband, "why

don't you and Percy go take one last look at the Morningdale stables? I know how you both enjoy horses.''

Dru opened and shut her mouth, stifling the protest which had risen immediately. While she did not enjoy the thought of Percy and George casting a proprietary eye over her stock, it would remove them from the room. George quickly agreed to his wife's suggestion and departed, dragging his unwilling son with him.

After the door was safely shut behind them, Lavinia leaned forward, lowering her voice as if sharing a great secret as she said, ''Actually, Drucilla, had it not been for poor Maude's actual suffering, I believe I would have felt forced to invent an excuse for our removal, for no mother worthy of the name could sit by and watch her beloved son remain in such danger.''

''Danger?'' Dru wrinkled her forehead in puzzlement. ''Is Percy in some kind of danger?''

Lavinia nodded vigorously. ''The worst kind,'' she hissed. ''I am surprised you have not seen it. But that unnatural partiality you show your cousin holds you blind to all her schemings.''

For a moment Dru blinked, for she could not believe that even her Aunt Lavinia could construe her distaste for Percival as ''unnatural partiality.'' Then she realized that her aunt had said ''her,'' and her brow wrinkled more.

''Aunt Lavinia,'' she said cautiously, ''are we talking about Matty?''

Again Lavinia's head nodded up and down.

''Matty?'' Dru gurgled. ''Matty is Percy's danger?'' she hooted at the thought. Her aunt was not pleased.

''I am glad to provide you such amusement, dear Drucilla,'' she said, her austere tone making it apparent that she was not at all glad. ''You may think the lures she has cast out to my son funny. I do not.''

''Lures?'' Dru tried her best to stifle her giggles. ''Matty and Percival? Oh.'' She stuffed her handkerchief to her mouth and with great difficulty regained her composure, avoiding her aunt's face, for she knew the look of outrage there would set her off again.

"I believe there is some misunderstanding, Aunt—," she began, but Lavinia interrupted her angrily.

"Percival is besotted with her," she said crossly. "My Poor Innocent has been caught in a web of that Jezebel's spinning, and our leaving is provident, for it will rescue him from her.

"Any woman would be honored to have your cousin," she continued, fixing Dru with a minatory eye which proved that young lady's undoing, for she dissolved in laughter again. "Honored," Lavinia repeated hostilely. "He is all a woman could ask."

"All a woman could ask—," Dru gasped, meeting her aunt's affronted eyes and making a heroic effort to stop her giggles. "All a woman could ask—oh, yes, Aunt Lavinia, I see why you must leave. I certainly do."

Lavinia eyed her with suspicion. "You have an unsuitable amount of levity in you, Drucilla. I have often warned you of it. You would do well to curb it if you hope to ever bring any man up to scratch. Gentlemen are not taken with ladies who laugh in their faces."

"I shall remember that, Lavinia," Dru murmured, dabbing furtively at her eyes and storing up these treasures for later laughter with Matty.

"Do," Lavinia nodded stiffly. For a moment they were silent, then she fixed her niece with a keen stare and said, "And when do you expect that to happen?"

"Happen?" Dru echoed, confused.

"Bringing your gentleman suitor up to scratch."

Dru blushed and hoped her aunt would think it an act of maidenly confusion. "Really, Lavinia, this conversation—," she began.

"But Drucilla," her aunt countered, her voice coaxing. "Surely you can tell me who he is now."

"Indeed I cannot," her niece replied truthfully.

"You *will* not," Lavinia snapped, and Dru remained silent, thinking wryly that one would not what one could not.

Lavinia tried another tack. "I suppose when you do marry, your mother and aunt will remove to live with you. As your mother says, your family is very close. Quite commendable that they go with you.

Then, to prevent the manor from standing empty, we would be glad—''

She got no further, for Dru interrupted her curtly, the distinct tremble in her voice containing no sign of amusement.

"Lavinia, I find such a thought insufferable," she said, taking no notice of that woman's outraged stiffening. "Morningdale Manor is my mother's home. It is Aunt Hester's home. They will not be leaving it. If I marry I shall visit here often to see that my mother and my aunt and the manor are all doing well. All must do well to remain in good condition for my future children, *true* Wrothton heirs." Looking at her aunt's belligerent face, Dru knew that if that meant having Old Peckingham, so be it.

"Well!" Lavinia exploded, and their conversation might have turned into a royal donneybrook if, with his usual good timing, Baxley had not entered to announce, "The Duke of Ratchford and Mr. Pettigrew."

"Pettigrew," Lavinia murmured, eyeing her niece speculatively. "Pettigrew."

The gentlemen entered, the conversation perforce turned to other subjects, and Dru's heightened color gradually subsided. Ruthlessly leaving Mr. Pettigrew to make what he could of her aunt's veiled titterings, she settled comfortably into a conversation with the Duke, secure in the knowledge that once the Hovingtons left, life would go on more happily.

What Dru did not realize was that since they were not gone yet, an unhappy incident might well occur before things grew merrier.

Out in the stables, a bored Percival listened with increased ill temper as his father put questions to the taciturn Matthew who could become amazingly deaf when it suited him. Not interested in horses himself, Percy was more intent on returning to the house and the ladies. When he saw the Duke and Pettigrew arrive, he tried to slip off, but his father called him back to admire a showy chestnut Matthew had taken the happy notion of selling to him since the animal was forever throwing out a splint. Matthew once had remarked disparagingly that it was hardly worthy of the name "horse," but none of that attitude showed in the groom's manner now as he praised the animal's hocks and chest, saying slyly that to have such a horse from the Wrothton stables would be to have something indeed. George, who considered himself a judge of horseflesh even if he was not one, agreed. As their discussion of the horse's merits deepened, Percy saw the doctor's gig drive off and, with a quick glance at his absorbed father, hastened from the stables and toward the servant's entrance to the Manor.

Upstairs, Matty was resting comfortably, the doctor having told her that in the next day or two her ankle should again be able to bear weight for short amounts of time, "although it'll be a while yet before you're dancing or climbing trees, Miss Matty." Assuring him that she could for the present live without either dancing or climbing, Matty was pleased with his verdict. As she reclined against the pillows, she heard a soft knock on the door and, expecting Dru, called, "You need not knock, Cousin. Come in."

The face which appeared around the door was not Dru's, however, and Matty suffered a shock when she saw it.

"Percy!" she said. "What are you doing here? This is my bedchamber. Go away."

But that he was not inclined to do. Closing the door carefully behind him, he advanced into the room, saying, "Dear Matty, I must speak to you."

Her eyebrows raised at the "dear Matty," and the lady, suspicious that he had been drinking, looked into his florid face and asked, "Does your mother know you're here?" His rising color answered her question. "No, I thought not. Percy, go away. My ankle hurts, and if you stay long my head will hurt."

"You joke," Percival assured her, smiling nervously and moving forward to stand near the bed, "but I am in deadly earnest. I must and I will speak to you."

Matty sighed. "Speak, then. But none of your long periods today. I am not up to it."

At that Percy possessed himself of one of her hands which had been lying quietly on the coverlet and, ignoring her surprised

108

pull-back, leaned forward saying, "Matty, you must know that I have always held you in high regard."

"WHAT?"

"High regard," he repeated, nodding. "Ah, Matty, I long to take you into my arms, to cover you with kisses—"

"Percival," Matty interrupted, her voice dangerously quiet, "when I was seven you covered me with a bucket of water. It made me very angry. But I prefer a bucket of water to your kisses."

"No, no," he protested, holding her hand more tightly as she tried to withdraw it. "You think I jest, but I do not. Matty, I want you to marry me."

"Marry—," the lady said blankly. "Marry—oh. Oh, Percy, you ridiculous creature. Unhand my hand and be gone."

"Say you'll wed me," he begged. "Say it and make me the happiest man on the earth."

"I will *not* marry you," she replied heatedly, "and that *should* make you the happiest man on the earth, for if we were to wed I would murder you within a week. Let go of me, Percy, and go." She managed to remove her hand just as a dry voice spoke from the doorway.

"May I be of some service, Miss Cresley?" Crandon Pettigrew asked as he took one step into the room.

Chapter XV

If Pettigrew's purpose at that moment was to discomfit the room's two occupants, he succeeded admirably. The lady, who had been

109

rather pale when he first opened the door, flushed rosily and retreated further under the covers until only her head was visible. The gentleman, whose complexion was already high, turned positively florid, his brow darkening. Not only was he pardonably annoyed at having his proposal so rudely interrupted, he was even more angered to find that the interrupter was "that fellow Pettigrew, damn his impudence."

"Sir, you interrupt," Percival said coldly, straightening from his position over Matty and drawing himself to his full height. Even then he was at a remarkable disadvantage in Pettigrew's presence.

"Well, thank goodness for that," Matty snapped. She glared at Percival, then at Pettigrew, noting with growing dismay that just behind the second gentleman was an open-mouthed Aunt Hester. Uttering a groan, Matty wryly reflected that it had been a most unsatisfactory day.

"My betrothed and I wish to be alone," Percival continued haughtily, and Matty stared at him aghast.

"Percy, do stop this nonsense," she begged. "We are not betrothed. I have told you we would not suit. Go away."

But Percival, finding his love's eyes fixed upon him just as Pettigrew looked amused and his aunt indignant, was beyond turning back. Grabbing the hand with which Matty clutched the blankets to her chin, he fell romantically to one knee beside her bed, beginning an impetuous speech which she listened to in open-mouthed amazement. Caesar, who had entered with Pettigrew and Hester, took instant exception to such behavior and barked loudly, then fixed his teeth in Percy's coat and began pulling the man away from his mistress.

"Dear Matty," Percy beseeched her as she struggled in vain to redeem her hand and as he struggled madly to shake off the dog, "do consider. You are not yourself. It is the pain in your ankle which makes you talk so. These past days I have known it is only your way of hiding your love which makes you appear indifferent to me." Forgetting for a moment the interested audience which stood beside the door, he pressed a passionate kiss into her palm. Matty, too well aware of them, tried to stem the tide of his fervor but could not.

"Think of all I could give you, Matty. Dresses. Jewels. A carriage. Fine sons—" Had he not chosen to add the latter, he might not have found Mr. Pettigrew's hand on his shoulder, felt himself jerked ignominiously to his feet, or heard the tear in his coat as the cloth ripped, caught between Pettigrew's pulling up and Caesar's pulling down. Glaring around at the person who had interrupted his proposal, he saw Pettigrew's face close to his and, dropping Matty's hand, swung wildly. Pettigrew threw him across his hip and sent him sprawling into a corner, upsetting a chair and knocking a Sevres vase off a small table. Caesar barked approvingly.

"I do not believe Miss Cresley is interested in your sons," Pettigrew said mildly, dusting his hands and readjusting his coat as he carefully avoided that lady's eyes. "And I believe you are distressing her when she should be resting quietly."

But Percival, usually a cautious man, was stung beyond endurance by hearing his proposal called "a disturbance." Rising, he turned beseechingly toward Matty. In a calmer moment her averted eyes would have told him to remain silent, but Percival was beyond rational thought. "I only want to share Morningdale Manor with you, Matty," he began eagerly. "I know how much you like it here; I have heard you say so any number of times—"

He got no further, for this time it was Aunt Hester, not Pettigrew, who interrupted him. That lady had watched the entire scene in growing outrage, and her fury now found an outlet in her nephew's unfortunate words.

"Morningdale Manor belongs to the Wrothtons, Percival Hovington," she reminded him angrily. "And I'd burn it down before I saw you share it with anyone."

Percival stared at her wildly, the words hardly registering. Then he moved toward Matty lying helplessly in bed, saying "Dear Matty, only think—"

Pettigrew, who had been watching the suffering lady, sought to forestall him. Unfortunately he slipped on one of the small hooked rugs which dotted Matty's room. The slip was just a step, but it was enough to cause the hold in which he held Percival to slacken momentarily, giving that angry young man enough maneuvering room to push his opponent off balance. The two swayed together for a moment, then fell. Their landing was cushioned by their happening to fall on Matty's bed, which gave way with a loud and resounding crash. The noise startled those taking tea below, and all hurried out of the library and up the stairs in search of the sound's cause.

Hester started forward gasping, "Matty, are you all right?," but her strongly lacerated temper was such that she could do nothing but ineffectually move back and forth between her niece and the gentlemen, pulling on Pettigrew's arm in a vain attempt to get him up and aiming an angry little kick at her nephew's backside, which did nothing to move him, either. All the time she was muttering, "I never! It's not the thing. Not the thing at all." Caesar did his bit by jumping on top of his mistress and yelping accusingly at the two men struggling to rise.

Pettigrew, deeply chagrined, quickly regained his balance and rose in embarassment. He tried to speak to Matty, but her averted face told him the lady was past listening.

Percival also tried to rise but had been more unfortunate than Mr. Pettigrew and found himself entangled in one of the dressing gowns which lay across the foot of Matty's bed. When his mother, Drucilla, and the Duke of Ratchford arrived on the scene, closely followed by the butler and several curious maids and footmen, he was trying unsuccessfully to remove a lacy bit of muslin from where it had fallen over one eye.

"Matty!" Dru gasped at the sight which met her eyes. "My dear, are you all right?" She hurried forward.

"Percival!" shrieked Lavinia. "My poor sweet boy! What have they done to you?"

"I say, Cran," the duke began, puzzled. "Been fighting, old boy? Not the thing to do, lady's bedchamber and all."

But before the babble which followed could reach epidemic proportions, it was silenced by one voice saying, with considerable feeling, "If you do not all leave immediately, I shall go off in strong convulsions. I swear it."

All eyes except Caesar's turned to the disheveled figure wrapped in the sheets and blankets of the now-broken bed. "Get out," she cried. "Get out. Get out. Get out." The dog seconded her impassioned pleas by growling menacingly at Percy.

"Matty—," Percival began, edging toward her, but before Pettigrew could stop him the lady's voice had halted his movement.

"Percy," she said dangerously, "my only regret at this moment is that I did not push you down the well when we were children." He took one more hesitant step toward her and her hand closed on a convenient broken board. "I will not be responsible for my actions if you come near me again," she snapped. "Get out."

"You heard her—," Pettigrew began, moving forward menacingly, but his action was stilled when Matty, with great loathing, continued, "And take him with you." Startled, he turned toward the angry lady in the bed and, dismayed to see tears sparkling on the ends of her lashes, took a hasty step forward.

"My dear Cleo—," he began.

"I am not your dear anything," Matty shouted angrily. "And don't call me Cleo." She dabbed at the tears that were beginning to spill over her eyelids and down her cheek. "And I am *not* crying. I despise weeping women." Whereupon she buried her head in her pillow and sobbed loudly.

Dru, bending over her cousin as she patted her comfortingly, turned like a small fury and herded everyone from the room. "Get out," she said fiercely. "Can't you see that she's upset? I don't know what you two did," she continued, fixing Percival and Pettigrew with an irate glare, "but I shall never forgive you for this."

"No, Drucilla, Mr. Pettigrew—," Hester began uncomfortably, but Dru, mistaking her aunt, did not let her continue, turning on that unfortunate man like a cat jealously guarding her only kitten.

"I might have known it would be you," she hissed. "To come here, upsetting my cousin. Oh, you have no shame."

"No, Drucilla, really—," Hester began, but the rest of her sentence was addressed to a closed door, for Dru, happy to have

113

them all out, had slammed it angrily and returned to comfort her cousin.

"Dear Matty," she said, trying with the anxiously whining Caesar to coax that lady's tearstained face from the pillows. "Do tell me what's wrong and I shall make it right again."

"Percival—," Matty wailed.

"Yes, dear Percival," Dru said warmly. "I too wish you had pushed him down that well."

"And Pettigrew—"

"That Pettigrew!" Dru snapped. "He had caused us nothing but grief ever since he moved into Green Corners. He is no gentleman, my dear, and you need not trouble your head with him."

"He is too a gentleman," Matty returned tearfully. "A true gentleman. And I never want to see him again."

Then, to her cousin's great astonishment, Matty the Brave, who saw something funny in everything and who might be expected to make a wonderful joke of a broken bed, turned her face to the pillow again and sobbed to her heart's content, causing Matty great relief and her cousin and Caesar great alarm.

Downstairs, events were not proceding any better. George Hovington, coming in from the stables, and Lady Jane Wrothton, arriving home after visiting an ailing tenant, arrived in the front hall just as the harrassed ensemble was making its way down the stairs, various voices raised in explanations and recriminations.

Jane paused, clearly startled by this unexplained uproar in her home, but Hovington, seeing that his son's coat was torn and that that gentleman sported what was rapidly becoming a bruising shiner, moved forward quickly, demanding to be told "what the devil is going on."

Jane, aware that a number of interested servants were lingering in the hall hoping to have that question answered too, firmly ushered all her guests into the morning room and saw the door shut before she would allow explanations to begin. Inviting everyone to be seated, she moved herself to a comfortable chair. When she was settled she bent a penetrating gaze upon those around her, mildly requesting to be told what had happened.

That quiet request brought an immediate uproar which she silenced by raising her hand. She sighed and looked inquiringly at her sister-in-law, saying, "Hester, dear, can you tell me what has been going on here?"

"It's Matty," Hester began, to be promptly interrupted by Lavinia's spiteful, "It always is."

But this time Hester would not allow aspersions to be cast upon her niece's character, and she glared balefully at the Hovingtons before she continued.

"Poor Matty," Hester said. "Tied to her bed by that unfortunate sprain. You know how trying that is for her, Jane."

Lady Jane nodded her agreement and Hester continued. "Mr. Pettigrew here"—and at that she broke off to honor that gentleman with a slight smile and an inclination of her head—"came to inquire how Matty had endured her jostling by coach this morning. Very thoughtful it was of him, too."

Pettigrew kept his lips firmly pressed together and avoided Ratchford's eyes as Hester again favored him with a smile. "And though it was highly irregular—you may say that, Jane, and you will be right, but I decided it was for the best—well, even though it was quite irregular, when he asked if he might see Matty, I told him I would take him up to her chamber to see if she was awake and if she felt like speaking to him. Which I did."

Sighing inwardly, for she still had no idea of what had happened, Jane waited, secure in the knowledge that if she let Hester talk long enough she would eventually unravel the mystery. Hester, enjoying her center-stage position, now pointed accusingly at Percival, who squirmed obligingly.

"When we arrived at Matty's room—and not a moment too soon, from what I could gather—we found that ridiculous Percival there before us, forcing his attentions on her in the most odious way."

"What?" George Hovington roared, glaring at his son.

"She entrapped him, George," Lavinia interposed venomously. "I told you how it would be. The woman is a siren. My poor baby."

"Matty? A Siren?" Hester was amazed at the thought. "Matty? What a fool you are, Lavinia! Your poor baby—as you choose to call that overgrown lump—is a cad. He is worse than that. He is common. There was poor Matty, unable to move from her bed, and there was your son—I should blush to admit it if I were you—there he was, leering over her—"

"Not leering," Percival protested weakly, but Hester was not to be put off.

"Leering," she repeated. "And when Mr. Pettigrew tried to recall him to his senses"—here she favored that gentleman with a third thin-lipped smile which almost overturned the Duke's gravity—"Percival so far forgot himself as to struggle with Mr. Pettigrew, who slipped on a rug after Percy pushed him. The two of them fell on Matty's bed, breaking it and throwing the poor girl into strong hysterics."

"Hysterics?" Jane blinked. "Matty?"

"Slipped on a rug, what?" the Duke murmured quietly for his friend's ears alone. "It's a good thing Jackson didn't see that." The frown on Pettigrew's forehead lifted slightly at his friend's jest but settled again as Percival leaped to his feet.

"I want to marry Matty, Aunt Jane," he said earnestly. "And she wants to marry me."

"The Jezebel—," shrieked his mother.

"She does not—," Pettigrew began, standing himself, but once again Jane motioned for silence.

"Hester?" she asked doubtfully.

"Matty," Hester pronounced with satisfaction, reducing her nephew to age five again with one of her famous stares, "told Percival that she is sure they would not suit. She told him to go away. And she told him that her only regret is that she did not push him down the well when they were children."

Lavinia's indignant gasp and George's angry growl did not affect her as she raised her eyes to the ceiling, continuing softly, "I do not know when I have been so in charity with Matty's thoughts."

"Well!" George exploded. "How dare she—that impertinent piece of baggage—Jane, I demand that Matty apologize to my son immediately."

116

"Apologize?" The word came incredulously from four pairs of lips.

Pettigrew swung in his direction, but it was Jane who spoke.

"Really, George," she said reprovingly. "I would think if any apologies are due—and I feel they certainly are—they should be made to Matty."

"What?" George rose from his chair, blustering wildly. "My son has been insulted and you think he should apologize to Matty? If that is how you feel we shall trouble you no further. Come Lavinia. Come Percival. The Hovingtons know when they're not wanted—"

"Ha!" Hester snorted.

Favoring her with a glare of great dislike, George stomped from the room, followed by his indignant wife and hangdog son. At the door Lavinia turned and said with deep frigidity, "I thank my lucky stars that my son has escaped from that crazy woman's clutches. How can you uphold her and wrong my innocent boy in this way—" She cut her speech short when she saw Hester's fingers close around a convenient figurine, for it had been only fifteen years ago that the latter had so far forgotten herself as to hurl just such an object at Mrs. Hovington. Judging it time to retreat, Lavinia did so with head high, merely slamming the door for emphasis as she left.

"Good riddance," Hester snorted, glancing at her sister-in-law and seeing again the two gentlemen whom she had for the moment forgotten. "I am sorry you had to witness this family quarrel, gentlemen," she began grandly, but the Duke hastened to assure her that it was already forgotten. Then, asking that she and Lady Jane convey his and Pettigrew's best wishes for a speedy recovery to Matty and their compliments to Miss Wrothton, he dragged his friend from the room, adding only that they would return to visit the ladies at a more convenient time.

"Such a gentleman," Jane murmured as the two departed, her eyes meeting Hester's in thoughtful speculation.

"And a duke," Hester agreed simply. "A real and genuine duke."

Chapter XVI

It was some time before Dru joined her mother and aunt in the morning room, and when she softly closed the door to Matty's chamber and descended the steps, she did so thoughtfully, a slight frown creasing her lovely forehead.

"How is Matty, dear?" her mother questioned, smiling at her daughter as she entered the room.

"I'm not certain," Dru replied slowly. "She's not herself. I believe the shock of her sprain and the night spent in a strange house must have worn her out more than we realized. And then that horrid scene in her chamber just now—if I were a man, I would call both Percival and that odious Pettigrew out. How could they?"

But neither her mother nor her aunt would allow her to continue slandering Mr. Pettigrew in this way, although Hester was quite happy to join in a round of condemnation of Percival and all Hovingtons, separately and together. Once her mother was convinced Dru now realized Mr. Pettigrew was not to blame for Matty's discomfiture, but had indeed been trying to alleviate it, her thoughts turned to making her niece more comfortable.

"I must send James to mend the bed at once," she said, reaching for the bellpull, but Dru stopped her.

"I wouldn't just now, Mama," she said hesitantly. "When I left her, Matty was quite vehement in her instructions that she is not to be disturbed. She said the bed is quite comfortable as it is and," her voice softened in astonishment, "that it is no more than she deserved for being such a fool."

"A fool?" Hester raised her eyebrows incredulously. "How can she call herself a fool? It was entirely that mushroom Percival's fault. A fool! I have called her many things over the years, but fool was never one of them."

Dru grinned. "I wish Matty could hear that," she said, quizzing her aunt. "I believe it's the nicest thing you've ever said about her."

Hester blinked at her niece, but before she could think of a suitable retort, Jane interrupted, saying, "The poor child is overwrought. I will give her a half-hour for quiet reflection and then I shall go up to her. She most certainly can't remain in a broken bed over night."

That matter settled, the three ladies drifted into silence, each absorbed in her own thoughts as they sipped the tea Baxley had procured for them. Finally Hester's thoughts found voice as she said, "How pleasant it is knowing the Hovingtons are no longer with us. I have not felt so well since their arrival in the neighborhood."

Dru nodded. "No more Hovingtons," she agreed as she sipped her tea, "and no more need for a ball. I believe the day has not ended so badly after all."

Two cups clattered in their saucers as two pairs of eyes stared at her in amazement.

"No more ball?" Hester echoed, her voice rising on each word. "And pray, why no more ball?"

Dru stared back at her aunt. "As far as I'm concerned, we used the ball as an excuse for the paint buckets and sheets in the house—our reason for not allowing our beloved relations to remain with us. Now they're gone and there's no more reason to go on planning this ridiculous party."

"Not ridiculous, Dru—," her mother began weakly, but her aunt's reply was much more spirited.

"Drucilla, you know we were planning a ball before the Hovingtons came," she said accusingly. "We had quite decided upon it. You cannot meet young men if you are never where young men are. Besides"—and here she gathered her shawls around her with an air of great self-satisfaction—"it is too late to call off the ball. I sent the invitations off yesterday. Already three of our neighbors have expressed their pleasure of acceptance."

"You what?" Dru asked. "Aunt Hester, it is too bad of you. Without a word to me—"

"I am not in the habit of asking your permission for my actions," her aunt replied regally.

"Of course not," Dru stammered, "but I would think—oh, never mind." She settled back in her chair and in a resigned tone inquired who her aunt had invited.

At that Hester grew quite animated. "Everyone," she assured Drucilla, causing that lady to groan aloud. Hester ignored her and began to tick names off on her fingers. "The Richleys, the Farthingtons, the Hermingtons, the Duke of Ratchford, Mr. Pettigrew—"

She got no further, for at the mention of Mr. Pettigrew, Dru straightened in her chair and gazed accusingly at her aunt.

"You invited that man, knowing that I despise him as I do?"

Hester waved her objection aside. "Don't be missish, my dear," she begged. "Of course I invited him. He is a close friend of the Duke's, and to invite Ratchford without inviting his friend would appear quite odd. Besides, he did offer Matty the hospitality of his house, and perhaps she will care to entertain him if you do not."

But that Drucilla would not allow. "No, do not foist him on Matty," she said. "I am sure that she has had quite enough of his insufferable presence."

Hester and Jane exchanged glances but decided not to continue that subject. Dru roused herself to ask for what day the ball had been set, and Hester replied happily that it was only a month away.

"There is so much to be done, too," she worried. "The menu to be planned, the chandeliers dusted, the silver polished, our gowns made—did I tell you, dear Jane, that I've engaged Mrs. Seldon from the village to do our dresses? She and her assistants will come for fittings tomorrow—and we must hire musicians, and I am not at all sure how to decorate the ballroom—and the weather. I do hope we can plan on a pleasant night."

Jane smiled at her plump sister-in-law, assuring her that she was sure that if anyone could contrive a soft spring evening, it would be Hester.

Looking gratified, that lady replied that she rather thought it possible now, for in her opinion the Hovingtons' departure had already chased a number of clouds away.

Even Dru could not help laughing at that, and, her good humor restored, she turned to her mother, saying, "For my part, I am glad I no longer need carry on this silly deception that I am in hourly expectation of an offer of marriage. It began quite by accident, but when it perturbed Cousin Lavinia so, I was unwilling to stop." She laughed. "Do you know that she left convinced that my suitor is Pettigrew? Can you imagine?"

Both older ladies smiled with her, but Hester, not catching her sister-in-law's warning glance, unwisely chose to assure her niece that she did not believe it was a deception, "for I shouldn't be at all surprised if you do receive an offer soon."

"An offer?" Dru repeated, the color rising in her cheeks. "I haven't the least idea what you mean, Aunt Hester. And I wish you wouldn't talk so. It quite puts me out of countenance."

Her aunt regarded her in amazement. "Don't know what I mean? Of course you know what I mean, Drucilla. You have always had keen intelligence. I am talking about the Duke of Ratchford, of course. He has obviously developed a tendre for you—and it's not the least surprising, I might add, for I had always thought you would make a lovely duchess."

"Really, Aunt Hester!" Dru said crossly. "You do the Duke a disservice by talking so. He has shown me no—no partiality—" She lost herself in her phrases, and her aunt raised her famous eyebrow.

"You don't mean that you believe him to be indulging in a mere flirtation, do you?" that good lady inquired.

"Of course not!" Dru exclaimed. "There is no flirtation. I am quite beyond flirting age."

"There is no such thing as beyond flirting age, my dear," her aunt assured her frankly. "I do not know what you are becoming so upset about. I understand all the London mamas have despaired of him, for none of them have been able to capture him in any of their traps, and here you, without even trying, catch him in your gentle snare."

Dru set her teacup down with a resounding clink, and there was a

121

dangerous glint in her eye as she rose from the sofa. "You speak of the gentleman as if he is a rabbit," she said hotly, "and he is not. Nor am I a hunter out setting snares for unsuspecting gentlemen to fall into. I am not flirting, I am not dallying, I am not interested in the Duke of Ratchford, and I heartily wish that you would quit busying yourself in my future."

With that she stalked out of the room and in a matter of minutes was one of two young women sobbing in her chamber.

Left alone in the morningroom, the two older ladies exchanged telling looks. "I believe we have two overwrought young ladies in the house," Jane said complacently.

"And I," Hester said, "believe that is very good for both of them."

Meanwhile, as those interesting proceedings occurred at Morningdale, the gentlemen who had visited earlier that afternoon rode slowly toward their homes. Occasionally Ratchford cast sidelong glances at his companion, but his earlier attempts at conversation having met with little success, he remained silent.

Presently he was startled as his friend's angry voice was heard.

"That crawling muckworm!" Pettigrew growled. "That sniveling turnip. To think that I permitted him to make me appear such a fool. And in Miss Cresley's bedchamber. I should have run him through."

"Oh, now Cran," his friend consoled. "You didn't permit him to make a fool of you exactly. . . . Besides, you couldn't run him through, old boy. You don't carry a sword. Nobody carries a sword anymore."

His friend glared at him. "The custom should be revived," he asserted. "With coxcombs like that in the world, no gentleman should be without a sword."

It struck the Duke that he had never before seen his friend concerned about how he appeared in the world's eyes. But then, he could not recall Pettigrew ever before being made to appear a fool. He again pictured his friend scrambling up from the broken bed, and not even his good breeding could prevent his smiling at the recollection.

Pettigrew caught the smile, and while his tone was less angry, his frown was still heavy. "Well, you may smile," he said. "Your delightful Miss Wrothton quite dotes on you, and you appear the shining knight while I fall into the role of court buffoon.''

"Fall into the role . . . ,'' the Duke choked. "I say, that's good.'' Then, realizing that his friend's brows had snapped together again, he straightened quickly, saying, "Not a buffoon, Cran. I'm sure Miss Cresley realizes you did not mean to break her bed.''

Pettigrew did not appear powerfully reassured by this thought. Instead he urged his mount to a canter, and the two rode hard for a while. When Mr. Pettigrew seemed to have ridden off some of his rage, he again drew his horse to a walk and the Duke pulled in beside him, a frown now creasing his forehead.

"I say, Cran,'' he began hesitantly, "what you said back there—''

Pettigrew, recalled from his own thoughts, waited. "What I said?'' he prompted as the Duke seemed unable to go on.

"About Miss Wrothton.''

"We were speaking of Miss Cresley.''

The Duke reddened but persevered. "No. No, you said Miss Wrothton dotes on me, and I was wondering . . . She is all kindness and politeness to me, of course, but I cannot tell . . . That is, she is all kindness and politeness to everyone—''

Pettigrew's brow lightened as he gave his bark of laughter. "That has not been my observation.''

The Duke's gaze was straightforward. "I believe that is my concern. I have seen well-bred ladies appear to hold the object of their affection in contempt so that no one will realize how much they care for him. I fear that Miss Wrothton is in love with you.''

"Good God!'' Pettigrew's laugh was loud and he regarded his friend through eyes dancing with amusement. "What a cloth-head you become when in love! Undeceive yourself, my dear. Miss Wrothton is not dissembling. She treats me as if she dislikes me because she dislikes me, I assure you.''

The Duke's face had brightened considerably at his friend's last speech, but there was one more thing he felt he had to know. "And in what regard,'' he asked with great delicateness, pausing as Pettigrew awaited his question with cocked eyebrow, "in what regard do you hold Miss Wrothton?''

"Oh, the highest regard," he assured the Duke, whose face fell. "But not the type of regard which need make your face fall so visibly. I hold her in the high regard I would hope to have for any woman my best friend plans to make his wife. I have no designs on her affections."

"You don't?"

Pettigrew laughed. "My dear fellow, do you think I want to spend my life with a woman who challenges everything I say, who is forever looking to get the better of me, and who has a tongue like a needle?"

The Duke grinned. "Yes," he said simply.

Pettigrew opened his mouth to speak, stared at his friend for a moment, then nodded. "You may be right," he said, "but not with that woman."

Relieved, the Duke spent the remainder of the ride to Green Corners expostulating on Miss Wrothton's many virtues, happily unaware that his friend was paying him no attention. That gentleman's thoughts were also at Morningdale Manor, but not centered on the divine Drucilla.

Chapter XVII

Two subdued young ladies joined their elder relations at the Wrothton breakfast table the next morning.

Matty, helped down the stairs by her thoughtful cousin, was unusually quiet. Not proof against the alternate scoldings and cajolings of her devoted Polly, she had at last been persuaded to move to another bedchamber while the bed in her allotted room was mended. James, the second footman, worked quickly and efficiently under

Baxley's austere eye, and she was soon back among her own things, but that did not lift the melancholy enveloping her.

Good Mrs. Waddington, the housekeeper who had plied both Dru and Matty with gingerbread men when they were small, was seriously alarmed and went at once to brew a cup of soothing herbal tea. Polly muttered darkly that it wasn't tea Miss Matty wanted but a good shaking, adding for good measure that she knew just the person to administer it, too. Mrs. Waddington, much shocked at such violent words, blessed herself and remonstrated, but Polly only harumphed and, maintaining a dignified silence, went upstairs to straighten Matty's wardrobe.

Matty, grateful that her faithful henchwoman was finally quiet, gazed unseeingly at the canopy which covered her recently repaired bed and thought wryly that her brother's prophesy was right; she had at last come to her own desserts. It was not a thought which gave her joy.

Caesar, as if sensing her mood, pressed his wet nose invitingly into her palm, but instead of delivering the pat he felt he so abundantly deserved, Matty removed the hand. Heaving a huge sigh for the sad life of man's best friend, he circled the rug slowly and lay down upon it, his head on his paws, there to dream happily of marrow bones and running rabbits. He slept contentedly throughout the evening and his mistress, not so lucky, tossed endlessly and envied him his slumber.

When Dru knocked on her door the next morning and asked if she would like support down to the breakfast table, Matty, looking far from fit, was tempted to say no. Yet a moment's reflection convinced her that not appearing for the meal would bring Polly in upon her again, asking many more questions and threatening to send for the doctor. Feeling unequal to that scene, she acquiesced to Dru's offer, slipping meekly into the wrapper her cousin held for her.

A quick glance in the mirror convinced her nothing Aunt Hester would consider indecent was showing, and then, leaning gratefully on her cousin, Matty made her way from her room and down the stairs. Thankful the staircase was wide and the midway landing a convenient spot to stop and rest, she was slightly cheered to find her ankle could already bear weight, and she assured Dru that she would soon be on her feet again. Dru, her arm around her cousin's waist and her mind rather further away, murmured, "I'm glad," and did not notice that Matty's cheerful tone was sadly forced.

Baxley, seeing the invalid and Dru at the bottom of the stairs, hastened forward to help them, full of anxious cluckings and "Miss Matty, should you be up?" After he threw open the breakfast parlor doors for them, he hastened to pull a chair out for Matty, and she smiled gratefully for his consideration. Lady Jane, noting that the cousins were not alike in appearance or temperament but that the bags under their eyes were identical, smiled to herself before solicitously asking her niece how she was feeling.

"Much better, Aunt Jane," Matty replied untruthfully. "I feel quite the thing again, thank you."

"Hmph," Hester snorted. "You look it, too." She was about to say more when she met Jane's reproving glance and subsided, not so much from a feeling of guilt as from surprise that her usually quick-tongued niece made no retort. In fact, she seemed not to have heard at all.

Meanwhile Baxley, having ascertained the young ladies' permissions to fill their plates, now placed before each a breakfast which would have done credit to the Prince Regent. Jane looked in amusement at the quantities of eggs, sausage, ham, and toast he seemed to think young women capable of eating. Knowing that at their best appetites he would have been disappointed, she was sure that today his hopes were definitely doomed.

"Would you care for tea, Matty?" Jane asked gently as her niece sat, fork suspended between mouth and plate, the bit of egg hanging from the fork in danger of landing in her lap. Matty started and the egg fell to the floor to be devoured by the eager Caesar, who had slipped in while Hester's attention was elsewhere.

"That beast!" Hester gasped. The dog grinned at her.

"A most helpful animal," Jane pronounced. "Better than a broom. Tea, Matty?"

"Oh yes, please," she said, reaching out her cup.

"Dru? " Jane asked, the teapot still in her hand. Her daughter was silent. "Dru?" That young lady started, dropping the scrap of toast she held in her hand. She bent to retrieve it, but Caesar was before her.

"A *most* helpful animal," Jane murmured.

Dru was looking at her doubtfully. "Did you say something, Mama?"

"Yes, dear," Jane smiled. "Would you care for some tea?"

Dru assented, but made no move to pass her cup. In fact, her mind seemed to drift elsewhere as her mother waited.

"Would you like it in a cup?" Jane asked finally. Dru hastily picked up the cup and saucer and, blushing, passed them to her mother as she murmured, "I'm so sorry, Mama. I don't know where my mind is today."

"I do," Hester snapped, "it's off with Matty's." Whereupon both young ladies blushed brightly, to her great astonishment.

"Well, I never——," she began, turning to her sister-in-law. "You'd think we had two schoolroom misses here——"

"Would you care for more tea, Hester?" Jane suggested, a warning in her eye. Hester recovered herself, looked at her nieces, opened and shut her mouth several times, and shook her head no.

Silence reigned in the breakfast room for several moments thereafter, broken only by the clatter of teacups on saucers and the thump of Caesar's tail as he encouraged his mistress to share her breakfast with him. Since she had no appetite, he was doing quite well when he could get her attention. Unfortunately her mind was elsewhere, and from time to time he heaved a sigh for the vagaries of humans who seemed to forget one's presence at the most inopportune times.

Hester regarded her nieces in amazement as she sipped her tea and turned once to say something to Jane. She found that fond mother watching both girls with such a delighted smile on her lips that she thought better of breaking the silence and went back to her tea and toast, keeping a wary eye on Caesar as he gravely watched each bit she raised to her mouth. At last she could no longer contain herself and, in a hearty tone a nurse might use with young and recalcitrant charges, said, "Well, we don't want to dawdle over breakfast today for we have much to do."

Three pairs of inquiring eyes turned toward her, and she doubted if two of the eyes' owners had heard what she said.

"Do?" Dru asked politely.

Relieved, Hester pressed on. "Yes," she said. "Mrs. Seldon will be here soon with the pattern cards and cloth bolts, and we do not want to keep her waiting, for the sooner she begins on our gowns, the sooner they will be finished."

"Gowns?" Dru frowned, and Hester, foreseeing trouble, decided to take the initiative.

"For goodness sakes, Dru, will you quit repeating every word I say?" she snapped. "Of course gowns—our gowns for the ball. I have told Mrs. Seldon to bring all the pattern cards she has and whatever cloths she feels suitable.

"I thought white for you," she continued mendaciously, "and pink for Matty."

"White?" Dru squeaked, appalled. "And pink?" Her voice rose even higher, for of all the colors in the world, Matty most detested pink. "I will not," she declared.

"What do you think, Matty?" Lady Jane prodded her niece gently, trying to recall her from her evident brown study.

"Think?" Matty asked, starting again.

"About the gown," Jane helped.

"Gown?"

"What Aunt Hester said," Dru supplied.

"Of course," Matty said absently, feeding the last of the toast to Caesar. "Whatever Aunt Hester says."

"Matty," Dru cried, "she says pink!"

"Pink?"

Matty was chagrined and looked at her Aunt suspiciously. "You wouldn't hold someone to something she agreed to when suffering the pain of a sprained ankle, would you, Aunt Hester?" she asked with a smile.

Hester gave her traditional snort. "It's not your ankle that pains you, miss," she retorted, but before that promising topic could be pursued, Baxley opened the doors to announce that Mrs. Seldon and associates were waiting in the upstairs sitting room. Hester rose at once, energetically adjuring the others to bestir themselves and not keep the modiste waiting. In all her bustling she did not hear Matty hiss to her cousin that she had a good mind to send Caesar after the tidbit of toast caught in the fringe of Hester's shawl. Caesar did not need such orders, however, for he had already seen the toast and was advancing on it with due speed, quickly claiming his prize and producing no more than mild hysterics in the bargain.

Upstairs, the voluble Mrs. Seldon was busily superintending her underlings in the laying out of various silks and satins the ladies might be tempted to choose for their ball gowns. A French emigré who had married an English soldier upon her flight from France, after her marriage she had found herself not in the heart of fashionable England, where she longed to be, but in a quiet village where the ladies most often required gowns more for visiting and attending church than for balls.

Her eyes sparkled and her mouth fairly watered at the idea of furnishing four such prominent ladies with the grand toilettes which might make her name known and furnish her with the entre of gownmaking for the Polite World, a position she had hungered after the past ten years. If she were successful and the ladies' fine friends clamored for her gowns, perhaps her doltish husband could be persuaded to remove from his stuffy little farm to the grand metropolis. If not—well, she gave a gallic shrug and thought she might post down to see him occasionally—when she was not so busy in London.

These were the thoughts revolving in her mind as she eyed the ladies for whom she would create her masterpieces. Realizing it was the dresses for the younger two which would make or dismiss her reputation, she studied them intently, her eyes narrowing as they fastened on the faces of those before her.

Where were the bright eyes, the sparkle, the youthful flush which should accompany the choosing of ball gowns magnifique? The sour expressions and wan looks on the faces of these two young ladies made it appear they would rather be elsewhere; indeed, it was the older women who seemed most excited about the preparations as they moved about the room picking up the edge of one bolt of cloth, inspecting the laces and braids which they realized could give a gown that certain cache or stigmatize it as overblown and gauche.

All this went through Mrs. Seldon's mind as she bustled about the ladies, studying them from this angle, then from that. Finally she nodded in satisfaction.

The youngest was a beauty, and it would be a pleasure to dress her. Believing that a gown was not a creation in itself but rather a setting for the wearer, the seamstress often compared her works to paintings. Yet, as she could not help confiding to one of her assistants, it was always such a relief to have a subject worth framing.

As for the older cousin—Mrs. Seldon's eyes snapped and she rubbed her hands with pleasure. Here was a challenge and one which could well make her name. Miss Cresley had an unusual beauty, so unusual that a less critical eye might miss it completely. Her lack of height was to be bemoaned, of course, but she had a fine bosom and a mass of auburn hair which, when dressed properly, could be the envy of any female. Mrs. Seldon decided she would talk to Miss Cresley's maid about her hair, for it should do her gown credit.

Here is a woman others might make look a spinster, but I, Antoinette Seldon, will make her an Originale Exquisite. Her bosom swelled at the thought.

Chattering continuously she set about measuring the ladies, calling out confusing figures to her assistant, who wrote them down religiously and never raised her eyes from the tablet. Her own enthusiasm for the visions she saw in the young ladies now under her hands helped them better endure what Matty darkly called her poking and prodding, and when she began to describe the gowns they would wear, she carried them away completely.

"For you," she said, regarding Matty critically and waving her hand toward her head, "for you, the look of the lady of mystery. You must pile your hair on your head and entwine it with an ivory ribbon, a ribbon to match those on your gown. But it must be done smoothly," she cautioned, shaking her head. "Do not make the mistake of curls, for curls will not become you. Smooth, like a Greek nymph.''

Matty, bemused that anyone could mistake her for any kind of nymph, Greek or otherwise, gazed dazedly at the little lady who continued her bubbling plans. "And your gown, mademoiselle. Ah, your gown." She paused impressively before picking up a bolt of pale green silk which Matty thought was the color of freshly unfurled leaves in spring. "This will be the gown," she said, "simply made, with a high waistline belted with an ivory ribbon. The skirt will flow—so—whispering as you glide about the dance floor. And the decollette, low—this low." Here she gestured a point which made Matty gasp and Lady Jane frown.

The seamstress gave one of her characteristic shrugs at the gasp and continued, unperturbed. "You will be *ravissante*," she promised, and Matty, with a grin, forebore to ask if she might be ravished as well. "A narrow band—oh, so narrow—of ivory lace will edge the sleeves and neck. And you will carry an ivory silk shawl embroidered with silk thread. Ivory silk slippers to match, a fan if you desire one, and mademoiselle—ah, you will be magnifique." She kissed her fingers to her lips in tribute.

"And you mademoiselle—" As she turned to Dru her eyes glowed. "You will do my gown honor by wearing it. For you, my piece de resistance. A rose gown with a white gauze overdress. For you also the high waist, the flowing skirt, and perhaps, a flounce around the hem. Yes? The flounce. And for you, too, the decollette." She gestured.

Lady Jane opened her mouth, but Hester, determined that Dru would attract the eyes of as many men as possible, silenced her with, "Would you have two such fine bosoms hidden from the world, Jane? Neither Matty nor Drucilla are unfurled roses, you know."

And Jane, who knew that she would indeed hide those particular bosoms, simply sighed, realizing that she would have no objection to such a gown on someone else's daughter and deciding that that was a good reason not to object to it on her own.

Finding no hindrances to her plans, Mrs. Seldon suggested slippers to match Dru's dress and a white shawl of the finest wool plus the Wrothton pearls—a singularly exquisite strand—as her accessories. "You will be the grande belle," she said simply, tears of joy rising to her eyes. "The grand lady."

Content with her plans for the younger ladies, she turned now to their elders. Finding that Lady Jane had decided on a simple gown of dove-gray silk, she did not try to dissuade her, for the lady was just out of mourning and Antoinette's quick eye showed that the silk was indeed becoming to Lady Wrothton. Hester, however, proved more difficult. That lady was determined to wear purple, and Mrs. Seldon, her hopes of a move to London riding on the ladies' backs, was just as determined that she should not. Heated discussion with much hand waving and raising and lowering of voices followed, and the two had just compromised on sapphire blue when Dru's maid scratched on the door. Upon admittance she informed the ladies that a gentleman had called and was waiting in the drawing room.

"Baxley told him you ladies are busy," she repeated conscientiously, for the butler, stiff-lipped, had stressed that point, "but he insists upon waiting."

With interest Mrs. Seldon noticed that that information did much to dispel the listlessness which had characterized Miss Wrothton throughout the morning. So, she thought, the beauty has an admirer.

"Who is it, Constance?" Dru asked hopefully.

"It's Mr. Pettigrew, Miss Dru. He insists upon seeing Miss Matty."

The dressmaker sighed at the crestfallen look on the lady's face but noted that the information did much to transform her cousin.

Aunt Hester suggested testily that he be sent away since the ladies were up to their necks in silks and likely to remain that way for some time, but Matty surprised the company by announcing that since Mrs. Seldon was almost finished with her, Constance could tell the gentleman that she would be down directly.

Dru, surprised, suggested to her cousin that after the scene in her bedchamber, it might be better not to make it so easy for the gentleman to apologize, but Matty replied lightly that her cousin knew she had never been one to hold grudges. Squirming guiltily under the seamstress's tape measure, Dru decided that Matty was right. Mr. Pettigrew had done little to ingratiate himself with Dru, but she knew his actions were not sufficient to make her dislike him as she did. Yet Matty, who had every reason to hold him in contempt, was ready to forgive him. She wondered how her cousin could be so broadminded.

Once released by Mrs. Seldon, Matty went to her room, dressed quickly, and was soon limping down the stairs, leaning heavily on the bannister and trying to resolve her whirling thoughts.

How should she act? That addlebrained Percival had made her appear a fool when Pettigrew last saw her. And what he must have thought to find such a gudgeon in her bedchamber looming over her in that revolting manner! She colored merely at the recollection.

Well, try for dignity, Matty, she cautioned herself and, squaring her shoulders and lifting her chin, she paused for a moment with her hand on the drawing room doorknob.

Inside, Pettigrew was experiencing much the same discomfort. Uneasily aware that he owed the lady an apology for the revolting scene in which he had taken part, he was at a loss about how to begin. Apologies were a new experience to him, especially when he was not sure how they would be received. There had been a great deal of anger in the young lady's eyes yesterday, anger and something he could not identify. He tugged at his cravat as if it were too tight, and his eyes riveted on the door as Matty slowly entered the room.

"Miss Cresley," he said, hurrying forward to pull a chair out for her. "How is your ankle today?"

"Improved," she said, gratefully accepting the chair and sinking into it. "I am walking, though slowly. The swelling is down somewhat." Then her own evil genius prompted her to mark demurely that she had found it necessary to get up, her bed having met with an unfortunate accident. Watching his color rise, she thought ruefully that that was so much for dignity.

Pulling again at his cravat, Pettigrew took a hasty turn about the room. "Miss Cresley," he began, "I would not for the world—"

"Of course—," Matty interrupted.

"But that Hovington—," he said with repugnance.

"Abominable!" Matty agreed.

"And that damnable rug—"

Matty's eyes sparkled. "I hope you weren't injured in your unfortunate fall!"

"Only my pride," he sighed.

"And then my faithful Caesar—"

"A Trojan of a dog!"

"Percy tangled in the bedsheets!" Matty giggled.

"Mrs. Hovington's expression—" Pettigrew gave his bark of laughter.

"And Aunt Hester's!" Matty agreed, wiping the tears from her eyes. Then she looked at the gentleman and started to giggle again. "Not to mention the expression of total chagrin on your countenance!"

"Or the total hopelessness on yours," he returned, and they were off again.

It was into this scene that a mystified Dru walked in search of Hester's sewing basket. "Mrs. Seldon forgot her shears and Aunt Hester asked me to fetch hers," she explained politely, gazing in amazement at the room's two occupants. At first glance she had detected tears on Matty's cheeks and was about to fire up in her cousin's defense when a closer look convinced her they were tears of laughter, and she wondered what the two could have found to be so funny. Bowing slightly to Mr. Pettigrew, she inquired politely about his health, and, after gravely assuring her that he was fine, thank you, he told her that he was charged with a message from his friend, the Duke of Ratchford.

"Sebastian has been quite busy with the workers he's employed to renovate his house the last few days, but he begs you will remember him, and he hopes to call upon you tomorrow."

Dru, who did indeed remember him, bestowed one of her most dazzling smiles upon Pettigrew and almost—but not quite—forgave him all his transgressions.

Chapter XVIII

The ensuing scene was one which, years later, would still bring Matty a reminiscent chuckle. At the time she could barely keep from bursting into laughter as her cousin and Mr. Pettigrew maneuvered and outmaneuvered each other, one intent on remaining for private conversation with Matty, the other just as intent that he should be on his way.

Delivering the Duke's message had done much to raise Pettigrew in Dru's esteem, but she had not so far forgotten their previous encounters that she had any intention of leaving her injured cousin to his mercies. Although she quickly retrieved the shears for which she had been sent, she showed no disposition of leaving the room again. Instead, she seated herself and inquired civilly—if with an evident lack of enthusiasm—after Mr. Pettigrew's health.

An amazed Pettigrew threw Matty a look of great appeal, but that lady, after grinning broadly at him, lowered her eyes and sat with her head down, her hands primly folded in her lap, as during the next half-hour her cousin and Mr. Pettigrew made labored conversation, each determined to outstay the other. Had either been able to see Matty's face, they would have been instantly suspicious, for the look of unholy glee there was impossible to hide.

As it was, Drucilla won the Great Library Skirmish, for she had reinforcements coming up from the rear.

Hester, irritated that she could not send her niece for such a small thing as scissors without having to later go in search of both her

135

niece and the scissors, soon appeared in the doorway ready to scold. Taking in the situation at a glance, she descended the library's two steps majestically, thanked Mr. Pettigrew for calling, told him they wouldn't dream of detaining him any longer when they were sure he had a great deal to do, and, hand upon his elbow, ushered him toward the door.

Thrown off balance by the realization that he had lost control of the situation—a feeling most uncommon for him—Pettigrew did rally slightly and, making a hasty bow to Matty, asked Miss Cresley if he might call upon her on the morrow for the privilege of taking her for a ride.

"For I'm sure your ankle is quite painful and you have no other way to take the air," he stammered, one eye cocked toward the lady's worthy aunt, who still held his arm in a firm grasp.

"Posted and riposted," Matty murmured, afraid to raise her eyes in case a glance at his bemused face would completely overturn her pent-up laughter. She thanked him primly for his invitation and, before either her aunt or cousin could intervene, told him that she would be quite pleased to drive out with him.

"I'm sure you're much less clumsy with your horses than on your feet," she assured him kindly, causing the gentleman, no mean whip, to grin appreciably and her aunt to gasp.

"Really, Matty," Hester scolded after the gentleman had been hustled out the door. "Why can't you learn to mind your tongue? I hardly knew where to look when you chose to allude to that regrettable scene in your bedchamber. A lady would never—why, I'm not sure what he must think—and him offering to take you driving, too—"

"Perhaps he thinks I'm not a lady," Matty suggested with what her aunt considered a deplorable lack of form. But before Hester could rise to such palpable bait, Baxley entered the room to inform them all that madame and the seamstress were waiting. The look of reproach in his eyes—for to keep madame waiting was, where Baxley was concerned, unforgivable—reminded Hester that she had larger fish to fry, and she chose not to reply to her unregenerate niece, contenting herself with an audible sniff as she passed by Matty's chair.

Matty grinned at Dru as they both rose to follow their aunt. "I do hope she doesn't assist Mrs. Seldon with the pinning," the former said as her arm encircled her cousin's waist. "If she does, I may spend the next hour on a cushion."

The two laughed and left the room. If Dru thought there was more spring in her cousin's limp, she attributed it only to Matty's indomitable spirit.

A half-hour later, when Matty said faintly that she must leave the seamstress's ministrations and go rest her ankle, the gleam in her eyes was met by an answering light in her cousin's, who generously— and quickly—offered to help the suffering lady to her room.

"So kind of you, my dear," Matty murmured as the two left. Once the door to Jane's chamber was closed, it did not surprise Dru to see her cousin's limp lessen nor to hear Matty whisper, "I know I should be better about these things, but to be continually turned this way and that, to be poked and prodded and measured so—it is more than I can bear.

"Besides," she added, and her face assumed a look of prim seriousness, "it was not only for myself that I asked to be excused."

"Oh?" Dru asked suspiciously. "If you mean to tell me that you did it all for my sake, I will thank you kindly, but don't think I'll believe it for a moment. Such a plumper."

"No, my dear, not for you," Matty assured her as they reached her bedchamber. Raising her eyes piously upward, and assuming the position of a gentle martyr, she said, "I did it for Aunt Hester."

"For Aunt Hester?" Dru repeated incredulously. "My dear, you must be feverish! Come lie down at once."

Matty grinned. "The way she kept holding those shears and gazing consideringly at my neck made me quite afraid she was contemplating murder. To be sure, Aunt Hester is a woman of strong principle, but I was not sure how long she could endure if I remained in her presence." At her cousin's gurgle of laughter, she gazed reproachfully at that lady. "Really, Drucilla, you know it would be in shockingly bad taste to have a murderer in the family."

"Especially if one were the murdered party," Dru murmured, placing a footstool for her cousin as she settled her into a comfortable chair.

"Especially," Matty agreed with a nod, and in that vein the cousins wiled away a pleasant hour, each politely pretending her thoughts were not elsewhere.

A great deal of attention followed Matty's exit with Pettigrew the following morning. Those servants who could not,- even on the flimsiest of excuses, find a reason to be in the hall when Pettigrew arrived did make it their business to be near a window or in the drive as the two drove off, the lady primly seated with her hands meekly folded in her lap and the gentleman staring straight ahead.

"I would guess that the Prince Regent himself never drove off with more interested eyes upon him," Matty said thoughtfully as the two bowled down the lane at a smart pace.

Pettigrew chuckled, and Matty realized that that was one of the things she liked best about this man; when she made what her brother Cecil irritably called her "obtuse and irrelevant comments" he understood perfectly, and never asked her to explain what she meant.

"Perhaps I should have allowed the horses to bolt," he suggested. "It would have added drama to the scene."

The lady tilted her head, considering.

"No," she decided finally. "I think it would have been far better if, instead of arriving so soberly clad, you had come for me in yellow pantaloons with a striped bombazine waistcoat and your shirt collars so highly starched that you could not turn your head. *That* would have been dramatic."

Pettigrew, who had not enjoyed her description of his raiment, answered forcefully, "*That* would have been ridiculous."

"Do you think so indeed?" she asked doubtfully, her tone at odds with the smile in her eyes. "I will have you know that I have been driven about by just such a gentleman, and his effect on everyone we saw was *quite* dramatic."

"I should think so!"

The lady opened her eyes wide. "My dear Mr. Pettigrew," she said, "my brother—who would be quick to tell you that he is much in the know on such things—assures me such attire makes a gentleman a Tulip of the Ton." At her companion's snort she added, "He says it is all the crack." There was a moment's silence while Pettigrew stared at her, wondering if he had been mistaken in the lady. She gazed at him demurely. "He did not take it at all kindly when I suggested such attire proved the gentleman to be cracked."

His quick bark of laughter and the momentary slacking of the reins startled his horses, and they broke into a run as he lowered his hands for a moment. The team was as quickly checked but not before Matty, in her best Aunt Hester imitation, recommended him to mind his horses. As a member of the Four Horse Club, his lips tightened slightly at that, but he agreed to do so meekly and the two drove in silence for several minutes, Pettigrew marveling that he had at last met a woman who did not feel it incumbent to talk when she had nothing to say.

Loath to break their companionable quiet, Pettigrew yet felt he must, and began, "Miss Cresley, there is something I would like to tell you—no, ask you—"

She turned inquiringly toward him and he realized that his cravat had grown too tight. He put one hand up to tug at it, and as he did so, one of his horses stumbled slightly.

"You want me to drive," she said promptly. "Of course."

"No, I don't want you to drive—," he began hotly, then noted the laughter in her eyes and grinned. "You have a way of doing that, don't you?"

She nodded. "My family will tell you it is my besetting sin." Visions of Aunt Hester rose in her eyes and she amended that to "*one* of my besetting sins."

"I'm sure your cousin would not say so."

"No," she agreed, "Drucilla likes me."

"And your Aunt Wrothton."

"Yes, Aunt Jane likes me too." There was a pause which she broke with a grin. "I see you didn't mention my Aunt Hester."

"I am sure your aunt likes you," he returned. "Indeed, she seems quite fond of you."

Matty smiled and, in an excellent imitation of that good lady, looked loftily down her nose and said, "Aunt Hester holds me in great familial regard. But"—and here she shook her finger at him in admonishment—"that does not blind her to my many faults."

He smiled his appreciation. "It is a pity you were born a gentlewoman, Miss Cresley. You were certainly meant for the stage."

Silence again descended as Matty watched the scenery passing before her eyes and as Pettigrew divided his attention between the lady on his right and his horses.

"Have you many?" he inquired mildly, and, startled, she gazed inquiringly toward him.

"Many?" she echoed.

"Faults."

Her ready gurgle of laughter rose in her throat. "My dear sir, too many to mention," she assured him with an airy wave of her hand. "Aunt Hester has a list. I believe it is bound, in four volumes. My brother Cecil has a similar list. I am, I have it on good authority, well past praying for."

"Do you wish them to pray for you?" he asked curiously, for while her tone had been light, a quick shadow had crossed her face.

She looked at him for perhaps half a minute and then, with a smile and shrug, half turned. "It can be quite lonely being an Original, Mr. Pettigrew," she began, looking away, then shaking herself impatiently. "I am sorry I said that, and I pray you will not regard it. I believe my ankle is making me quite mopish. I am not usually so, I assure you." She looked up into his eyes and at the expression there looked down again. "I believe we should be getting back. I am feeling quite tired."

But Mr. Pettigrew showed no disposition to return. He continued driving north at a spanking speed.

"Mr. Pettigrew," Matty said, "I would like to return home." There was no answer. "Mr. Pettigrew, where are we going?"

"Gretna Green," he returned shortly, looking straight ahead.

"Gretna Gree—," she gasped and sat up very straight. "Mr. Pettigrew, if this is your idea of a joke it is a very poor one. Please turn your phaeton around immediately." At the determined look on his face, her voice rose sharply and she stomped her good foot. "Mr. Pettigrew, either turn this phaeton around or set me down. Immediately."

Much to her surprise—and a good deal to her consternation—he drew in his team and pulled them to a halt. Turning toward her he said, "Well?"

"Well?" she echoed.

"Are you going to get down?"

"Oh!" She was exasperated. "You abominable man! You know with my ankle as it is that I cannot walk home."

"Then Gretna Green it is—," he began, gathering up the reins.

"Nevertheless!" she said, reaching for footing in an effort to spring down, "Nevertheless, I believe that I had better try."

At that he put his hand on her arm, and Matty thought his tone rather pleading as he said, "Miss Cresley, wait. I am making such a mull of this. Gretna Green didn't enter my head until a few moments ago when you talked about being an Original; if Sebastian could see me now he would laugh himself sick. I pray you'll never tell him what a gudgeon I am—I used to pride myself on my control—of course I will take you home. But first—that is—dear Cleo—I mean Miss Cresley—will you marry me?"

She stared at him amazed, and two bright spots of color burned in her cheeks.

"Mr. Pettigrew," she began, her voice shaking, "I do not understand. If you are making sport of me—I assure you, sir, I have never been closer to strong hysterics—"

"Not even in your bedchamber?" he quizzed her, but at the lady's indignant look he quickly changed his tone, saying, "My dear Cleo—I mean Matty—I mean Miss Cresley—I assure you—how could you even think that I am making sport of you? We are agreed I am not a gentleman, but I didn't know that you held me in such low regard."

Now it was Matty's turn to be thrown off-guard. "It isn't that," she cried. "You must know it is not!" Then, catching the gleam in his eye, she stiffened and averted her face so that he could not see the troublesome tear coursing down her cheek. "You are bamming me, sir," she accused. "I have told you that I am an Original, past praying for. I have been on the shelf for years. Ask Aunt Hester. Ask Cecil. Ask anyone. And now—for some reason unknown to me, you choose to tease me like this. I thought you were my friend—" Her voice, wholly suspended by tears, failed her.

"Good God, Cleo—," he began, perturbed, his efforts to take her in his arms hampered by the firm hold he must keep on the reins.

"Don't call me that!"

"My dear Matty, don't cry," he coaxed, succeeding in getting one arm around her shoulder. "How can a woman of your superior understanding be so foolish?"

"I'm not—," she fired up, but he continued.

"Can't you believe a man could want to marry you?"

She shook her head woefully.

"My dear, my dear. I love you, Matty. And if that is to make you the butt of a joke, Miss Cresley, then the joke is on both of us. Now *will* you quit behaving as if your wits have all gone begging and look at me?"

She raised her eyes to his, and he leaned over to kiss her, letting the reins slacken so that the horses started forward, throwing both the phaeton's occupants off-balance.

"I believe I may have to take you in hand at that." With a smothered oath, he checked the team as Matty murmured, "You are too cowhanded by half, my love—I mean Mr. Pettigrew—I mean—"

But the "my love" had elicited a crow of delight from the usually urbane gentleman, who continued to press his suit. "Does that mean yes, dear Cleo?"

"No, it does not," Matty returned crossly. "And don't call me Cleo. It only means—it means—it doesn't mean anything at all!"

"Ah, but it does," the gentleman said, fetching up a heavy sigh as he turned away from the lady. "It means you are toying with my affections." Matty refused to rise to that bait, instead imploring him

142

to consider carefully and to see that they would not suit. He would not agree.

"I haven't evaded Parson's Mousetrap for these many years without considering carefully, my love," he said, enjoying her obvious fluster. "We will suit perfectly."

"We will?" Her tone was doubtful.

"Of course. I am not a gentleman and you are not a lady. If that's not enough, we're both slightly mad."

But instead of drawing the smile he had hoped for, his love grew more serious. "I am, of course," she acknowledged, "I work quite hard at it. But you—no, it will not do."

"Matty," he said firmly, halting his horses as he turned toward her, "do you love me? Yes or no?"

"Well, I—"

"Yes or no."

"Yes—no—that is—a woman my age does not fall in love!"

"Could you slip into it, then?" he coaxed and she regarded him with an angry glare.

"I am perfectly serious!" she said.

"Oh, Matty, so am I," he replied with a rueful shake of his head. "Why can't you realize I'm serious? Matty, I love you."

"Why?"

"What?"

"Why do you love me?"

He sighed. "Because you are the most infuriating, outrageous, totally entrancing woman I know. Because I am comfortable with you, because we share jokes no one else knows are funny. Because not loving you is impossible."

"It is?" she ventured shyly.

"It is. And you are going to marry me." There was a long silence, and the pleading note crept back into his voice. "Aren't you?"

The silence lengthened. At last Matty said thoughtfully, "I think that you should ask my brother for my hand."

"Ask your brother—"

"He will grant it to you, of course, with great hallelujahs. 'Her

143

hand and all the rest and welcome'—I can hear him now. Then I think you should make me a proposal in form—on your knee, bring a pillow if you like. Proposing in an open carriage! Really, Mr. Pettigrew!

"Yes," she continued dreamily, "I would like you to propose on your knees. I, of course, will turn you down several times, but you will persevere. Perhaps you will go into a decline, and refuse to eat. You will write odes to my eyes and I, remorseful, will accept you at last—"

"Cleo, you wretch—"

"I believe it would be nice if you showered me with presents," she continued. "A ring that even Aunt Hester considers vulgar. And a Cinderella carriage with blue—no, pink velvet—cushions and the wheels picked out in pink—"

Mr. Pettigrew put an end to his love's flights of fancy the only way he knew how, but from the way their lips lingered she did not seem to mind. Unfortunately, his mind elsewhere, he again let the reins slip, and the horses again started forward, one of them glancing over its shoulder as if to assure itself their real owner was driving. Glad that none of his Four Horse Club compatriots could witness the whipster-style he had employed this day, he gathered the team together but held them to a brisk walk, the better to keep one arm around his unprotesting love's shoulders.

"I will apply to your brother—," he began hesitantly, at which his love sat bolt upright and said, "If you do I shall send Caesar to sit on you forever."

"I'm glad," he murmured, relieved, and at her look of inquiry added apologetically, "I have met your brother."

"And you still wish to marry me?"

His eyes reflected the laughter in her own. "Against my better judgment."

"I suppose we will have to tell him."

"Well, no," he replied promptly. "We could invite him to the baby's christening and see if he got the idea."

"Baby's christen—" Matty gasped. "Mr. Pettigrew!"

"Crandon," he corrected her firmly, and, drawing her back onto the shoulder she had just abandoned, he pretended ignorance. "Of course the baby must be christened, my dear. You don't want the child to grow up a heathen, surely?"

"Mr. Pettigrew. Babies—"

"Ah," he nodded wisely. "You do not understand about babies. I will explain it to you, never fear."

"Of course I know about babies," Matty exclaimed crossly. "It is just that—"

"That gentlemen do not talk about such things to ladies—"

"That's right."

"But my dear, I have it on good authority that I am no gentleman!" His eyes gleamed and she laughed, and the next few miles agreeably slipped away with two sensible people involved in a great deal of nonsense. Finally Matty ended that when she asked, her brow creased, "Did you really mean to drive to Gretna Green?"

"Well, no," he admitted. "I haven't enough blunt in my pockets to get us halfway to York. It was just at that moment—when you looked just so—" The thought of it made him kiss her again. But Matty was not to be deterred.

"Perhaps Gretna is a good idea," she said slowly.

"Cleo!" her love exclaimed.

"It would get it over quickly," she explained.

"Well, if you want it over quickly—" His tone was stiff.

"It's what my family would expect of me," she added with a wide smile. "You must know I'm too ramshackle by half."

"I'll remember that," he promised. "But I do not intend to marry you over the anvil; you may be ramshackle, but I am a high stickler."

"A high stickler," she scoffed. "Kidnapping ladies in an open carriage!" Then she regarded him speculatively and in a dulcet voice said, "If we are married in London my brother will hold an engagement party in our honor. Perhaps he will have several parties; he would not want to appear backward in any attention. All his worthy friends will attend. *All* of them. Then Aunt Hester will invite *her* bosom friends. They are all a great deal like her, although

145

few have her sweetness of temper. You will no doubt find that enjoyable."

Pettigrew started and she murmured, "Just so."

"Your brother's friends—?"

"Extremely worthy."

"And your aunt's friends—"

"Delightful gorgons."

There was a pause.

"We shall go north," he said with decision.

"To Gretna Green."

"To Grantham."

Matty blinked. "Grantham?"

"My aunt has an estate there," he explained. "I am sure her rector will be delighted to marry us by special license."

"Delighted?" Matty asked doubtfully.

"Amenable."

She stared at him. "Is your aunt like you?" she asked finally.

He grinned. "Now how am I to take that?"

Her smile answered his own. "Is she highhanded like you?"

"*I* am merely in control," he returned. "My *aunt* is highhanded"

Matty laughed. "I shall like her excessively," she said with great conviction. "I already do."

Chapter XIX

Drucilla was one of those watching from a window as Pettigrew drove off with her cousin, but her sentiments were not those of curiosity or excitement felt by others in the house; indeed, she was suffering from pangs of guilt, feeling that if she had realized how beneficial a ride might be for Matty, her cousin would not now be consigned to that odious man's company. She vowed to make it up to her cousin later, then turned from the window to her mirror to put the finishing touches on her toilette.

Had Dru been in possession of her customary good sense, she would have noticed that from the first Pettigrew's manner toward her cousin was markedly different from the deplorable lack of manners he exhibited whenever she came in contact with him. Indeed, if she had been seeing the world as clearly as she usually did, it would have occurred to her that her cousin did not find the arrogant gentleman nearly as repugnant as she did.

But during their growing up, the cousins had shared such identical assessments of their acquaintances that in her present vague state of mind it did not occur to Drucilla that Matty's feelings could ever vary so completely from her own.

That the vagueness with which she moved through the world just now could be attributed to a mild-mannered man with smiling eyes and a deprecating manner went without question in the mind of every gentlewoman in Morningdale, although Drucilla would not for the world admit it and took great comfort in the thought that neither her cousin nor her aunt and mother had any idea that the reason she always found herself sitting by a window or listening for arrivals in the drive was because she was awaiting a visit from the Duke of Ratchford.

Nor was she admitting to herself as she dressed that the reasons she chose to stroll in the garden in a becoming chip hat and a soft dove-gray cape which matched her eyes was because she lived in moment-to-moment expectation of the Duke's arrival. As she left her room to descend the stairs, she stole one last glance in the hall mirror, then told Baxley that she would be in the garden "in case anyone should want me," assuring herself that she was only leaving a message in case her mother or aunt should require her help.

Baxley replied, "Quite so, Miss Dru," and bowed primly, as aware of the meaning of the young lady's message as she was herself. Accordingly, when the Duke of Ratchford appeared at the door a half-hour later, Baxley, his face wooden, informed the gentleman that he could not answer for the older ladies' whereabouts, but he believed Miss Matty to be out riding with Mr. Pettigrew and Miss Drucilla to be taking air in the garden. Thanking him pleasantly, the Duke ignored his later offer to ascertain Lady Jane's location and walked briskly around the house to Morningdale's not-inextensive gardens. There he found Dru bending over a bed of freshly cultivated earth and searching for the small green sprouts she expected there. Her cheeks were rosy from brisk walking, and several tendrils of hair escaped the charming hat. The Duke believed he had never seen anyone more lovely.

At his approaching step she glanced up, then straightened and smiled happily at him. "Good morning, my lord," she called. "I am awaiting my daffodils' pleasure."

"Indeed?" he said, returning her smile and wishing ruefully that he could tell her that it was the daffodils who should be awaiting her pleasure; he wanted to say that not even their bright glory could add anything to the scene now before him; he wanted to say that she was Spring and the earth could in no way match her radiance.

Instead he said, "Indeed?" and wondered again why the fine art of flirtation was completely beyond him.

"Would you care to walk with me?" Drucilla ventured as he seemed inclined to stand smiling at her, and he at once fell in beside her as they started down the path. As they walked they spent an agreeable half-hour in pleasantries, the Duke inquiring after Drucilla's health, the health of her aunt and mother, her cousin's ankle and being. Dru in turn asked him how the work on his estate progressed, and he launched into a description of the work being done. Before he realized it, more time had elapsed than he had planned, and he checked himself, saying, "I have allowed my tongue to run on and have forgotten the real reason for my calling." At her look of inquiry he smiled and said, "Miss Wrothton, I have come to take my leave of you, for I am on my way to Bath and must be in Reading before nightfall. I dare not linger."

"Your—leave?" Dru faltered and was unaccountably relieved

when he assured her it was for a few days only, "a trip down to visit my mother, who takes the waters there."

"I hope she is not seriously ill?" Dru inquired, her ready sympathy aroused, for she could imagine no other reason one might retire to Bath at this time of year.

"Nothing that a change in scene won't cure," replied the Duchess's undutiful son with a grin. "Since my father's death six years ago, my mother's only comfort has been the certain knowledge of her impending demise, a knowledge she is forever sharing with her nearest and dearest, as well as her furthest and most disliked. As she enjoys excellent health, we happily do not expect that impending event for many years, but whenever she becomes bored, death is once more impending."

"I understand," Dru said, meeting the smile in his eyes with one of her own.

"My mother is an intelligent and delightful woman," he assured her earnestly. "And I would let her decline in peace in Bath right now except that I have some news to discuss with her which I believe will do much more good than the waters in ending her boredom. Indeed, I expect it to bring her posting into the country in a very short amount of time."

"A miraculous recovery, then?" Dru murmured, and he agreed with a grin.

"It must be a wonderful piece of news," Drucilla said politely. "Are you at liberty to disclose it to me, for I admit I find myself quite curious. Such a miracle cure should certainly be written up for medical science."

But the Duke only laughed and said he was not at liberty to disclose his cure now, adding as her face fell that he hoped to share it with her shortly.

"Upon your return?" Dru asked hopefully, her curiosity now fully piqued.

"Sometime after my return," the Duke temporized, and with that Dru had to be content, realizing it would be impolite to continue to press the Duke on a matter which clearly was none of her concern.

She did not allow herself to dwell on why she found herself so interested.

Changing the subject, she walked with him back to the house where he took her hand, and, with great punctillio, kissed it, bringing a slight blush to her cheeks. Bowing slightly, he took his leave, walking jauntily off to the stables with a bemused Miss Wrothton staring after him. Realizing how she must look standing there, Drucilla gave herself a sound shake and walked slowly inside, her calm face at odds with the confusion behind it.

It was just like the Duke to call to tell her he was leaving, her thoughts ran, but what did it mean? Was there a special significance behind it, or was he only being his polite self, fulfilling an obligation? The gentleman had enjoyed many a London season among more beautiful ladies than she, she thought woefully. How could she imagine she could kindle a spark where others had failed?

"What a fool you are, Drucilla Wrothton!" she told herself sternly, going upstairs to dispose of her cape and hat and to smooth her hair. "He is just being kind, like the gentleman that he is."

And that thought so dismayed her that it was some little time before she roused herself to leave her chamber to join her mother and aunt in the drawing room where each was comfortably ensconced in a chair before a crackling fire, obstensibly engaged in needlework but spending much more time discussing the upcoming ball.

Upon her entrance, Hester cast a keen glance toward her niece, then, as if satisfied by what she saw there, returned her stare to the embroidery she held and with studied casualness asked, "Was that the Duke of Ratchford I saw riding off from the stables a few moments ago?"

Her mind elsewhere, Dru did not catch her aunt's tone and merely nodded, saying the gentleman had come to call.

"How odd that he did not call inside as well as out," her aunt pursued. "Usually so attentive to all the conventions—a most unexceptional young man—and how he came to know you were in the garden—"

But Drucilla did not wish her aunt to think how the Duke might have known she was in the garden, so she changed the subject, explaining that his lordship was on his way to Bath and had only stopped to take his leave of them, thus fulfilling his promise to call.

"Fulfilling his promise—," her aunt murmured speculatively, but before that interesting tidbit could be pursued further, wheels were heard in the drive, and Dru moved quickly to a window to see who had arrived.

She was in time to see Mr. Pettigrew hand her cousin down from his phaeton, and her swift gurgle of laughter bubbled out as the odious man bent to kiss Matty's hand.

"And pray, what is so funny, Drucilla?" her mother inquired mildly, to which the daughter replied, "Oh, it is the drollest thing, Mama. It is Matty returning with Mr. Pettigrew, and I believe she has charmed him completely, for he is kissing her hand, for all the world like a gentleman. I'd as lief be kissed by a toad, but Matty is remaining calm—" She broke off as she saw the gentleman return to his horses and heard her cousin's voice in the hall, and in waiting for that lady to enter, missed the complacent looks exchanged by the room's two older inhabitants.

In a moment Matty was with them, in such good looks and such high spirits that Aunt Hester was moved, with much arching of her eyebrows, to suggest that her niece should perhaps go driving every day.

Matty's look was demure and her voice tranquil as she replied she would like nothing better, again occasioning an exchange of speculative glances between the two older ladies. Dru immediately offered to take her out the following day, then bore her cousin off to divest herself of her cloak and bonnet and to rest her fast-healing ankle.

Until the drawing-room door clicked closed behind them, Lady Jane and Hester sat quietly, but once the cousins could be heard ascending the stairs, Hester put down her embroidery and, in a tone of self-congratulations, said, "My dear Jane, I believe we've done it. I never doubted that we could get Drucilla eligibly betrothed, but to think of firing them both off at this late date—oh, it is too wonderful. I believe I shall write Cecil immediately to apprise him of the happy news."

"Oh, Hester, no!" Jane protested, startled, a note of urgency creeping into her voice. At her sister-in-law's surprised look, she began a hesitant explanation. "They are hardly betrothed yet—and Cecil—while an estimable man, of course—well, he would likely be so foolish as to post down here immediately to make Mr. Pettigrew's acquaintance. And my dear, you know how he sets up Matty's back—there's no telling what harm he might do."

Much struck by this piece of good sense, Hester nodded. "You're right, of course," she agreed. "We must exercise the greatest caution. It is only when I think of our triumph—"

"Hardly *our* triumph, Hester," Jane interrupted, amused. "I do believe Matty and Dru have had a great deal to do with it."

But Hester waved that aside. "No, Jane," she said firmly, "We shall bring it off. It is our foresight in planning this ball which will do it. When the Duke sees Drucilla in her gown—and when Pettigrew sees that even Matty can look presentable—that seamstress is a miracle worker, Jane. I believe I will make her the fashion."

"Really, dear, you make Matty sound like a positive antidote," Jane began reprovingly, but Hester, caught up in the visions of her matchmaking victories, was not listening.

"I'll tell you what, Jane," she burst out, interrupting her sister-in-law's gentle conversation. "I'm so sure that we will have two offers—one for Matty and one for Drucilla—within a se'en-night following the ball that if we do not I will eat the feathers on my purple hat."

"Your purple hat?" Jane replied faintly. "But my dear—really—" Then she paused and regarded the other lady mischievously. "I would like to see that, dear Hester. I have never liked that hat."

Upstairs, the two objects of the elder ladies' conversation were conversing on their own, Drucilla having followed her cousin into Matty's chamber as that lady removed her cloak and settled herself in her favorite armchair, her ankle resting on a stool before her.

"And tell me, Matty," Dru was saying, "was Mr. Pettigrew his usual arrogant self today?"

Matty's eyes sparkled. "Well, I'm not sure I'd say arrogant,

Dru—perhaps—no—well, perhaps overbearing. I have never seen him more so.''

"Such a pity," her cousin sighed. "How he and the Duke of Ratchford can be such friends . . . But perhaps he is not so insufferable with his male cronies. The Duke tells me a number of London ladies also find Mr. Pettigrew very attractive, but I think that is only Ratchford's partiality for his friend speaking. Still, he might be quite handsome if he weren't so arrogant. Do you think so?"

Matty, who hadn't been attending, started, and said, "I beg your pardon?"

"Do you think Mr. Pettigrew might be handsome if he weren't so arrogant?"

Matty cocked her head as if considering, then agreed. "I daresay he might be.''

"He seems to find you quite attractive," Drucilla teased and mistook her cousin's blush for distress at the idea. "I daresay it would do him good if you broke his heart," she continued lightly, "but I don't believe he has one, so it would waste your time to try."

"Oh, I would never break Mr. Pettigrew's heart," Matty assured her, then changed the subject, amused at her cousin's lack of perception and wondering what that lady would say when the news were broken to her.

Chapter XX

The Duke of Ratchford arrived in Bath the following day and stared out the windows of his coach as the coachman made his way to the house the Duchess had rented for her stay there. That was not difficult for it was not the resort's busy season, and the Duke wondered with a grin what ever had possessed his mother to repair to such a spot at this time of year.

"She'll make herself sick if she's not careful," he thought, smiling at the memory of the last time the lady had arrived in Bath to drink the water. She had taken one large swallow, pronounced it terrible, and thereafter made a miraculous recovery which allowed her to go about in Bath society without ever resorting to the beneficial drink again.

The ancient butler who opened the door to the Duchess's establishment was delighted to see the Duke and, with the familiarity permitted an old retainer, urged him to visit his mother immediately before changing his clothes.

"For she'll be that glad to see you, my lord, I'm sure," Harris burst out in a fit of confidence. "Regular moped to death she's been—" Then, realizing what he had said as the Duke's eyes twinkled in sympathy, the old butler drew himself up and said, "That is, the Duchess has not been feeling at all well lately, and we hope the journey to Bath will do much to restore her spirits."

"Yes, but Harris, why Bath?" the Duke asked, putting to the servant the question which had been most puzzling him. "At this time of year? Surely she doesn't really intend to drink the waters again?"

"Oh, no, sir," Harris assured him most emphatically. "I have heard her say a dozen times that she has no intention of poisoning herself with a bunch of illtasting minerals."

The Duke's grin was one of appreciation. "I can hear her myself," he agreed, then returned to his former question. "So why Bath?"

"Well—," the butler hesitated, the need to unburden himself warring with his sense of what should and shouldn't be said in the Upper Halls.

Understanding that, the Duke patted him kindly on the arm and said, "Come come, Harris, I am family."

"Just so, sir," Harris replied gratefully. "Well, of course you realize I can't be sure—'' He peered anxiously at the Duke, who nodded. "And you know I wouldn't for the world speak out of turn—'' Again the Duke nodded to assure him.

"Well, sir, what I think it was was your Aunt Margaret," he said, letting it all out in a burst of confidence.

The Duke's look of puzzlement increased. "Aunt Margaret?" He repeated. "Don't tell me she's here too!"

"Oh, no, sir," Harris said, smiling at the Duke's evident relief. "I'm just saying that I think it's because of your Aunt Margaret that her ladyship and her ladyship's household are here."

The Duke sighed and, leaning his back comfortably against the wall, folded his arms and stared at the old butler in resignation. "I believe there is more to this story than I first imagined, Harris," he said. "Please begin at the beginning."

Harris was only too happy to do so, for there had been no one other than the housekeeper with whom he could talk, him not feeling it was good to encourage the footmen to think themselves better than they were by confiding in them.

"It's really not that confusing, my lord," he assured the Duke, who did not look convinced. "There was her ladyship several weeks ago feeling rather hipped, and she says to your Aunt Margaret—who was visiting at the time—that her health is quite indifferent and she wonders if a change of scene would do her good. 'Perhaps I will go to Bath and drink the waters,' she says, for I heard her as I was bringing in the tea tray. You know her way, sir—I'm sure at that time she had no intention of coming to Bath.''

The Duke's eyes met Harris' with a smile. "I believe I'm beginning to understand," he murmured. "Correct me if I'm wrong, Harris, but Mother said she thought she would go off to Bath as a way of eliciting Aunt Margaret's sympathy, and what must my forward speaking aunt do but point out to her that she did not like the waters and could not be brought to drink them if she were there.''

The butler nodded in agreement. "But that was not all, sir," he said. "I believe Mrs. Murphy and I might have quieted her ladyship's indignation over that slur upon her intentions had not your aunt—an estimable woman, I'm sure, but perhaps a bit quick of tongue—added that nobody comes to Bath this time of year and that her ladyship would be much better off if she would just brace up and quit quacking herself."

"Brace up?" the Duke repeated faintly. "Aunt Margaret told my mother to brace up? And to quit quacking herself? Oh Lord!" The look on Harris's face showed he was in complete agreement.

"So what must Mother do but pack up immediately and head for Bath?" the Duke said. "Of course. Thank you Harris. I understand now."

"Yes, my lord," the butler replied with his most stately bow. "I was sure you would." Then, in perfect agreement, the two men walked down the short hall to the morning room at the back of the house where the Duchess of Ratchford reclined upon a sofa by the fire, her invalid pose at odds with her well-filled frame. When Harris opened the door to announce her guest, she raised languid eyes to him, but at the first sight of her son that attitude left her, and she rose excitedly, moving forward to greet him.

"Sebastian, my love," she cried, offering him a cheek to kiss. "You here? And to what do I owe this unexpected visit?"

"Unexpected, Mama?" he chided her, bestowing a peck on her cheek before allowing her to lead him back to the sofa where she again resumed her languid air, drawing her shawl around her shoulders and reaching for the smelling salts which were never far from her. "How can you say so when you send me a letter informing me you have entered a sharp decline from which you do not intend to recover? Do you think I have no family feeling?"

The Duchess at fifty-four was a tall, handsome woman whose unlined face was graced with a prominent nose and heavy-lidded eyes. She now gazed suspiciously at him from under those lids and said, with considerable asperity, "Having paid no attention to my ill health in the past, I cannot think why you would expect me to expect you at this point. One of these days I shall be dead and then you will all know I was as sick as I said." The thought seemed to give her satisfaction.

Her son, who loved her dearly, raised her hand to his lips and said, "I pray that will not be for many years, Mama. I would hate to see you deprive your grandchildren of the doting I'm sure you'll give."

"Well that's all very well," the Duchess began roundly, before all he had said could sink into her thoughts, "But no one pays the least attention to my illnesses, and your Aunt Margaret—my only sister, at that—goes so far as to say I *quack* myself—did you say GRANDCHILDREN?"

The Duke grinned.

"Grandchildren?" she repeated, sitting bolt upright and staring at her son in disbelief. "Do you mean after all these years of cajoling you, praying for you, pleading with you—"

"Nagging me—"

"That you have finally taken your mother's advice and found a young woman to marry?" A terrible thought crossed her mind. "She's not one of the Americans you met on your travels is she?"

The Duke's grin grew larger. "No, Mother, she's not," he assured her. "She's an English lady just as you've always wished."

"Just as I've always wished..." the Duchess replied, drawing heavily on her smelling salts to refresh herself. "Just as I've always wished... Oh Sebastian, I had quite given up hope."

"Indeed you had not," replied her undutiful son, his eyes twinkling. "Forever sending me word of this girl or that heiress, and dragging me off to Almacks when I was in town—given up hope indeed!"

The Duchess ignored that and, patting his hand expectantly, smiled at him. He smiled back. "Well?" she prodded.

He looked puzzled. "Well?"

"Sebastian, you are just like your father! The most exasperating man who ever lived—who is she, Sebastian? Where is she?"

"Of—of course. Her name is Fanny Flarue, and she is one of the leading actresses on the London stage."

"Fanny Flarue—" His mother clutched one hand to her heart and with her other raised her smelling salts to her nose. "Fanny Flarue—," she repeated faintly. "An actress. An Actress. But you said—you said—'' She looked up into the dancing eyes before her and her indignation grew as he burst into shouts of laughter.

"JUST like your father!'' she stormed. "That you could do this to me with my delicate nerves—''

"If you could have seen your face—,'' her son choked.

"Coming here to tease your poor mother with this dreadful hum—raising my hopes and then shattering them like that—it is too bad of you, Sebastian. Truly it is. I suppose I shall never have grandchildren. What woman would have you with this sadistic streak—''

"Oh, Mother, not sadistic,'' her son protested.

"Yes, sadistic,'' she repeated bitterly. "Coming here raising my hopes, saying you're to be married when you aren't to be married at all—''

"But I am,'' he assured her. "At least I hope I am. That part of the story is very real.''

She regarded him with suspicion. "We shall try this again, Sebastian,'' she said stiffly. "Tell me about your young woman; and if you dare to say Fanny La-something-or-other, I shall go off in strong hysterics, and you shall know until your dying day that it was you who killed your mother.''

Such threats did not seem to seriously discomfit her son, who patted her hand coaxingly and said, "Oh give over, do, Mother. It was only a tease, and one I must say I think you deserved, with all the young ladies you have been pushing at me the last twelve years.''

Now it was her turn to protest. "Oh, surely not twelve, dear. And I wasn't *pushing* young ladies at you—that would be vulgar—'' Then she realized she was wandering from the subject and with great dignity settled her shoulders and said, "But you have not yet explained yourself. Who is she and where is she?''

For a moment the Duke didn't seem to know where to begin. Then he said hesitantly, "You know I've been seeing to one of our smaller estates, fixing up the house, which was in bad need of repairs. She lives near there. Her name is Drucilla Wrothton, of the Wrothtons of Morningdale Manor.''

"Wrothton,'' the Duchess mused, "Wroth—never say she is Jane

Wrothton's daughter?'' At her son's nod of acquiescence she cried, ''My dear, I never thought you to have such good sense! I do believe I've even met the girl—although it would have been several years ago—what with the death of Jane's husband and then her son they have not been in company for some time—and a loss it has been to society, too, for we have too few gentle ladies—Jane Wrothton's daughter! Well!'' She sat for several moments engaged in her own thoughts, then turned to the Duke and said, ''Now, my dear, you must tell me all about your young lady. What did you say her name was again?''

''Drucilla,'' the Duke supplied, amused at his mother's reaction. ''And what can I tell you, except that she is lovely, and kind, and comfortable—easy to converse with, and intelligent—not in a superior sort of way, you understand, but just so quick to follow what one is talking about—and not forever expecting one to dance the pretty as so many females seem to do—she's—she's—'' He floundered and looked at his mother appealingly.

''Why Sebastian,'' that good lady smiled, reaching out to touch his cheek. ''I believe you really are in love with this girl.'' At his nod she dusted her hands briskly and said, ''Now that is beyond anything wonderful. When is the wedding?''

Her son was startled. ''The wedding?''

''Of course the wedding,'' his mother replied. ''Don't tell me you haven't set a wedding date yet? How am I ever to see those grandchildren if you're going to be so slow doing your part? What must Drucilla think if you won't talk about a date for the wedding?''

Ratchford cleared his throat. ''Well, you see Mother—,'' he began. ''That is—well, Miss Wrothton would probably think it amiss if I did ask her to set a wedding date right now, seeing as I have not yet asked her to marry me.''

''Not asked—not asked—not asked her to marry you?'' The lady again raised her smelling salts to her nose. ''You are your father's son,'' she murmured. ''It is enough to make me despair.''

''Oh, not again,'' he quizzed her, but she fixed him with a stern stare and asked why he had not asked the lady for her hand when he was so obviously besotted with her.

"I don't want to rush her, Mother," he tried to explain. "She has an aunt already doing that. We really haven't known each other that long—I know she is pleasant to me but I don't know that she loves me—well really, Mother, a man doesn't just up and pop the question overnight!"

"Sebastian, Sebastian," his mother groaned. "You are thirty-four years old; thirty-four years is not 'overnight.' Of course the girl loves you. If she has any sense at all—and I am sure she has a great deal of sense, from all you've said—she must love you. Why are normally intelligent men such ninnies when it comes to women?"

She glared at her son, who looked somewhat embarrassed and went to stand by the fire, his hands behind his back.

"I don't want to risk her saying no, Mama," he said, and at his tone she went to stand beside him, one hand reaching up to smooth the hair at the base of his neck.

"She would not, my love," the Duchess said quietly. "I am sure of it." There was a moment's silence as the Duke's thoughts flew to Morningdale Manor and as his mother cogitated a plan, which she had in short order and rather startled him by announcing.

"You must sweep her off her feet," she said with swift decision. "Procur a special license and carry her off to the nearest clergyman—"

"Mother!" exclaimed her shocked son. "For thirty-four years you've preached propriety to me and now you want me to elope as if I'm one of the characters in some of those ridiculous novels you're so fond of? Really!"

His mother looked at him wistfully. "It was just an idea."

"A bad one!"

She sighed. "All right, my very conventional son; if you won't marry her out of hand, we'd best begin the conventional way as soon as possible. When may I meet your future wife?"

He grinned. "If you promise not to call her that on presentation, you might join me at Maplehurst in several days, secure in the knowledge that when your presence is known you will be invited to the upcoming Wrothton ball, and you can meet her there without making a large production of it." A thought struck him and he regarded his mother anxiously. "You *can* meet her without making a large production of it, can't you Mother?"

The Duchess threw him a look of great scorn. "Of course I can," she said. "When have I ever made a great production of anything?" Then, seeing that her regrettably honest offspring was about to tell her, she forestalled him by saying, "Did you say a ball, my dear? How delightful that will be. I believe it will do me much more good than the horrible waters they have here. I tell you, Sebastian, I don't know how people drink them—" She met the smile in his eyes as she looked up and, with a great deal of shrewdness, said, "You knew that, didn't you, my dear? In that way you are also very like your father. How I miss that man—but there!" She gave herself a shake. "We have much to talk about before you leave tomorrow, and I have much to do if I am to follow you soon. Dinner is at 7:30; you will want to change, and—" She paused a moment, and at the break of her speech her son, who had been moving toward the door, looked back inquiringly.

"Mama?" he asked at the look of dismay upon her face.

"It just occurred to me!" she said, sinking slowly into a chair. "When you marry I shall become the Dowager Duchess!"

Comprehension at once lit his face. "The youngest Dowager Duchess ever, Mama," he said gallantly, returning to kiss her hand. "And, I am sure, the prettiest."

She smiled with gratitude, then a gleam which matched the one in his eyes entered her own. "You must make me a promise, Sebastian," she said, and he readily agreed. Belatedly he asked what he had agreed to.

"Only this," his mother returned. "Since it is you who will soon be making me a dowager duchess, it seems only fair that you will also—soon—make me a grandmother. Promise?"

Her son smiled down at her. "I'll tell you what, Mama," he said, "I shall take it up with my duchess as soon as we are married."

"Just like your father," the lady returned with a reminiscent nod. "How I envy your wife!"

Chapter XXI

Preoccupation pervaded Morningdale Manor in the following week. Lady Jane and Hester, involved in their arrangements for the ball, had little time to notice that Dru and Matty were present in body but absent in thought, and when they did notice, it was without surprise. A lifted eyebrow and a swift smile were all they exchanged, and those were quickly hidden when the young ladies turned inquiring eyes toward them.

Dru, whose thoughts had centered on Bath for several days, found them closer to home with the Duke's return, and she was only too happy to take her cousin driving each day to raise that young woman's spirits.

If they just happened to drive east more often than not, and if the road east led by the Duke's estate, and if they just happened to tool up the drive to see how the work being done there progressed, who was to care? Matty did not. In fact, she seemed quite interested in the progress, although she neglected to tell her cousin that Mr. Pettigrew was thinking of buying this estate from his friend, since it was only one of the Duke's many properties, and a rather small one at that, compared to the Ratchford familial seat.

Since Drucilla was not in possession of this piece of knowledge, she did not understand why the insulting Pettigrew was forever present, and she stiffened each time she saw him in discussion with Ratchford. However, upon the Duke's swift smile at sight of her, she

162

simply forgot the more obnoxious gentleman and did not remember him again until the cousins were driving home. Then her conscience smote her, and she apologized to Matty for leaving her to bear Pettigrew's conversation while she herself was so much more delightfully entertained.

Matty largely forgave her, and Dru, intent on maneuvering her phaeton past a clumsy coach, did not note her cousin's quizzical glance; nor did she catch the gleam in Matty's eye before that good woman folded her hands in her lap and remarked mildly that she did not find Mr. Pettigrew so forbidding after all. Indeed, she ventured, she began to think him quite human, and she hoped that someday Drucilla might overcome her dislike of him.

Dru, impressed by her cousin's greatness of spirit, reached over to squeeze Matty's hand, saying, "Your kindness does you credit, cousin. I only hope Mr. Pettigrew appreciates the condescension you are showing him."

Visions of her crushed efforts to condescend to Mr. Pettigrew rose before Matty's eyes, and the kindly cousin found herself seized by a coughing spell which made Dru quicken the team's pace, for she thought it would be a terrible thing if Matty should fall ill only four days before the ball.

The same cough afflicted Matty the following afternoon as she informed Mr. Pettigrew of the great condescension her cousin believed her to be showing him. The height of the gentleman's eyebrows and the chagrin which covered his face were more than she could bear.

He fixed her with a stern glare and, his color slightly high, said stiffly, "I am glad you find it so amusing, my dear Miss Cresley."

Matty bit her lip. "I really do," she assured him, "especially when I see how you appreciate my kindness."

"Your kindness?" he repeated incredulously. "Condescension *and* kindness?"

"Indeed yes, sir," she said demurely, tucking her hands into her muff and fixing her glance on the toe of her left boot. "Drucilla is *convinced* that being seen with me must vastly improve your consequence."

"Improve my—" She peeped up in time to see a muscle twitch at the corner of his mouth.

"Aunt Hester thinks so too," she added for good measure, whereupon his lips tightened, and they rode in silence down the road, a silence broken only by the rhythmic sound of the horses' hooves.

After several moments Matty remarked airily that it was a good thing she had such a large spirit, for a smaller woman might have been sadly put out of countenance being driven about by a gentleman who chose to entertain her with sulks and an occasional grinding of teeth.

The gentleman's harsh features relaxed as he murmured, "Too, too kind of you."

"Isn't it?" the lady replied brightly.

He stared at her, then burst into laughter. "Cleo, my love, it amazes me that you have reached your age with no one having murdered you."

She drew back in mock alarm. "But what did I say?" she inquired, the plaintive note in her voice belied by the laughing eyes she turned toward him.

"Wretch!" he returned. "What clankers you tell. I might believe that your cousin feels driving out with you gives me consequence, but that your aunt agrees—pitching it a bit too strong, my dear!"

"Oh, but it's true!" she assured him. "These days I am a pattern card of propriety in Aunt Hester's eyes." Assuming her perfect imitation of that lady's haughty tone, she touched him lightly on the arm and said, "Really, my dear, to be seen in the company of any Wrothton, no matter how remote the connection, cannot help but raise one in the eyes of the world."

"Does the remoteness of that connection extend to the Hovingtons?" he teased.

Matty grinned in approval. "Precisely what I asked her. Whereupon I lost some of my pattern-card respectability."

"Shocking," the gentleman said. "I see there is nothing for it. I shall have to take you away before you become past praying for again. Will tomorrow be too soon?"

Matty, who had been enjoying the passing scene, turned inquiring eyes toward him.

"Too soon for what?"

He smiled and heaved a mock sigh. "My love, you can be remarkably caperwitted for such an intelligent woman."

Blushing rosily, Matty informed him that it was not proper for him to call her his love, whereupon the gentleman replied that if she expected him to call her Sebastian's love, she would have to wait all day for he had no intention of doing so.

Matty gazed at him consideringly, then touched his arm. "Mr. Pettigrew, there is something I feel I should know—that is, there is something I would like to ask you."

Surprised at her serious tone, he covered her hand with his and said, "Of course, my dear. What is it?"

She gazed straight into his eyes. "Does insanity run in your family?"

His bark of laughter exploded on the air, and he promised she could soon judge for herself when she met his Aunt Agatha in Grantham. They rode in companionable silence while Matty turned their conversation over in her mind.

"Did you mean it?" she asked finally, and at his surprised look explained. "About eloping tomorrow?"

He appeared to consider. "Well, I had nothing better to do tomorrow," he said at last. "This is humbug hunting country, and a man gets so bored."

"And you thought eloping would alleviate your boredom?"

He grinned. "My dear, I am convinced that eloping with you, and the life after that elopement, may be many things, but none of those things will be boring."

"Well!" Matty said silkily, "am I to understand that you wish to marry me simply to keep you from being bored?"

His grin broadened. "You would be a great noddy to understand any such thing, and well you know it. If my only purpose in eloping were to escape boredom, I could more easily achieve that end by spending an afternoon with your Aunt Hester." At her look of inquiry, he continued. "Spending tomorrow with her would not be boring, but neither would it be much fun."

Recalling the air of distraction which enveloped her aunt as the ball date drew nearer, Matty had to agree, adding, "It certainly wouldn't. Especially since my darling brother is due to arrive tomorrow."

"Your brother?" Pettigrew was startled.

Matty's disgust was evident in the decided shake of her head. "He and his loving wife are coming to share in the glory of a ball at Morningdale Manor. At least, that is their ostensible purpose. It is my belief that their trip is prompted by my aunt's dark hints that there is something afoot between us—"

"Afoot? Between us?"

"My aunt," Matty said crossly, "is a great deal too busy about my business. She is obsessed with seeing me wed."

"A most intelligent woman, your aunt," Pettigrew interjected promptly. "Behold in me a man determined to see that she gets her wish."

Matty glared at him for a moment, then turned slightly away so that she could still glimpse his face while he could not see hers.

"You will enjoy meeting my brother," she assured him. "He will, of course, wish to know your exact intentions toward me. And he will want to know your expectations. He will ask if you have a fortune of your own or if you are hanging out for mine." She noted with satisfaction that her love's complexion was beginning to rise, and her eyes twinkled as she continued, her tone mendacious. "He will insist on a large Westminster wedding, and he will want to give me away—"

"With great relief, I'm sure—," Pettigrew interjected.

The lady ignored him. "He will want to know if you will love me forever, and no doubt he will huff out his cheeks as he informs you he will stand for no ill treatment of his sister—"

"I will assure him that I shall love you right up until the moment I wring your neck—"

Her tone was dulcet. "You will no doubt enjoy that interview?"

"I look forward to it, my dear," he assured her. "I regret

extremely that I will be away when your estimable brother arrives at Morningdale.''

At that Matty started. ''Away?'' she questioned, for she had expected him to support her during Cecil's trying presence.

''I'll be on my way to Grantham,'' he said.

''Oh.'' She digested that. ''Will I be accompanying you?''

He paused and rubbed his chin thoughtfully. ''Well I do hope so, Cleo. I would appear such a cake, eloping by myself.''

''I would like to see that,'' the lady murmured wistfully, but before she could go further, Pettigrew put an end to her conversation by pulling his team to the side of the road and, oblivious to the grinning farmboy walking by, proceeded to kiss her soundly.

''Crandon, really,'' she protested after a suitable interval. ''This is a public road.''

His eyes twinkled as he suggested finding a private lane, but the lady would not agree, informing him roundly that he was quite impossible and that he had crushed her bonnet beyond repair.

''I thought I was quite ingenious,'' he reproached her. ''I believe I've found the perfect way to quiet you when I am tired of conversation.''

She eyed him warily. ''I did not know you find my conversation so boring.''

''Oh, not boring,'' he assured her. ''It is just that when you make such absurd remarks—well, there, I feel that I must do it again,'' and the lady, nothing loathe, gave herself up to an embrace, secure in the knowledge that it would not do to struggle with a madman.

''You really are insane, you know,'' she said presently, her head leaning on his shoulder as they made their way back to Morningdale.

''Quite,'' he replied cheerfully. ''There's nothing to it but to marry me immediately before word leaks out and they clap me up in Bedlam.''

''Now there's an idea—'' She pretended consideration but hastily recanted as he leaned toward her, his purpose written in his eyes. ''No, Crandon—I mean Mr. Pettigrew—I mean—don't you dare,'' she snapped. ''I just got my hair tucked back under this blasted bonnet and I don't care to have to do it all over again.''

"I like the way you say Crandon," he replied. "I was beginning to wonder if you found my name so hard to pronounce."

"No, Mr. Pettigrew, I do not," Matty answered primly. "It is just that I do not consider it proper for me to make use of your Christian name at this time."

"Would half-past two be a better time?" he inquired in an innocent tone which the lady met with silence. "Would you prefer to make use of an unchristian name?" he asked finally and was rewarded with her burst of laughter.

"Really, I wish you would be sensible," she scolded him, "for if we really are to go dashing off to Grantham tomorrow—"

"My love, I said nothing about dashing—"

"Then we must make some plans. How am I to get my clothes out of the house without raising suspicion? And of course I shall have to bring Caesar along—"

"Bring Caesar?" Pettigrew asked incredulously. "You really expect to elope with that great beast?"

"What's one more great beast?" she twinkled up at him, but all her further cajolings could not move him on the subject of the dog.

"He stays at Morningdale, Matty," he said firmly. "Your cousin will look after him until we return."

She remained doubtful, but at last consoled herself by remarking that it would not be so long after all, since they must return for the ball.

Again Pettigrew's voice rose. "The ball? We are eloping, and you are thinking of some trumpery ball?"

On this point Matty was firm. "I came to Morningdale to see Drucilla through this ball and I shall do so," she said. "I will assure her of that in the note I leave—"

"The NOTE?" The decibel level of Mr. Pettigrew's voice matched the height of his eyebrows. "You are going to leave a *note*? My dear Mathilde, why do we not just issue invitations—Miss Cresley and Mr. Pettigrew request the honor of your presence at their elopement—"

"Don't be silly," she snapped. "No printer could have them ready in time."

He was not amused. She tried again. "Do you really think I could go off for several days without leaving word?"

"Yes."

"Now who's being caper-witted? They would be in a rare taking if they had no idea where I'd gone. What would they think?"

"That you've been kidnapped by gypsies," he returned promptly. "That you'd gone to join your countrymen in the defense of England. That your cousin Percival came by night and stole you away. That—"

"That will be enough," she supplied. "I will leave a note. A discreet one."

"Ha!"

"Bah!" she replied, folding her arms across her chest and glaring up at him.

A reluctant grin broke as he gazed down at her militant pose. "Most unladylike," he reproved, but she ignored him, spending the rest of the drive wondering if it would be best to slip her necessary clothes out of the house in a bundle that evening, to be thrown to him over a wall at midnight (a scheme the lady favored), or if she should be more conventional and simply pack them in a picnic basket and say he was taking her on a picnic. The gentleman favored the latter idea.

"You have a very unromantic soul," she informed him, to which he agreed with a grin. As the manor came into view, they decided on a 10 a.m. departure, a time Matty felt would put them out of the house well before her brother's arrival but after Dru had left for her morning ride. One final thought struck her.

"You do have a special license, don't you?" she inquired suspiciously, to which he patted his coat pocket, not telling her that he had been carrying it there the past three weeks.

As they pulled up to the manor and he helped her down from the phaeton, Matty raised her eyes to his and in a not-unhopeful voice asked, "Are you sure you wouldn't rather come in the dead of night and steal me away by raising a ladder to my window?"

"It is my heart's desire to do so, my dear," he returned promptly, "but I have lent out my last ladder, not knowing I'd be needing it.

However, if you would care to make a rope of bedsheets and lower yourself from the window—''

Dru, opening the door just as Pettigrew drove away, could not determine what it was he said which had sent her cousin off into such giggles, nor would Matty tell her. And Matty, pleading a sore ankle as a reason to rest alone in her room, escaped to that chamber, there to sit and dream.

"This is insane, Matty,'' she told herself as she peered at her reflection in the mirror, then giggled aloud as she realized she did not mind.

In accordance with their plan, Matty did not descend to the breakfast table the next morning, and although Dru was surprised to hear Polly's announcement that her mistress was too tired to appear, she did not attend to the maid's dark mutterings about Miss going off on a picnic when she was burned to a socket and should be staying in her bed like a woman of sense. Dru said mildly that she rather thought a picnic might relax Matty, and beyond charging Polly with a message that she would look in on her cousin when she returned, she thought no more about it as she trod happily off to the stables for a ride which just might take her down a path the Duke often traveled in the mornings.

After having Polly procure a large picnic basket loaded with food for her and Mr. Pettigrew, Matty wisely sent her faithful henchwoman off to the village on an errand, making sure that Caesar accompanied her. The dog looked at her sorrowfully as he left the room, almost as if he sensed a trick, and Matty was moved to remove one of the picnic sandwiches for him, much to Polly's dismay.

"You do spoil that beast, Miss Matty,'' said the scandalized maid, but Matty only laughed and said she always had a soft spot in her heart for a beast.

After Polly and the dog departed, Matty regretfully unloaded the chicken, ham sandwiches, and cakes the cook had so thoughtfully provided. Stuffing them into the bottom of her wardrobe, she then packed the few necessities she would need, tied on a straw bonnet the green ribbons of which matched her morning gown, and, grabbing up her cloak, limped from the room and down the stairway to the main hall, where she promptly encountered her Aunt Hester intent on a visit to the kitchen to confer with an already distracted cook about the hundredth change in the menu.

"Going on a picnic, I see," Hester began, eyeing her niece curiously, for at sight of her Matty blushed brightly.

"Yes, Aunt, Mr. Pettigrew and I are going to explore the old abbey ruins," she began, then remembering her injured ankle added, "that is, we are going to visit the ruins, we won't do much walking about—that is—" She stumbled to a stop but noted with a bit of a twinkle that her aunt did not seem to find her any more incoherent than usual.

"Mr. Pettigrew, hmmm?" Hester repeated, smiling like a cat left in the pantry with the cream pot. "And what goodies has cook packed for you?"

She started forward to peer into the basket, but her startled niece held the lid firmly closed as she backed away. "Oh, the usual things," Matty replied vaguely as her aunt stared at her in surprise. "Chicken, sandwiches, cakes, and—oh, I believe I hear Mr. Pettigrew coming now. Good-bye, Aunt! Have a pleasant day!" And with that she hastily made her departure, only to sit on the steps for several minutes until her true love arrived.

When he drove up he raised his eyebrows to see her sitting there and asked mildly if there was no room at the inn, or if she were so eager to be off that she was considering walking out to meet him. Matty replied crossly that it was neither and that if he had no interested relatives to elude when taking flight, he might realize other people did and appear when he was needed instead of several minutes late.

"I would say that eloping does not improve your temper, dear Cleo," he remarked as he took the picnic basket from her, but when she started to take it back and say that if he had second thoughts she was quite prepared to go back inside, he answered by picking her up and depositing her firmly on the phaeton seat.

"Entirely too hot at hand, my dear," he said, "and caper-witted besides."

The lady gave an excellent imitation of her aunt's snort. "You call me caper-witted and you turn up for a trip to Grantham in your open phaeton? I'd say that was the pot calling the kettle black!"

But that was met with a grin and the information that the phaeton was only for a drive to the Blue Boar, where a coach awaited them, "since I rather thought that arriving at your door in a coach and four might arouse unnecessary suspicion."

Matty glared at him. "It puts me so out of temper when you're right!" she said, then grinned. "One would almost think you had done this before."

"Practice makes perfect," he agreed cheerfully, and his lady, deciding that she could not discomfit him, chose instead to ignore him. She did that so well that after several miles he felt compelled to inform her that it was not considered good form to ignore a husband until *after* one had wed him. She was about to reply in kind when she spotted a coach toiling toward them. Something about the color of the driver's cape made her stare, and after one startled gasp she considerably astonished her love by slipping to the floor of the phaeton.

He started to pull his team in, but her hissed, "Drive on, drive on, and don't you dare look down," made him set the horses in motion. It was only after the coach had passed that Matty again joined him on the seat.

"A remarkable performance," he said in an amused tone. "Extremely entertaining. But do you intend to do so each time we meet a coach?"

Matty smoothed her skirt and straightened her bonnet. "I do if the coach contains my brother," she replied bitterly. "Wouldn't you know that on this day of all days that slugabed would choose to arrive at his destination early?"

"Your brother?" Pettigrew repeated. "I thought he wasn't expected until supper."

"He wasn't," Matty almost wailed. "You can't count on him for anything."

Pettigrew grinned at her tone and reached over to squeeze her hand. "Come now, love," he reproved. "It isn't as though he'd come chasing after us as if we were two children yet wet behind the ears."

Matty stared at him. "You don't know my brother, do you?"

"But surely no man of sense—"

She repeated the question. "You don't know my brother, do you?"

Pettigrew's grin deepened. "Should I be quaking in my boots? Do you think he'll call me out? Will it be small swords or pistols? I hope he doesn't plan to make it a killing affair—"

"Oh, *will* you be quiet?" his goaded love returned. "Of course he wouldn't call you out; I daresay you're a much better shot than he is. But what he will do is kick up a dreadful dust and arrive in Grantham out of temper and—"

"I doubt that," Pettigrew interrupted smoothly, but Matty was not assured.

"Haven't I just been telling you?" she asked. "He'll come after us and—"

"And he won't know where to look."

The two exchanged glances, and Matty brightened as she enthusiastically hugged Mr. Pettigrew's arm. "By all that's famous, you're right!" she crowed. "Wouldn't it be wonderful if he dashed off to Gretna Green in hot pursuit? Oh, I feel better already."

He was about to chide her on her lack of sisterly feeling when the Blue Boar came into sight, and in the next few minutes the topic was lost as the picnic basket was transferred to the coach and instructions were given for the safe return of the phaeton. As she started to mount into the coach, Matty caught sight of all the luggage tied on behind and chided Mr. Pettigrew for the amount of clothing he seemed to consider necessary for an elopement. She was shocked when he replied calmly that one of the trunks was hers, him not having much dependence on her ability to pack all she needed in a picnic basket.

Scandalized, Matty demanded to know if he had purchased clothes for her himself.

"Well I couldn't ask Sebastian to do it, could I?" he replied, his tone deceptively reasonable.

"Oh!" Matty said, her eyes stormy. "You are absolutely impossible."

"Past praying for," he agreed.

There was a long pause. "Well," she said at last, "aren't you going to tell me what you bought?" Her grin met his answering bark of laughter, and peace was restored as the two rode in amiable silence until Pettigrew asked Matty what news she had left of her elopement.

"I was very brief," she replied. "I wrote 'Dear Dru, I have eloped with Crandon Pettigrew. Will return for the ball. Love, Matty.'" He nodded his approval, but his brow darkened slightly as she added there had been a postscript.

"A postscript?" he asked suspiciously.

Matty smiled. "I told her to treat Caesar extra gently and to be sure and take the chicken and sandwiches out of the bottom of my wardrobe before they drew mice!"

"The chicken and sandwiches?".

"Well, you didn't think Cook would send us on a picnic with an empty picnic basket, did you?" she demanded, and he laughed again.

"Matty, I love you," he said. "I never thought I'd find you."

"Nor I you," she replied, then blushed, adding railingly, "and if we don't change the subject soon we are going to become quite maudlin."

Whereupon her intended drew out a traveling chessboard and they spent the next few hours locked in that game of skill.

Chapter XXII

Matty was correct when she said her brother and his wife were not expected until early evening, and upon their arrival the Cresleys were left waiting in the morning room for several minutes while Baxley and one of his underlings went in search of Hester and Lady Jane.

The former was run to earth in the kitchen, where she was driving the cook to surreptitious nips at the cooking wine with her continual "suggestions" for refreshments for the ball. Lady Jane was found supervising the hanging of the ballroom's new draperies; but upon being told that her guests had arrived, she left that task to the excellent Baxley and immediately made her way downstairs, arriving at the morning-room door just as Hester emerged from the kitchen. The two entered the room together, Hester remarking that had they expected dear Cecil so soon, she was sure Matty would not have gone off on a picnic but would have waited to welcome her brother.

"A picnic?" Cecil repeated, surprised. "Isn't it a bit early in the year for a picnic?"

Hester gave him an arch look and said, "Now, Cecil, surely you remember that in a certain person's company one can feel quite warm on the briskest day?"

Cecil looked incredulous and his wife blushed while Jane smiled at everyone and handed around cups of tea.

It was into such a domestic scene that Drucilla walked moments later, the Duke of Ratchford at her heels. The two had met while riding, and Dru had hit upon the happy notion of inviting him back to Morningdale for a light luncheon.

At the sight of one of her less favorite cousins, she wondered if it had been a good idea, but she politely presented the Duke to Cecil and his wife, saw Ratchford comfortably seated with a cup of tea at hand, and then excused herself to change from her riding habit into a morning gown. However, all intentions of changing were banished when she reached her room and found Matty's note propped against the pillows on her bed. She paled as she read the brief message written there, then sank shakily onto the bed and read it again.

"Eloped!" she gasped, her hand stealing to her cheek in a nervous gesture she had had as a child. It could not be! While she believed it would be just like her cousin to choose such an unconventional means of marriage, she could not believe that that young

175

woman would go willingly to wed a man such as Pettigrew. At that thought her eyes narrowed.

"He has tricked her!" she said aloud, rising from the bed and slapping her riding crop against it with considerable spirit. "He has tricked her, and I will not have it! That—that—that—" Words failed her, and for the first time in her life Dru wished she had paid more attention to the stableboys' conversations throughout the years. She was sure that in their vocabulary must be the very word she was seeking.

She was out the door of her room and down the stairs before she even realized it. It was only when she sped into the morning room in search of the Duke that the five pairs of eyes turned inquiringly toward her made her stop abruptly.

"Oh, I forgot—," she began, then collected herself and, turning to the Duke with a smile and pleading eyes, said, "that is, I forgot that you wanted to see our newest foal—"

"Now, dear?" her mother interrupted mildly. "It is almost time for luncheon. Wouldn't you rather change now and walk down to the stable later?"

"Oh, no!" Dru protested with a vehemence which surprised all those present. "That is—I mean—I believe we should do it right now, Mother. Right now." She fixed her eyes imploringly on Sebastian, and that gentleman, although he had not until this moment heard of a new foal, rose nobly to the occasion, saying, "I thought you had forgotten, Miss Wrothton. I would indeed like to see the foal. Now."

He was rewarded with a swift smile which changed to a look of horror when Cecil remarked that he too would enjoy seeing the newest piece of horseflesh, since he considered himself a rather knowledgeable judge of such animals and since he would be happy to trade opinions with the Duke anytime.

"Oh, no!" Dru blurted, turning to face him and filling him with indignation at finding his presence so unwanted. Then, aware of the surprise on the faces of all her relatives, Dru tried desperately to retrieve the situation, saying, "That is, of course you may see the foal Cecil—but not now," she added hastily as he began to rise. "That is—that is—"

"I believe Miss Wrothton is trying to say that too many people might frighten the mare," the Duke interposed smoothly, to which the lady heartily agreed. Not waiting for further argument, she grasped Ratchford's arm and hurried him from the room, leaving several shocked people behind. Yet once the door was shut after them, Dru made no move toward the entrance. Instead she led the mystified gentleman into the library, closed the door, and, turning dramatically toward him, said, "My lord, you must help me save my cousin. Please say that you will!"

At her look of entreaty, the Duke promptly agreed to do so. "With the greatest will in the world," he replied with his best bow. "Of course we must save Miss Cresley. Of course." He paused and cleared his throat apologetically. "One thing, Miss Wrothton—I mean—that is—what are we saving Miss Cresley from? Is she ill?"

Dru fixed him with a tragic stare. "Worse," she whispered. "She has been kidnapped by that viper Pettigrew."

"Kidnapped?" The word burst from the startled gentleman. "I say, Miss Wrothton, that's hardly Crandon's style." He stopped to peruse the note she thrust into his hand, and at sight of it his brow cleared.

"Ah, eloped," he said, as if a great mystery had just been solved. "They've eloped, Miss Wrothton. That's not kidnapping!"

"Ha!" Dru snapped her fingers at his protestation. "He has taken you in, too! I don't care what the note says, my lord, I know my cousin and I know she would never voluntarily go off with such a dreadful man. He has flummoxed her—and I don't know how, for Matty is usually so sensible—but however he has done it, I won't allow him to ruin her—"

Engrossed in her tirade, Dru missed the look of amusement that passed over the Duke's face as he pictured the unlikely scene of his friend Pettigrew trying to ruin the indomitable Miss Cresley.

"I must go after her," Dru continued earnestly. "I must find her and bring her back before they are found out and her reputation is ruined. How provoking of Cecil to arrive early—it is just like him!

He must not know or he will sermonize forever, and Matty will never have a moment's peace. Oh please," she said as she turned imploringly toward him. "Please, will you come with me to find them? We must leave immediately!"

Ratchford opened his mouth to expostulate, thought of something his mother had said, and closed his mouth again, patting his breast pocket as he pointed out that Matty and Pettigrew were old enough to know their own minds, and that he rather thought an elopement suited both of them. At Dru's burning look of reproach he capitulated, saying that since he was convinced that if he did not take her she would go without him, he would be happy to escort her.

"Thing is," he began apologetically as she brightened, "don't have my carriage. Felt I should mention it," he excused himself as her face fell again.

But Drucilla was a determined young woman, and she soon swept that consideration aside, saying, "We shall take my phaeton, and since they can't have been gone more than two hours, we shall come up with them quickly, don't you think?"

Ratchford, who had a very good opinion of the horses his friend would be driving, kept such thoughts to himself in an effort not to erase the look of hope in Drucilla's eyes. Instead he nodded noncommittedly and watched with interest as the lady seated herself at the desk and began to write.

"I must tell Mama what is happening so she won't worry," she explained as she signed her name to the hastily scrawled note. Feeling somewhat guilty, she added that she hoped her mother would be able to fob her aunt and cousin off until they all returned, "for by then we'll have thought up some explanation for our absence."

The Duke wryly shook his head and murmured, "Women always leave a note" as he followed her from the library. The lady did not hear him for her mind was elsewhere, intent on the task ahead. Halfway down the passage to the side door which led to the stables she checked and, excusing herself, asked the Duke to wait for her by the door while she fetched something from upstairs.

Scurrying up the steps, she hurried to Matty's room and opened the wardrobe. Grabbing an old shawl which hung there, she used it to hold the picnic lunch Cook had earlier prepared for her cousin. She saw no reason to let it go to waste when she and the Duke would be missing luncheon and would doubtlessly get hungry.

As she turned from the wardrobe, Dru met a disconsolate Caesar, who had returned from the village with Polly and was now standing sadly by the door as if he knew he had been left behind. He whimpered piteously and Dru paused only for a moment before saying, "Come along, old fellow. We must find Matty."

At that the dog ceased his whining, and his tail began to wag madly as he raced ahead of Dru down the back stairs to the door where the startled Duke eyed him questioningly.

"He will help us find Matty," Dru explained, "and besides, she asked me to look after him, and the only way I can do that is to take him with us."

The Duke blanched at the idea of riding bodkin with a giant black dog for who knew how many miles, but he forebore comment and, taking the shawl which Miss Wrothton informed him was their lunch, followed her and the dog out of the house and to the stables, wondering dazedly if he would soon wake to find he had been dreaming—or rather, he amended wryly—suffering a severe nightmare.

Years later Ratchford would pale at the remembrance of the occurrences of the next twenty-four hours, but he was often heard telling his grandchildren that one must sometimes endure great trials to win a prize worth having.

The great trials he had to endure began with Caesar and grew at the Blue Boar, for the Duke—unlike Drucilla, who was convinced that Pettigrew would carry her cousin to Gretna Green in an open vehicle—was sure that the gentleman would trade his phaeton for a carriage as soon as possible. He only wished that he might do the same, for Caesar, settled between the Duke and Drucilla, seemed to fancy himself a lapdog and rode with one front paw on each of their laps, his large head alternating from the lady's leg to the gentleman's.

A quick step into the Blue Boar convinced the Duke he was right, and he emerged from the modest hostelry smiling, only to find his companion in deep argument with a gentleman recently descended from the coach Ratchford had heard approach while he was inside. With a sinking feeling he recognized the form of Percival Hovington and hurried forward. Caesar, who had accompanied the Duke into the inn, also saw Percival, and, recognizing a man for whom he had a great dislike, advanced growling, much to Dru's delight and Hovington's dismay.

"Get away from me, you beast," Percy shouted, kicking out at the dog, who retaliated by grabbing his pants leg and refusing to relinquish it. Dru crowed, "It serves you right," but the Duke quickly put his hand on the dog's collar and, after convincing him that a bone would be better for his teeth than cloth, ordered him up into the phaeton, where he settled beside Drucilla and contented himself with an occasional bark in Percival's direction.

"*Most* improper," Hovington reiterated, and Drucilla, who had heard that remark before the Duke's return, shrugged in disgust as she told him to go away. That he would not do, and he turned to Ratchford, saying, "I have just been telling my cousin Drucilla that it is most improper for her to be riding this distance in an open phaeton with a man—and with no groom up behind. You would not find her cousin Matty doing so."

The Duke grinned, his hand sweeping toward the now dignified Caesar, who sat like a statue on Ratchford's half of the seat. "Tell me, Hovington," he said, "what do you think we might be doing in Miss Wrothton's phaeton with that large mutt along?"

Percy was not to be put off, although the Duke did his best to do so, even going so far as to say—with a speaking look at Dru—that he was sure Hovington was right, and Miss Cresley would not drive a distance in an open phaeton. Unfortunately, Drucilla so far forgot herself as to blurt out, "You mean they changed to a carriage?" and the aghast Ratchford could only stare at her in reproach.

Now no one had ever said that Percival Hovington was quick-witted; but it was often noted that when he did get an idea in his head, he worried it to death. The idea which entered his head now upon seeing the Duke's frown and Drucilla's hasty blush was that something was being kept from him, and he determined to find out what it was.

" 'They,' Cousin?" he repeated, blustering up at the lady who glared down at him. "And who do you mean by they?"

"No one, Percival," Dru returned. "No one. Thank you for your advice on ladylike conduct. I shall take it to heart. Come, my lord Duke, we must be off." The Duke agreed devoutly and hastened to climb into the phaeton, but Percy detained them by putting a heavy hand on the reins.

"But we were talking about Matty—," he cogitated slowly. "Then you said 'they'—" He stared up at the harassed faces before him, and enlightenment came. "It's that cur Pettigrew!" he cried. "He's kidnapped Matty!"

"Not kidnapped." The Duke was stung to a strong defense of his friend. "They've eloped. There's a vast difference."

Percival did not appreciate the distinction. "Eloped!" he yelped while Drucilla looked accusingly at Ratchford, who blushed at his own indiscretion.

"Eloped!" Percy repeated. "I cannot believe it. I will not believe it. That dog, that cur, that damned b—"

"Sir," the Duke roared, "there is a lady present!"

Recalled to his surroundings, Hovington colored brightly and bowed stiffly to his cousin as he apologized. "It was my strong feelings upon hearing this unfortunate news which so led me to forget myself," he huffed. "The thought of my dear Matty misled by that—that—" His voice trailed off as the Duke fixed a minatory eye upon him.

"Eloped!" he repeated again, shaking his head as he did so. "Eloped! But how—where—"

"Gretna Green," Ratchford replied with great promptitude, bringing him a reproachful glance from Dru. Percival started for his coach, intent upon giving chase, and it was unfortunate that at that moment the landlord, with the happy thought of finding another sovereign dropped in his palm for his helpfulness, emerged from the inn with just-remembered information about the "gentleman and lady who set off for Grantham."

The Duke cursed softly under his breath, wondering what in his past life had led to his being the recipient of such bad luck in the present; Drucilla stared at him in surprise and Hovington in puzzlement which soon turned to anger. Ratchford was comforted, however, when the lady beside him threw her arms around his neck, saying, "I didn't think you'd betray them." He had just freed an arm from where Caesar leaned on it to return her hug when the lady realized what she had done and drew back stiffly, begging pardon. Before he could assure her that he had enjoyed it above all things, Percival was beside the phaeton again, demanding his attention.

"Grantham, sir?" he sputtered. "They have gone to Grantham and you would have sent me chasing geese to Gretna Green? You would make me a figure of ridicule while you conceal information about your unhappy friend? I should call you out sir, I swear I should."

The Duke gazed down into his angry face and replied with some asperity that Hovington was quite capable of being a figure of ridicule without any help from him. He added that if Percy hoped to challenge the Duke to a duel, Ratchford would be only too happy to oblige him. Before their altercation could grow, Dru interrupted, crossly suggesting that her cousin "go home and mind your own business. I don't know what you're doing here anyway," she continued in exasperation, "although it does seem that ever since childhood you have had the most uncanny ability to be where you are unwanted."

He glared at her, his dignity wounded, and replied that he was on his way to Morningdale since he felt the future lord of the manor should be present at all festivities there. That remark so incensed Drucilla that she favored him with a short but pithy description of the circumstances under which he might find himself at Morningdale; since that was "when horses fly," she seemed to find the idea highly unlikely.

"Now go away, Percival," she ended. "We have business in Grantham."

"I too have business in Grantham," he returned stubbornly, causing Dru to exclaim in disgust as she gave her team the office to start. That sent her cousin, who had been leaning against the phaeton's wheel, into the dust. Helped up by the interested landlord, he sputtered angrily and jumped into his carriage, commanding the postboys to "follow that phaeton." When informed that a new team was needed for continued travel, he swore roundly and sat fretting as the horses were poled up. By the time the new team was in place, Drucilla and the Duke had disappeared from sight. He shouted, "Grantham!" at the postboy who asked his direction, then sank back on the carriage cushions as the coach lunged forward. His frown deepened as he sat there reliving his wrongs at the hands of the infamous Mr. Pettigrew.

Never in his indolent life had anything provoked Percival Hovington to such a fury that he would risk life, limb, or the disarrangement of his cravat. But his mother's opinion notwithstanding, he considered himself in love with his cousin Matty, and he worked himself into a fine passion as he assured himself that this abduction—for he refused to believe it could be anything else—was more than a body could bear. He puffed out his chest at the idea of calling the scoundrel to book and told himself that once the villain was dispatched, Matty would be his.

In that manner he whiled away the first part of his journey, envisioning himself a hero. He did not dwell on his inability to handle either the sword or dueling pistol well, for he had once seen Pettigrew perform at Mantons, and if his memory did not deceive him, the gentleman had been quite good. His brow darkened when he remembered that the man was also accounted an expert swordsman. Feeling his courage flag briefly, he regained it by picturing Matty's admiring face when he—never mind how—saved her from her abductor.

Meanwhile, the objects of such hot pursuit were nearing Grantham. An hour and a half behind them came Dru and the Duke, the former grimly holding her team in check so they would not tire too quickly. The gentleman beside her, who had almost had his nose bitten off when he offered to drive, watched her feather a corner and sank back onto the phaeton seat, beguiling the time by alternately watching the determined lady at his side, convincing the friendly Caesar that he was not a lap dog, and picturing Crandon Pettigrew's face when the three of them burst in upon him. The latter thought made him chuckle, although he would not tell his companion why he laughed. Folding his arms across his chest, he settled himself more comfortably on the seat and grinned as he wondered how he had ever thought a trip to America exciting when such adventures were awaiting him at home.

Chapter XXIII

Inside his carriage, Percival Hovington was growing increasingly fretful at the thought of the villainous Pettigrew damaging Percy's intended bride's reputation, and he leaned his head out the carriage window, adjuring the coachman to ''drive faster, you fool, drive faster.''

The coachman, who had his own grim opinion of which of them was the fool, nodded sullenly and began to spring 'em, throwing his passenger back into the coach with a heavy thud. Percy righted himself and rubbed his head angrily, his temper more injured than his person.

The past few weeks had been trying ones for Percy. His usually doting parents so far forgot he was the light of their lives as to carry him off to his sister's dull home and had scolded him soundly for imagining himself in love with the disgraceful Mathilde Cresley when they had practically secured a far more compliable—and infinitely richer—heiress for him. When he pointed out that the wealthy Miss Brown had a squint and no conversation, his father had adjured him to consider her fortune and not to nitpick about more trivial matters. Upon his setting his chin and saying sulkily that he absolutely would not have Miss Brown, his mother was so overcome by his ingratitude that she took to her bed with the vapors, moaning that never had she thought to nurse such an ungrateful monster at her breast.

Percy's stubbornness had seen him through the laments and accusations they hurled at his head; indeed, he had rather enjoyed standing up to them, imagining himself a romantically persecuted figure who would win out for love. That his love was not returned was not something which he allowed to trouble him greatly, for he still believed Matty's refusal to be due to maidenly confusion and not to any great aversion to his person. He did not believe for a moment that she had eloped with Pettigrew; he was sure the dog had spirited her away, and he could not wait to come up with them. Occupied with visions of a grateful lady falling into his arms and covering him with kisses, he was not prepared for the sound of splintering wood or the sudden careening of his coach before it landed abruptly at a quite awkward angle in a ditch. He heard the squeals of frightened horses and the accusations and counter-accusations of the coachman and postboys and tried unsuccessfully to right himself within the carriage. That he could not do, and when the off door was finally wrenched open and an anxious coachman peered in to inquire if he was hurt, Percy could hardly speak, so angered was he to find such an accident befalling him. He was even more frustrated when, after being ignominiously pulled from the coach by several postboys, he found that a wheel had come loose and one of the horses had been injured in the ensuing confusion. Snatching his hat from his head he threw it to the ground with great violence, then stomped on it for good measure. To the interested postboy who had watched this little tantrum he shouted out a demand that he "do something, at once." The postboy, who could think of nothing else to do, grinned, further enraging his worthy patron, but the boy did not seem unduly concerned about it.

Things were not progressing much more smoothly at Morningdale Manor, for when Drucilla and the Duke failed to return to the house when luncheon was announced Lady Jane asked Baxley to send one of the footmen down to the stables to fetch them. At her request, Baxley cleared his throat and ventured to suggest that such action would be futile, since Miss Drucilla and the Duke of Ratchford had ridden off from there some twenty minutes earlier.

"Ridden off?" Jane repeated, her soft brow furrowing at that information. "Well that's certainly strange! I wonder what ever possessed them—"

Her thoughts were interrupted by a blustering Cecil, who fixed Baxley with a commanding eye and demanded to be told where they had gone. The butler fixed his gaze on a point just right of the gentleman's ear and with great dignity replied that he could not say, him not being so forward as to question Miss Drucilla's movements.

Cecil, wondering suspiciously if that was Baxley's way of giving him a setdown, thought deeply and concluded that something was being kept from him. "I suspect that something is amiss here," he pronounced with great authority, "and I demand to be told what it is." He gazed around him in expectation but met only four pairs of confused eyes, and his temper mounted as he realized no one else seemed to know what was happening either.

"I don't think anything is really amiss, dear—," his wife ventured, but he cut her off, saying, "My sister jaunters off on a picnic with a man I've not met more than once in my life, and then only to exchange bows—my cousin drags a duke off to the stables to see a horse but then doesn't see the horse and instead rides off with the man—and you say there is nothing amiss? You are a goose, Amabel! Such behavior is highly irregular, even for my sister and cousin, and I demand to be told the reason for it!"

His wife subsided at being called a goose, and with a wry look Lady Jane realized he was now waiting for a reason from her. Since she had none, she found it difficult to answer and turned a look of inquiry on Baxley, who bowed and informed her that before leaving with the Duke, Miss Drucilla had spoken to that gentleman in the library.

"The library?" Jane echoed. "Now what do you suppose—" She gazed at Hester and her guests and smiled as she rose. "I'll just slip into the library for a moment—," she began, at which they all rose to go with her. Suppressing a sigh, she smiled at Baxley and murmured, "We will all be slipping into the library, it seems. Would you be so good as to inform cook that luncheon must be set back half an hour?"

He nodded his assent and held the door as she and the others passed through it. Feeling a great deal like a mother duck with three anxious ducklings, she led them into the library where she quickly spied two pieces of paper lying on the desk. Picking up the one with her name on it, she perused it quickly, then turned to the other and read it also. Her daughter's note was as brief as Matty's, and Drucilla's read, "I have gone to rescue Matty from her elopement. Ratchford accompanies me. We will return by nightfall. Please don't worry, and don't tell Cecil."

At the last sentence she smiled in despair, for how was she to keep the information from Cecil when he, his wife, and Hester were standing expectantly in front of her? Wishing that she had the imagination of her daughter or Matty, she tried desperately to think of a suitable story but was saved the effort when an impatient Hester twitched Dru's note from her loose grasp.

"Oh!" Hester gasped. "Oh! Oh! Oh!" She tottered to the nearest chair and sank into it.

"Well put," her sister-in-law murmured dryly, then turned back to Cecil who was regarding her sternly. "It seems Matty and Mr. Pettigrew have cloped," she said with a calm she was far from feeling, "and for some reason known only to her, Drucilla has seen fit to go after them. The Duke accompanies Dru." Ignoring the explosion of wrath which had escaped Cecil's lips, Jane rose and with great firmness suggested they all go in to luncheon.

"Luncheon?" Cecil and Hester repeated incredulously, while Amabel stared in wonder. "Matty and Drucilla have run mad and you suggest luncheon?"

Jane sighed. "I do not believe that either Matty or Dru are mad, and I do believe that our best course of action would be to wait for their return. Surely you see that?"

A quick look at their faces convinced her they did not. Indeed,

Cecil was turning such an alarming shade of red that she wondered if he would soon remember to breathe.

"Wait for their return?" he sputtered, his outrage apparent as he took an angry turn about the room. "Wait for their return? Upon my word, Aunt, I cannot believe that you are taking this news so calmly! My only sister—my headstrong, foolish sister—runs off with a man I do not know, and her cousin—your daughter—so far forgets herself as to go after her without a by-your-leave to me, when I should have been informed immediately. It is too much. I will not have it. I should have locked Matty up years ago, and I swear I shall do so this time. I will not have her making the Cresleys the laughingstock of England!"

That was too much for Jane, and the normally gentle lady drew herself up to her full height as she faced her nephew and said, "How dare you talk so about your sister! If anyone makes the Cresleys the laughingstock of England it will be you, with your wild talk of pursuing your sister and locking her up in Yorkshire, for all the world as if she were mad! If you had a particle of sense in your head, you would let her lead her life and you would stay out of it. You have not even considered the fact that Matty and Mr. Pettigrew may be very much in love and very right for each other. For years you've scolded her because she refused to marry, and now that she is ready to do so you want to call her intended out—an action which is both reprehensible and illegal! You condemn Drucilla for setting out after them, yet here you are prepared to do the same thing. Let me tell you, Cecil, that I see no need for this entire family to be careering over the countryside to rescue a lady who I am sure has no need or desire to be rescued!"

Surprised at such vehemence from his normally quiet aunt, Cecil stood for several moments merely goggling at her. "Well!" he said at last, returning glare for glare. "Well!" Then he slammed out of the room and stamped off towards the stable in a state of high dungeon. Jane stared at the closed door and heaved a sigh of vexation before turning to the round-eyed Amabel and the moaning Hester, who kept repeating, "The ball! The ball! What will we tell our guests at the ball?'' Lady Jane sighed but remained silent, feeling that that was the least of her worries at the moment.

As he stomped off to get his carriage, Cecil Cresley assured himself that he was—and always had been—a reasonable man. Within a short time he had convinced himself that it was an overturning of his aunt's nerves which led her to speak to him in such a forthright—and surprising—manner. A sober man whose regard for his family—and especially for his sister—was as real as he was capable of, he was sincerely shocked to hear of Matty's elopement and even more aghast at the accusations his aunt hurled at him. Her charge that he was much more likely to make the Cresley's a laughingstock rankled as had her suggestion that he let Matty live her own life.

"Everyone knows females ain't capable of that,'' he spluttered while waiting for his coach to be brought out. "I don't know what Aunt Jane was thinking of—it must have been the shock—if only I'd taken a firmer hand with Matty when she was growing up—although how I was to do so, when she was the most reprehensible and headstrong piece of baggage I've ever seen—if only she'd listened to me—'' He muttered on and on until his coachman approached to ask their destination. Realizing he hadn't a clue, he looked bitterly at the man for a moment, then said, "Gretna Green, I suppose.'' The coachman was considerably taken aback and begged to inform his master that the Cresley team, already tired from their day's journey, would never last for even the first leg of such a trip. Cecil frowned heavily before remembering that the Blue Boar kept good cattle in its stables and would be able to furnish him with a team for the first part of the distance. He ordered the coachman to drive there, and when he alighted for a mug of ale—for, as he was quite aware, he had missed his dinner and was not happy about it—the loquacious innkeeper informed him that it had been quite a day for visitors.

Cecil stared at him for a moment before inquiring about the visitors, and the landlord, pleased to have hit upon a subject which found favor with his patron, was only too happy to tell him about the first gentleman and lady who had arrived in a phaeton and left for

Grantham in a carriage; about the second lady and gentleman who had arrived in a phaeton several hours later and left in the same vehicle, also making speed for Grantham; and about the nasty-tempered gentleman who had followed the second lady and gentleman in his carriage after poling up new horses.

Who the third gentleman was, Cecil could not imagine, but he was greatly interested in the first two couples who had arrived at and departed the inn, bound for Grantham. Why Grantham he did not know, but laboring under a strong sense of ill-usage, he felt it was just like his sister to make for a destination there was no reason to go to. Upon learning all the innkeeper knew, he dropped a few coins into that worthy's hand and, swinging himself back into his carriage, ordered the coachman this time to make for Grantham. As he did so he wondered again who that third gentleman might be and how many guineas it would take to convince him that it was to his advantage not to spread the events of the day abroad.

He was to learn the identity of the third gentleman much sooner than he wished, for as his coach rounded a sharp curve in the road, he was surprised to find his coachman pulling up, and when he peered out the window to see what had caused this slowing, he perceived a gentleman standing in the road waving his arms, the carriage in the ditch beyond him mute evidence to the accident which had occurred some moments earlier.

As he gazed at the agitated figure looming larger by the second, Cecil had the faint feeling that he had seen the man before. He stared with disfavor at the many-caped coat and high shirt collars worn by the apparent dandy, but it was when his glance traveled to the scowling face above the pitifully awry neckcloth that he suffered a jolt and allowed a soft groan to escape him.

"Well, Hovington, still cow-handed, I see," he said to the gentleman rapidly approaching the carriage door, and at that unexpected greeting Percival's already high color rose.

"It wasn't me," he began blustering, "it was that rascally coachman—and a loose wheel—" Then more important matters returned to his mind, and he wrenched open the carriage door and began to crawl in.

"Come to rescue your sister?" he inquired, and at Cecil's hot, "And what do you know of my sister?," he nodded in satisfaction and stuck his head out the coach window to command the Cresley coachman to drive on. That worthy, recognizing Mr. Cresley's cousin, did so, much to Cecil's disgust. Considerably stung, he inquired who Hovington thought he was to be ordering Cecil's servants around, but Percy just looked at him and said that if Matty was to be saved, one of them must be a man of action.

"Well!" Cecil spluttered, "man of action indeed! May I ask by what right—"

"No, you may not," Percival spluttered back, "for it's obvious to me that if you were any kind of brother, your sister would not be in this regrettable situation right now. That is why I am going to rescue her from that cur Pettigrew, and that is why I am going to marry her as soon as I have dispatched him from this earth."

"Marry?!!" Cecil's eyes seemed to start from his head. *"Marry?* Why you overgrown mushroom—what makes you think I'd allow you to marry my sister?"

Percy, who had whiled away the afternoon before his unfortunate accident in picturing himself as a hero, huffed out his chest and said, "What makes you think I would ask you for your permission?" However, upon seeing his cousin's hand tighten on the cane that gentleman always carried, he thought better of his answer and suggested in a milder tone that it would be the best thing for them all under the circumstances.

Cecil was not mollified and gave it as his opinion that there could be no circumstances under which such a marriage would be the best thing. Then it was Percy's turn to huff, "Well!", and the two spent an unpleasant afternoon debating who had the most right to call Mr. Pettigrew out and who was most responsible for Matty and her future happiness, the idea that the lady might be very able to take care of herself never occurring to either of them.

Beyond them on the road to Grantham the two occupants of Miss Wrothton's phaeton were having a much more agreeable afternoon. True, Drucilla felt Ratchford was not taking the proper view of his friend's perfidy, and the Duke in turn believed that they would arrive in Grantham to find Miss Cresley a willing participant in an elopement, not a kidnapping. Aside from those differences, however, they found much to agree on during their ride, such as the fact that it would be much more comfortable if she called him Sebastian and he called her Drucilla, and the belief that phaetons were never meant to carry two adult persons and one gigantic dog. Of the three, only the gigantic dog did not seem to mind.

They also agreed that they were hungry and, when Ratchford bent down to pull out the shawl which had contained their lunch, they were in agreement that it had been a great deal too bad of Caesar to eat it when they were conversing. They taxed him with that bit of infamy, but he fixed such large and innocent eyes upon them that both were forced to laugh. "You'd think he hadn't eaten for a year to look at that face," the Duke said, and Drucilla agreed, noting that Matty had trained him well.

"Well, not too well," the Duke amended and they laughed again. Settling back to where he could get a better view of her face, Sebastian smiled as he said, "You think a great deal of your cousin, don't you, Drucilla?"

"Indeed I do," she answered warmly. "Matty is the best relative—in fact, the best friend—one could ever have. I don't know what I'd do without her."

"A very special woman, in fact."

Dru nodded. "Very special. She is intelligent, kind, funny, wise—"

"Just the type of woman any man would be lucky to marry."

"Yes," Dru agreed, then turned to look at him suspiciously and to ask just what he was getting at.

Ratchford smiled. "My dear Drucilla," he said gently, "it seems to me that you are describing the woman Crandon has been looking for all his life—"

"Oh, no!" the lady protested. "I know he is your friend, my lord, but I believe your partiality for him blinds you to his faults—"

"And I believe your dislike for him blinds you to his good qualities," the Duke interrupted, and as the lady dropped her hands to stare at him, he gently took the reins from her and urged the horses forward again.

"But—," Dru began, shaking her head. "But—"

"Tell me, Drucilla," he invited, "What kind of woman do you think would appeal to old Cran?"

"We-ell," Dru cocked her head as she considered, and he thought it a good thing that his hands were engaged in driving. "We-ell," she said again, "If I were to think of it at all, I would expect Mr. Pettigrew to seek a sweet young London miss whom he could mold as he wished, someone who would say 'Yes, Crandon' and 'No, Crandon' as he told her, and who would treat him not as a husband but as a lord and master. Someone who would not give him the least argument—"

Her further comments on Mr. Pettigrew's perfect wife were cut off by the Duke's shoulder-shaking laughter. "Oh, Drucilla," he assured her, "that is just the type of wife Cran could not tolerate. I should know—we've run from such sweet young things often enough together."

At her look of inquiry he reached out one hand to take hers in his, but Caesar misunderstood the motion and obligingly raised his head for a pat, thus intercepting the Duke's touch. "I can certainly understand why your cousin did not take this beast on *her* elopement!" he said with feeling, at which Dru laughed delightedly. "But Sebastian," she said, "*we* are not eloping! Caesar is our chaperone — and a very good one, you'll admit."

"Oh, I'll admit it, all right," he murmured, putting his hand back on the reins. "A very good one!"

Silence started to fall between them, but his earlier comments were lodged in Dru's mind, and hesitantly she asked him what he had meant about running from "sweet young things."

"Oh," he said, somewhat embarrassed. "Perhaps I shouldn't have said—it's just that—well. You see, Drucilla, both Crandon and I have done the pretty for a number of social seasons, and because we are rich we have found ourselves much in demand among the doting mamas set on making splendid matches for their lovely daughters. I don't know how many girls I've met just like the one you described for Crandon, but I do know this—they become tedious very quickly. It is a tiresome thing to be admired for your fortune.''

"Oh, my lord,'' Drucilla assured him earnestly, "I cannot believe it is your fortune which attracts ladies to you. That is—'' She realized what she had said and blushed becomingly. The Duke smiled.

"Thank you, Drucilla,'' he said gravely. "That is perhaps the nicest compliment I have ever received.''

She looked up, caught the warmth in his eyes, and gazed down again quickly, absently patting Caesar's head as he rested it on her lap. Finally she ventured, "Then what is it—that a man—like your friend Pettigrew, that is—looks for—in a woman?—''

A slight smile played at the Duke's lips. "Well,'' he began, "when a man—like my friend Crandon—passes the first stage of youth, he finds himself wishing for a companion, someone to share his home and his thoughts and his life.''

Dru looked up. "You think that Mr. Pettigrew and Matty have found that together?''

He nodded, then reached out to softly touch her cheek. "I like to think I've found that too,'' he said. "I like to think I've found it in you.''

"Oh Sebastian—,'' she began, and he, mistaking her high color for maidenly confusion, started to apologize profusely.

"I didn't mean to pop it at you like that,'' he said. "I'm rather afraid I've made a mull of it—Drucilla—my dear Miss Wrothton—that is—would you do me the honor of becoming the Duchess of Ratchford?''

Dru met his eyes and held them. "I don't really care to be a duchess—,'' she began, but at his look of despair hurried on, "but I would above all things like to be your wife.''

Within a moment the Duke had the team halted and, mindless of the huge Caesar, pulled the lady into his arms in an embrace he had wanted to give for the last hour.

"Oh, blast that dog!'' he said finally as an interested nose succeeded in separating him from the lady. "*Will* you change places with him so that I might be sure of an arm full of you next time I reach out for a hug?''

Dru blushed but was only too happy to oblige, and for several minutes she found herself too occupied to even remember why she and the Duke and the indulgent Caesar were seated in the phaeton on the road to Grantham. When she did remember, it was to adjure her love—quite reluctantly—to gather up the reins and drive on, ''for we know that Percival is behind us, and we aren't quite sure what we'll find ahead.''

Ratchford, who at the moment did not care about either in front or behind, nevertheless acceded to the lady's wishes, and they were off. When he asked her if she cared for a large wedding, she replied she couldn't think of that now while her cousin's future remained so undecided. The Duke acquiesced and said no more, merely patting his coat pocket for a moment before enfolding both of Drucilla's hands in one of his.

Chapter XXIV

Meanwhile, the objects of everyone's search were quietly drinking tea with Pettigrew's Aunt Agatha near Grantham. That lady, whose sharp eyes belied her frail form, was at the moment critically surveying her nephew as she informed him that five minutes of conversation with Matty convinced her the lady was too good for him.

''You're a lucky dog, Crandon,'' she observed tartly. ''If I were

Miss Cresley I wouldn't have you. Such a bright young woman can surely do better.''

That pronouncement sent poor Betty, who served as Agatha's companion, into agonies of embarrassment, during which she fluttered, ''Oh, Agatha—she didn't mean—that is to say—'' Eyeing her with disfavor, Agatha sternly told her to hush.

''I never could abide wailing women,'' she told Matty. Then for good measure she stared defiantly at her nephew and said that since she had been reading his pedigree for him for years, she had no intention of stopping now.

Poor Betty grew even more inarticulate, wringing her hands in dismay, but Pettigrew, far from being offended, smiled wickedly at his aunt and agreed with everything she said, although he did add mildly that Miss Cresley was not such a young lady after all. That brought him a glare from his beloved, which he blandly ignored as he continued to say that she was also quite mad in the bargain, and it was in one of her less lucid moments that she had agreed to marry him.

Matty swiftly returned that she thought the haste in their marriage was to keep his madness from becoming known, and Betty goggled at such unloverlike talk. Agatha snorted happily, glad her nephew had chosen a woman with both spirit and humor.

''You'll do, my dear, you'll do,'' she approved, passing Matty a second cup of tea and a freshly baked macaroon. ''I like a woman who speaks her mind. Can't abide these milk-and-water misses of today who say, 'Yes, sir' and 'No, sir' to everything a man says. After all, my dear,'' and here she leaned toward Matty and lowered her voice as she glanced toward her nephew, ''men say such *foolish* things.''

Matty and Pettigrew burst into laughter, and Matty agreed delightedly while Betty again wrung her hands at her outspoken companion's opinions. Seeing that, Agatha told her she might as well take herself off, because she intended to go on talking just as she liked, and she didn't want any Friday-faced companion around to make her uncomfortable. Pettigrew frowned at his aunt and said gently that indeed he thought Miss Betty might like to lie down upon her bed for a while since he knew that to be her afternoon custom. Casting him a look of gratitude, she clucked her way out of the room, torn between staying to hear the details of The Great Romance (for so the romantic lady had dubbed Matty's and Crandon's relationship in her mind) and leaving before Agatha turned her tongue on her again. Fear gave way to romance, and she left the three to enjoy a comfortable coze while she repaired to her chamber, there to compose herself with the aid of her vinaigrette and rose water.

After tea was completed Agatha settled back in her chair, banged her cane on the floor, and fixed her keen eyes on the faces of the two before her. "So you want to get married," she said, "and you've come here to do it. Well, I don't say that I mind. But I'd like to know why."

"Because you're the only one of my family I care to have at my wedding, dear Aunt," Pettigrew answered promptly, and though she snorted, the old lady looked gratified. "And because," he continued, a twinkle in his eye, "you're also the only one of my relatives who keeps in her employ a clergyman who does all that she says without question."

At that her cackle of laughter exploded, and she nodded approvingly at her nephew. "That's why I like you, Crandon," she said. "You're the only one of my relations who says what he thinks."

Then she paused and rested her chin upon the hand which held her cane. "But not even I can persuade the Reverend Tyler to marry you without banns."

"You can if we have a special license," her nephew returned, drawing that paper from his pocket.

Saying that he had more sense than she'd ever given him credit for, Agatha took the paper and perused it, murmured, "He still won't like it," and rang the small bell sitting on the table beside her. The butler appeared promptly, and she requested that he send someone to fetch the rector at once—on a matter of grave importance.

"Grave importance?" he inquired politely, casting a most interested glance in Matty's and Crandon's direction.

"Yes," Agatha said wickedly. "Tell him I've decided to repent of my worldly ways. That ought to bring him on the run."

Pettigrew laughed, but as the butler shut the door behind himself, Matty's brow wrinkled and she asked why the Reverend Tyler wouldn't care to marry them by special license.

Agatha waved the question away. "He's an old woman, my dear," she said crisply. "He has a studied dislike of anything the least little irregular. I am a constant trial to him—his cross to bear in this life, but he hopes for reward in the next." She nodded pleasedly and murmured, "Quite," as Crandon gave his bark of laughter, then continued confidently, "But never fear, child—he'll do as I say for all of that. He always does."

The complacent look on her face made Matty feel slightly sorry for the little clergyman, for she did not doubt that Agatha always got what she wanted. However, since what Miss Pettigrew wanted was also what she wanted, she did not dwell on the state of the clergyman's feelings. Instead, she was caught up in the conversation of the two witty people who shared the room with her and joined with enthusiasm in the telling of her first encounter with Crandon, a performance which made Agatha crow with delight.

So it was that when the Reverend Tyler arrived out of breath, having been roused from his afternoon nap and expecting to find his patroness in the depths of repentance and remorse—a condition he had often prayed would descend upon her—he found her instead ordering wine to toast a future bride. When all that was expected of him was explained, the holy look on his face rapidly gave way to one of harassment and anger; and Matty thought amusedly that the fierce grip he maintained on his prayer book might not all be laid at the door of religious fervor.

"Really, Miss Pettigrew," the little man huffed, "I came as quickly as I could—without even stopping for tea—because I believed—I was led to believe—that your immortal soul was in need of my support and guidance. I spared no thought for my own comfort in my haste to come to your side to succor and console you.

"But when I arrive, what do I find?" His voice rose as he considered the magnitude of it. "What do I find?!! I find you drinking wine and telling stories and expecting me to perform one of God's holy sacraments on command. You tricked me, Miss Pettigrew," he said stiffly, pulling himself up to his full height of five feet and swelling out his chest in a way which strongly reminded Matty of a pouting pigeon. "You tricked me, but God is not deceived. He will not be ordered about on your command, and neither will I."

Had she been more conciliating, Agatha might have calmed the reverend's feathers with a few words of contrition. Over the years she had indeed pushed him to great lengths, and at present, past injustices were swiftly pouring into his mind. Unfortunately, Agatha was not a woman to—as she told him—suffer fools gladly, and she showed no regard for his feelings, adjuring him to quit his theatrics and get on with the wedding. This made the little man angrier, and among mutterings of "highly irregular," "tricked me again," and "no regard for my feelings", he began to list reason after reason why the ceremony could not be performed immediately. All were overborne by his patroness who, rapidly bored with his temper and what she considered hysterics, finally asked him quietly if he liked the living she paid him.

The reverend paused, an arrested look on his face, and eyed her miserably. He had worked himself to a point from which he could see no honorable return, so, clutching his Bible to his breast, he faced her squarely and said, in his best Sunday-sermon voice, "You threaten me, Miss Pettigrew, but it will not do. I have served you well and long and had hoped to continue to do so for years to come. But I serve One even higher than you, and He calls me to stand for what is right and good, and not irregular."

Agatha muttered that she wondered at the patience God had to employ such a man on his errands, while Matty, who had remained silent through the whole performance, astonished all those present by bursting into laughter. The look of outraged dignity the Reverend Tyler bent on her did nothing to ease her giggles, and Pettigrew, harassed at finding his plans so nearly overturned, begged her to hush as he took the clergyman aside and spoke earnestly to him.

The ladies, agog at the conversation, could catch only snatches of it such as, "I understand the principles which lead you to put the right above all else—" and "But you can see that under the circumstances it is not irregular at all. Indeed, it is the rightest and best thing you could do.''

The Reverend Tyler, who had begun by shaking his head adamantly at everything Pettigrew said, did not seem to shake it nearly so much now, and when Crandon finished his speech with a promise of a large contribution "for the parish poorbox," the clergyman was heard to say—albeit stiffly—that it was only his concern to do the right thing, and now that he fully understood the circumstances he would indeed perform the ceremony.

Matty, fixing her betrothed with a minatory eye, started to ask just what he had said to change the man's mind, but Pettigrew merely grabbed her hand, saying loudly, as if she were deaf, "There, there, my dear, don't worry. Crandon will take care of you." As he patted her shoulder he grinned into her indignant eyes and whispered, "I'll tell you after we're married."

Then, to forestall questions from Agatha, whose curiosity was also at its peak, he quickly asked her to ring for Betty and the butler to serve as wedding witnesses. She did so reluctantly, but her desire to see her nephew wed before Tyler changed his mind again overcame her interest in how the wedding had been accomplished, and with a shrug she decided she could wait ten minutes to find out. What was ten minutes, compared to the lifetime she had spent waiting to see Crandon caught in wedlock's web?

Thus when the witnesses were assembled the ceremony was begun, and it was half-completed when a loud knocking was heard at the outer door. Matty was amazed when the clergyman jumped and turned pale at the sound. He cast a frightened look at Pettigrew who, straight-faced, encouraged him to hurry, "for they must be here, and you know what that means."

The Reverend Tyler blanched and had just reached the point where he asked if anyone present knew of any just cause or impediment why the two should not be joined together when the parlor doors burst open and Drucilla ran in, preceded by Caesar and followed at a more leisurely pace by the Duke.

Reverend Tyler grew even more white, and Pettigrew, seeing that, strode forward, grasped the arms of the indignant lady and the surprised gentleman, and thrust them from the room. Their energetic tattoo on the parlor doors was immediately heard and, settling his shoulders against those doors, Pettigrew turned to the surprised and bemused faces before him and bade the clergyman, "Hurry, or all is yet lost."

Caesar, who had not been ejected, was delighted to see Matty again and set up a barking which Agatha said would waken the dead if they hadn't already been roused by the ferocious pounding. Unfortunately, since Caesar chose to bark right under the parson's prayer book, that volume clattered hastily to the floor as the worthy took refuge on the nearest chair.

Matty threw a harassed yet laughing look at Crandon as she tried simultaneously to assure the clergyman that the dog was harmless and to get said dog to hush. Pettigrew met her look with a grin and the suggestion that she hand the parson his book so that they could get on with the wedding.

Agatha, whose mouth had been opening and shutting rapidly, blinked and did just that, adjuring the Reverend Tyler to get on with it since she wasn't likely to know what it was all about until it was over.

So it was that Mr. Crandon Pettigrew and Miss Mathilde Cresley took each other for better and for worse, in sickness and in health—in Grantham and in Bedlam, Matty was heard to mutter—until death did they part; with Pettigrew holding the parlor doors shut, with a clergyman standing on a chair as he finished the service, with Aunt Agatha restoring her nerves with a little red wine, with Betty fainted dead away in the stalwart butler's arms, with Caesar barking, and with Matty laughing so hard she could barely say, "I do."

Once the final vow was repeated, Crandon moved swiftly toward his bride. He took her in his arms just as Dru's hearty assault on the no-longer-barred door sent her sprawling into the room. The Reverend Tyler took a step back when he saw both Drucilla and the Duke, hurriedly accepted the pounds Pettigrew held out to him, and inched his way cautiously to the door, giving the two newest arrivals a wide berth. At the door he paused, inquired heroically if he should send for the constable and, upon being assured that he should not, hastened from the room, only sticking his head back in to shout, "I will pray for you."

Matty, Agatha, and the Duke, who was helping Dru to her feet, stared after him, astonished. Pettigrew smiled, first after the vanished minister, then at his new bride, and finally at his bemused friend.

"What, Sebastian, you here?" he asked gently. "Have you met my Aunt Agatha?"

The Duke, thoroughly confused, bowed automatically to the lady in question.

"And my wife, Mrs. Pettigrew?" Crandon continued, which made the Duke start and Drucilla wail.

"Oh Matty, you haven't!"

"Congratulations, my dear Miss Cres—I mean, Mrs. Pettigrew—," the Duke began.

"Oh, Sebastian, how can you?" Dru asked. "Matty, Matty, Matty. Not Pettigrew. You're too good for him."

"Precisely what I said," Agatha agreed with satisfaction, liberally helping herself to the wine. Then she sharply commanded her companion to stop making such a cake of herself, for, once revived, Miss Betty began sobbing loudly about housebreakers and heathens.

"They aren't housebreakers, you ninny," the old lady said, declining to comment on their standing as heathens. "They're a duke and a Miss—Miss—"

She looked inquiringly at Dru, who was now in Matty's arms, and it was Matty who supplied, "Wrothton. My cousin."

"Wrothton," Agatha repeated triumphantly. "Matty's cousin. Now that we're all acquainted, let's sit down and have some wine. We have a great deal of toasting to do."

But Dru ignored her, saying desperately to her cousin, "Oh, Matty, we've come to save you and we're too late. But you needn't stay with him. You can come back to Morningdale with us."

Matty laughed and gave her cousin an affectionate shake. "But Drucilla, my love, I *want* to stay with him. I told you not to worry. I don't *want* to be saved." At her cousin's incredulous gaze, she grinned and flashed her love a quizzing smile. "You've always known I have horrible taste."

Her love, smiling back, handed each lady a glass of wine and, with a sympathetic grin for Dru, added, "Besides, she's mad, you know."

At that Dru fired up, and Pettigrew hurriedly assured her that he was joking. After a moment's study of her face, he stuck out his hand and said cajolingly, "Come, Miss Wrothton, let us cry friends. For now that I've married your cousin and you're to marry—" A quick glance from his friend and the blush on the lady's face made him hurriedly change that to, "That is, we are sure to be seeing a great deal of each other. Who knows, you may even come to like me."

"Well, maybe tolerate him—," Matty struck in consideringly, and Dru smiled reluctantly, finally taking his hand as she looked up into his face.

"I do not see what my cousin or Sebastian—I mean Ratchford— sees in you," she said, coloring rosily, "but I shall try to see it too. If you will stop baiting me."

"No more baiting," Crandon promised.

"And if you will be good to my cousin."

"Very good."

"And if—"

But here Agatha took charge. "And if," she pronounced, "you will tell us what whisker you told that pompous Tyler to change his mind about marrying you."

Looking guiltily at Matty, Crandon smiled and demurred.

"I knew it," his new wife said resignedly. "You told him something about me."

He nodded.

"Something terrible," she continued with conviction.

He grinned.

"Well, we'd just as well hear it," she said with a sigh. "Did you tell him I'd been kidnapped? Cast off? Left abandoned in a cruel world?"

"I told him you were mad," Pettigrew said, drawing every eye toward him, astonished. He sipped his wine.

"Mad??" Matty exploded incredulously. "You actually told that poor man I was *mad*? And he consented to marry us? You, sir, have gone too far!"

Amazed that his lady appeared seriously discomfitted, he hastened to assure her that he had not pictured her as mad at all times but only when the least little thing occurred to overset her reason. "It accounted for your laughing at that inopportune time," he said, "and you shouldn't fear, for I made you a heroine."

Matty continued to glare as he told her soothingly, "I told him your mind was overturned in the service of our country. I told you were once an English spy, but that women being such delicate creatures"—here three explosive 'bahs' from Matty, Dru, and Agatha made him grin appreciatively—"you finally cracked under the strain, and needed time and the companionship of one who loves you to make you well again.

"I assured him that our betrothal was of a long but secret standing, and that he would indeed be doing the right and good thing—right and good being very important to him—if he married us at once. I told him that even at this moment Bonapartist agents might be on our trail to carry you off and imprison you in an asylum where I could not reach you."

Noting that his entire audience was staring at him, fascinated, he continued.

"I told him that once we were married I could protect you, who had served your king and country so well. He was touched. I almost cried myself." He sipped his wine again, then rose to pour himself another glass.

"Oh!" Matty interjected tartly. "Touched, was he? I would like to touch you, sir. Touched! By your story and the large purse you promised him!"

Her love raised his glass to her. "I admit that helped," he said. "But then, when there was the loud knocking on the door, and you two burst into the room—" Here he turned and raised his glass to Ratchford and Dru. Sebastian grinned back. "It was a very nice, although unexpected, touch. But what can you do when women must always leave notes?" He paused, and the smile on his face grew. "Did you see the parson's face?"

Agatha and Matty dissolved in laughter. "And when Caesar barked under his nose—"

"And he jumped onto the chair—"

"No wonder he edged past us to get to the door," Dru marveled.

"Bonapartist agents!" the Duke choked, amazed. "What if I ever meet the gentleman again? What shall I say?"

"Say you are mad," Matty struck in. "Plead temporary madness. Say you are a double agent. Say whatever you like."

"Or don't meet him again," Crandon suggested, pouring his friend another glass of wine. That delivered, he went to perch on the arm of Matty's chair, and it was just as he put his arm around the lady that Hovington and Cecil walked into the room.

"Unhand that lady, sir!" Percival cried, visions of the daydreams which had beguiled his afternoon rising before his eyes. But before he could carry his theatrics further, Caesar, who recognized an enemy when he saw one and who retained in his mind the memory of the man who had knocked down his mistress' bed, hit him full-force, then growled ferociously as he settled comfortably on the downed man's chest. He looked around to see if Matty was going to spoil sport, but she was busy laughing and seemed to have no immediate intention of doing so.

"Unhand that gentleman, dog," Sebastian murmured, sending all those seated in the room into gales of laughter. The gentleman left standing, however, was not amused.

"Matty, for goodness sake, call that beast off and let Hovington get up," he said testily, his exacerbated temper adding to his harassment. "You're as much a hoyden at thirty as you were at thirteen. Past praying for, my dear. Past praying for."

"I'll have you know, sir, that you speak to my wife," Pettigrew said sternly as he rose, forestalling Matty's answer. Then his face relaxed into a smile. "And there is at this moment a clergyman praying for her."

That last statement again threw all those seated into laughter, much to Cecil's disgust. Turning to the Duke, he stiffly informed him that he had hardly expected to find a man of his standing embroiled in such an affair.

The Duke mendaciously disclaimed all responsibility, stating he had simply accompaned Miss Wrothton on a drive and that she had kidnapped him to Grantham.

"Kidnapped you?" Dru gasped. "Well, I never."

The Duke's face fell. "Does this mean you're not going to hold me until I marry you?"

"Well! I didn't—I never—," Dru sputtered, and Pettigrew, promptly forgetting his promise not to bait her anymore, struck in to ask if she really thought she could toy with a man's affections that way, carrying him off and then not making an honest man of him.

Before she could reply, the loud groans emanating from Percival Hovington grew so intense that Matty called Caesar to her and asked Percy solicitously if he had really been hurt.

But once relieved of the dog's weight, Hovington showed no inclination to rise, merely lying on the floor groaning. "Married. She's married. Oh Matty, Matty, why didn't you wait for me?"

Agatha regarded him critically for a moment, then announced that she wanted that young jackanapes removed from her carpet immediately.

Stung, the "young jackanapes" rose to one knee, proclaiming that his life was ruined and he might as well End It All.

Cresley told him irritably not to be such a fool, and Agatha snapped that she was sorry she could not offer him a sword.

Matty, seeing that he was genuinely upset, rose and went to take his arm, helping him to his feet and assuring him gently that his life would be ruined only if they really had wed, "for we would not suit, Percival; I am convinced we would not."

He continued to regard her through tragic eyes until she finally asked him to quit staring at her as Caesar did when she refused to let him bury a bone under the bed. That comment hurt him so that he uttered another of his loud groans and flung out of the chair into which Matty had so recently pressed him.

"You have no feeling for me," he charged. "You all laugh at me and when I offer you my heart you make mock. Well, I am going. I am going. And I wish you joy in each other, for I see now that you deserve him."

Matty watched him go, then turned to Pettigrew, her eyes twinkling. "Well, I don't think I ever did anything *that* bad," she observed, but before he could reply Percival was back.

"Forgotten something?" Ratchford inquired mildly.

He hunched a shoulder and glared at them all impartially. "I don't have a carriage."

"Well, take mine," Agatha offered, eager to be rid of him. "Take mine and be off, and good riddance. My carriage is at your disposal."

He bowed stiffly and was gone. Agatha severely eyed Cecil still standing in the middle of the room and, turning to Matty, informed her that she rather thought Matty had some shockingly loose screws for relatives.

"Precisely what I told her about my family," Pettigrew murmured, and that seemed to please his aunt, for she merely told him that turning her up sweet would not help. Then she turned to Cecil and asked if he intended to remain rooted to her floor or if he was going to use the good sense God gave him and sit down.

Matty, noting her brother's angry flush, fanned the flame by dulcetly informing her hostess that indeed she should not blame Cecil, for she truly did not believe God had given him any good sense at all.

Agatha's resulting cackle did nothing to relieve Cresley's ill humor.

"Really, Matty," he snapped. "You are impossible. Going your own way, following such odd starts, and now eloping. I am embarrassed that we share the same name."

"But you don't, sir," Pettigrew corrected him. "Your sister and I now share the same name. And I am not embarrassed at all. Indeed," and here he raised Matty's hand to his lips and looked lovingly into her eyes, "I am quite pleased."

"Confound it, man, I don't even know who you are!" Cecil cried, snatching his hat from his head and smashing it to the floor. "If I've met you more than once in my life I don't remember it, and that a chance meeting at a London club. Yet my only sister runs off with someone I can consider nothing but a total stranger to me, and you all act as if I—the head of my family—should accept it as if she'd brought home another stray animal.'' He looked at his sister and sighed deeply. ''Ah, Matty, where did I go wrong?''

He seemed so perturbed that Matty took pity on him and assured him that she knew he had always tried to guide and protect her but added that when their ideas of what makes a good life were so different, they were bound to disagree.

''But to elope,'' Cecil said despairingly. ''What will people say?''

''As to that,'' Ratchford said, breaking in unexpectedly, ''I imagine they will say that Miss Cresley has made an excellent match. For you must know, Mr. Cresley, that Crandon Pettigrew has been considered a prime target of matchmaking mamas for these past fifteen years.''

''So long?'' Matty murmured provocatively, causing her love's lips to twitch.

''And consider, man,'' the Duke continued bracingly. ''Who is to know that Miss Cresley's marriage did not have your full approval unless you tell them? For all the world need know, you arrived in time for the ceremony.''

Mr. and Mrs. Pettigrew looked at their friend in wonder as that aspect of ''this business'' sank into Cresley's mind. He seemed much struck by it and made no complaint when Crandon, setting down his wine glass and rising, suggested that they go elsewhere and discuss his circumstances.

''I am sure we can use my aunt's library for that purpose,'' he said, taking his new brother-in-law's arm and marching him out of the room. ''Once you know how I am situated, perhaps you will find you can like the marriage better.''

''Well!'' Matty exclaimed, staring after them in amazement. ''I like that! I think it might help if I discussed his circumstances, too!'' And she followed them out of the room determinedly, promising that she would not be left out of any such interesting conversations.

Agatha, seeing that the excitement had ended, informed the room at large that she was an old woman and not used to such goings on and that she would retire to her room now to recruit her strength. Leaning heavily on her companion's arm, she made her stately way out of the parlor and toward the stairs. If Betty suspected that she was much more likely to recruit her strength with sherry and Mrs. Radcliffe's newest novel rather than a nap, she was much too meek to say so.

Left alone, Dru glanced at the Duke, who was watching her intensely.

"Well," she sighed.

"Well."

"I seem to have bungled this completely."

"Oh, not completely," he assured her.

"No?" She smiled rather tremulously. "I dash off to rescue a cousin who doesn't want to be rescued, embroil you in my scheme, leave a note which no doubt has all of Morningdale Manor in an uproar and all for what? All for naught." She sighed disconsolately.

"Not all for naught," the Duke said, joining her on the sofa.

She gazed at him in surprise. "What do you mean?"

"I was wondering," he said after a slight pause, "if we could convince the Reverend Tyler that it is extremely important that two Bonapartist agents become husband and wife tonight."

"What?" Dru blushed rosily, stuttering. "But how—are you sure—I wouldn't for the world trap you into anything—my mother—the banns—"

Smiling lovingly at his usually coherent bride-to-be, he pulled a piece of paper from his pocket and spread it before her eyes. She stared at it for a moment, reading incredulously. "A special license?" she breathed. "But—"

"I took the liberty of procuring it on my recent trip to Bath," he explained. "Actually it was my mother's idea."

"Your mother's?" Dru asked, amazed.

He nodded. "I'm not sure she meant it, but she suggested I marry you immediately so that she may see her grandchildren before she dies."

Dru blushed again at the mention of grandchildren, but her

forehead puckered as she considered his words. "But—your mother doesn't know me—"

"My dear," Sebastian assured her, "the fact that I want to marry you makes my mother love you already. She has been despairing of me for years, hounding me to find someone to share my hearth and home and family. Especially family. Although she only wanted one son herself, Mother thinks I should have many children. Before she dies." He cocked an eyebrow and regarded Dru quizzically. "I hope you don't mind?"

The lady was heard to murmur that she did not mind the idea at all, and then, aghast at her own forwardness, she blushed again and inquired solicitously if the Duchess enjoyed ill health.

"Immensely," the Duchess's undutiful son replied. "She enjoys ill health immensely. Actually, I have no doubts that she will live to see her great-grandchildren. My mother is as healthy as a horse, but whenever she is bored or faced with something she particularly does not wish to do, she informs the household that she is ill and that any shock to her system or unpleasantness would no doubt send her across death's door. It works very well for her. And she is such a lamb in general that we let her get away with it, except for one of my aunts, who insists on informing my mother that she is not at all ill and would be wise to stop quacking herself. You can imagine how well my mother likes that!"

He smiled again and Dru smiled back, and the Duke dismissed his mother's health from his mind as he inquired again if his love was willing to marry him that night. So sure was he of her answer that his face fell when the lady, looking away, shook her head slowly from side to side and informed him that she could not.

"Cannot?" he echoed, feeling as if a horse had kicked him in the lower abdomen. "But Drucilla—my dear—I thought—that is, I had hoped—" He stood abruptly and took a quick turn around the room before returning to stand before her, his face and manner stiff. "I am sorry, Miss Wrothton," he said, the words coming thick between tight lips. "I obviously misunderstood your actions, and I pray that my precipitous manner has not given you a disgust of me—"

He was allowed to go no further, for Dru, staring at him in

amazement, grasped one of his hands in both of hers and said, "Dear Sebastian, whatever do you mean?"

Now it was his turn to look amazed, as well as confused. "What do I mean?" he started, then thought deeply. "Well," he said cautiously, "what do you mean?"

Dru gave his hand a coaxing tug, and he willingly took the seat beside her as she smiled into his eyes, one of her hands reaching up to touch his cheek before she allowed it to drop back into her lap. "Dear Sebastian," she said quietly, "all I meant is that I cannot marry you in this out-of-hand fashion. I did not mean that I do not wish to marry you. Indeed, I can think of nothing that I wish more."

He stared at her for a moment, comprehension growing as a lopsided grin started small and grew across his face. "You will still marry me?" he repeated, and at her happy nod he stood and danced around the room. "She'll marry me!" he shouted at the stern portraits that gazed down at him from Agatha's walls. "She'll marry me!" he told the Dresden shepherd and shepherdess who adorned the mantelpiece. "You'll marry me, you'll marry me, you'll marry me!" he said to Drucilla as he swooped down upon her and lifted her in his arms to twirl her laughing and breathless about the room with him. "I say, life is good! You'll marry me!" And he kissed her, long and fervently, as they collapsed together on the sofa.

At last Dru raised her head and laughed into his eyes. "I had hoped for a little more enthusiasm," she told him, and his lopsided grin grew again.

"Oh, Drucilla," he begged, "why won't you marry me now? We'll have Cran and your cousin Matty as witnesses, and we'll tie it up right and tight here with that funny little fellow of Cran's aunt to say the vows. Please say you'll marry me tonight. Please."

It took a great deal of resolution, but that Drucilla would not do, explaining as gently as she could that she could not bear to disappoint her mother and aunt, who she was sure would be heartbroken to miss her wedding. "And think of your mother, too, Sebastian," she told him. "If she has looked forward to your marriage as much as you say, surely she would like to see the ceremony take place."

The Duke, about to protest, was moved as much by his intended's words as by the pleading look in her eyes, and his strong sense of responsibility persuaded him to agree that he was sure she was right. He added, however, that his mother was not far away, and he saw no reason to wait much longer than it would take to gather the appropriate relatives together. Dru, who had no desire for a large wedding, although she knew her Aunt Hester would have a great deal to say about it, agreed, and the two spent the next half-hour agreeably discussing the merits of the English countryside or a trip abroad for their honeymoon.

It was the sound of rain on the windows that interrupted their agreeable little chat, and it was several minutes before the soft spitter/spatter penetrated Drucilla's consciousness. In the back of her mind she knew the sound, and when the memory connected with the sight of raindrops on the windows, she half-rose in dismay, crying out, "It's raining!"

The Duke, confused to have his pleasant time so abruptly interrupted, gazed vaguely toward the window and murmured, "So it is." Then he turned his eyes toward his fiancée. "It is no cause for alarm, Drucilla," he reassured her. "It often rains in the springtime!"

"Yes, of course it does," she cried, "but how are we to get home? We have only my phaeton, and we cannot drive all the way back to Morningdale Manor in the rain! My mother and aunt will be so worried! Oh, what are we to do?"

The Duke, puzzled for a moment, suggested that they borrow his friend Crandon's carriage, but when that suggestion was put to Crandon, Mr. Pettigrew told them they might take it with the best will in the world, except that he and his new wife had dismissed the carriage, thinking to borrow his aunt's for their return home. That vehicle, of course, had left earlier carrying the irate Percy and was no longer available. Matty, catching sight of her cousin's face, suggested that the two ask Cecil for the loan of his carriage, but when he was applied to he informed all sourly that one of his horses had pulled up lame two miles out of Grantham, and he had sent his coachman out to inquire about horses for hire. He was informed that a new team would not be available until morning, and, he added, since he was a careful man who would not take his own carriage out on unknown roads on such a rainy night, he certainly would not lend that carriage to a cousin whose hurly-burly behavior had led her into such an irregular situation.

Both Drucilla and the Duke fired up at that, and Matty was heard to say that he was a good one to talk about irregular situations and hurly-burly actions, but before those promising embers could be fanned to flame, Agatha Pettigrew entered the room to inform them all that earlier that afternoon she had taken the liberty of dispatching a groom to Morningdale to inform the Wrothtons that the two cousins, her nephew, and the Duke were her guests for the night.

"And what about me?" Cecil blustered. "Am I not to be your guest, too?"

Agatha regarded him with distaste. "Who *is* this?" she demanded of Crandon who, well versed in the way she played forgetful when it suited her, merely smiled and reminded her that Cecil was Matty's brother and therefore deserving of her hospitality.

Agatha sniffed and, with a loud aside in which she informed Matty that it was a pity one was not allowed to choose one's relations, she informed them regally that Cecil could stay, but he was not to try her too far. That so incensed the subject of her condescension that he stomped from the room vowing that he would not trouble them with his presence if someone would only be good enough to show him the room in which he was to lay his head that night. Agatha, taking him at his word, was only too happy to do so, and Cecil soon found himself ensconced in a back bedroom which had a chimney that smoked and a view of a brick wall from its only window. Feeling extremely ill-used, he settled down with a bottle of port provided by the thoughtful butler and spent an evening cataloging the misadventures of his sister since her birth two years after his. It was a very long list.

Chapter XXV

A merry group gathered in the breakfast parlor at Agatha Pettigrew's the following morning, for Cecil overslept and did not join them, and Betty, still recovering her sorely tried nerves, elected to have another tray in her room. Banter flowed as freely as the coffee and tea, and Agatha looked with delight on the happy faces surrounding her.

It was otherwise at Morningdale Manor, where two of the ladies present appeared heavy-eyed, and one evidenced traces of weeping, Amabel having spent the night with visions of Cecil's lifeless body being found in a ditch somewhere between Morningdale and Gretna Green. Miss Pettigrew had neglected to mention that he, as well as the others, was her guest for the evening.

The ladies had received Miss Pettigrew's note in the drawing room the night before, where they had sat making polite if labored conversation as they waited for the others to return. The note, meant to reassure them, had actually raised more questions than it had answered for the three women, and while it told them that Matty and Drucilla were safe, Hester spent a great deal of time wondering if Miss Agatha Pettigrew of Grantham was a fit chaperone for the two wayward young ladies.

"Because she's no doubt a relative of that fellow Pettigrew," she said darkly as she paced around the room, "and at the moment I don't consider that a recommendation for anyone."

Jane pointed out fair-mindedly that before the elopement they had both thought Mr. Pettigrew the perfect gentleman for Matty, and she was still of that opinion, but Hester refused to be placated.

"You may sit there very calmly if *you* choose to do so," her sister-in-law said, "although I don't know how you can when Drucilla and Mathilde have so far forgotten themselves as to go jauntering about the country like a couple of loose women—yes, loose women, Jane," she repeated as that lady began to protest. "There's no point trying to wrap it up in clean linen. But I cannot remain calm when Matty's picnic takes her to Grantham, Drucilla drives off with a duke and a dog, Cecil charges off after all of them, and the cook is being so inconsiderate as to refuse to change the menu one more time for tomorrow night's ball."

That brought her to her other consideration, and she sank into a chair wailing, "The ball, Jane! The ball! What will we say when Drucilla, in whose honor this ball is given, does not appear at it? What will we do? Oh, what will we do?"

Jane refused to join her in her moanings. "We don't know that Drucilla and Matty will not return for the ball," she pointed out, her face a bit pale but her tone calm. "Indeed, I am sure they will. Drucilla and Matty may at times be—impetuous—but they are certainly not thoughtless. They'll be here."

"But what if they're not?" Hester wailed again. "Perhaps we should cancel the ball!"

"Cancel the—" Jane gasped at the thought. "Really, Hester, you must get hold of yourself. It is much too late to cancel the ball. If for some reason Dru and Matty cannot return in time, we shall simply fob our guests off with a story. We will tell them the girls were called away—no, that would not do." She thought deeply for a moment, then brightened. "I've got it! We'll say they have chicken pox!"

"Chicken pox???" her sister-in-law repeated. "At their age? Rather we announce to the world that Matty eloped and Dru went after her! Chicken pox indeed!"

But Jane only repeated "chicken pox" firmly and said that that would be their tale if they needed it, which she for one did not believe they would. Then, because she did not care to discuss the matter further, she suggested that they all retire, "since there will be much to do tomorrow and we will all need our sleep if we are to finish the preparations and enjoy the ball."

Amabel was heard to sob that she could not enjoy anything while her dear Cecil lay dead somewhere upon the road, which so incensed Hester that she forgot her own lamentations in adjuring Mrs. Cresley not to be such a goose. "For if there's one thing Cecil has in excess it's good sense," she said, "and you can be sure that he's put up snug at an inn for the night and will return tomorrow demanding clean clothes and his dinner."

Amabel did not believe her, of course, but she was so in awe of her husband's Aunt Hester that she managed to restrain herself in that woman's presence. Once in her own chamber, however, her imagination again took over, and it was a very watery pillow from which she arose in the morning.

Hester escorted the young Mrs. Cresley up the stairs and then took to her own bed with a severe headache, and Lady Jane, who had remained in the drawing room on pretense of wishing to speak to Baxley before she retired, found herself at the long windows looking out at the moonlit night, a position she remained in long after the last log in the fire had been reduced to smouldering embers.

So it was that when the three gathered for breakfast that morning, none could be said to be in her best looks or the best of spirits. Consequently the meal was a silent one, broken only by Amabel's occasional sniffles and Hester's more frequent sighs. Jane, who was trying valiantly to appear as if nothing was amiss, finally gave up her struggle to down a piece of toast and with a last swallow of tea rose and stood facing her melancholy relatives.

"Come now, if you're finished," she said, her brisk tone belying her actual feelings. "There's much to do today." And with that she sent Amabel off to the kitchen to inquire after Cook's last minute needs, and Hester out to inspect the chandeliers and silver in case any last minute polishings were required. She herself met with her housekeeper and the good Baxley to answer questions they might have and to issue last minute instructions as to the setting of the tables and the disposal of the ladies' and gentlemen's cloaks, etc.

Thus occupied the morning sped by, and each woman soon found herself at a different task, one leading to another, so that each was involved elsewhere and did not hear the arrival of the elegant coach which deposited a stately white-haired lady at the steps of the manor. Her knock was answered by the second footman, Baxley being occupied in the lower regions of the house, and having shown the lady to the morning room, he set off to find either Lady Jane or his superior. From his expression it was quite plain that he would prefer the former, Mr. Baxley having inspired him with an awe none of the Quality could match.

The last time he had seen Lady Wrothton she had been in the kitchen, and so he headed there just as Amabel entered the hall from the library, a vase of flowers in her hands as she made her way to the morning room. There she was so startled to find such a superior-looking stranger that she almost dropped the vase but recovered it in time to see it safely deposited on the mantel before inquiring shyly if there was anything she might do for the waiting lady.

"Well, you might tell me where I could find my son." The woman's tone was dry as she eyed the flustered face before her. "I am the Duchess of Ratchford."

"The Duchess of—" Amabel turned quite pale as she swept the lady a hasty curtsey, stuttering that the Duke was not there.

"Indeed?" The lady's brows rose at the young woman's obvious confusion. "Do you perhaps then have an idea of where he might be? And are you by any chance Miss Drucilla Wrothton?"

Amabel disclaimed being Drucilla with such haste that the Duchess's brows rose higher, and the ready twinkle which was never far from her eyes took up decided residence there as she inquired if she might then see Miss Wrothton.

"Oh no!" Amabel gasped. "You can't!"

The Duchess stared at her.

"That is—you see—Drucilla isn't here either. Nor Matty. Nor Cecil—" At the last thought, the young Mrs. Cresley burst into tears and considerably astonished her noble guest by rushing from the room just as an older lady entered it. That woman stared after the departing figure in surprise, then turned to greet the Duchess with a friendly smile.

"Well, Victoria," she said, "I see you have met my nephew's wife."

"Jane!" the Duchess said in delight, "how good it is to see you again. We have missed you in society." Then she gazed at the door Amabel had so recently passed through and inquired delicately, "About your nephew's wife—is she quite—that is—"

Jane smiled. "Amabel is at present lingering under the totally unfounded belief that her dear husband must at this moment be lying lifeless somewhere on the road between here and Gretna Green. Other than such flights, she is really a charming young woman."

"Lying dead—," Victoria repeated faintly. "Of course." Her face showed that she did not understand at all but was much too polite to inquire further, and Jane, feeling unequal to the task of explaining it all at present, let it pass as she asked her guest to be seated. The Duchess sank gracefully into a chair, and upon being asked to what they owed the pleasure of her company, she smiled her attractive smile and said, "I have come looking for my son."

"I rather thought that might be it," Jane murmured as Her Grace explained that she had arrived at Maplehurst the previous night to find him away from home, "although his servants expected him momentarily—well, I finally went to bed last night on the expectation of awaking to find him at breakfast in that morning, but when he did not appear I inquired of his valet just where he had gone the previous day, and that toplofty man—my son keeps such loyal servants, my dear, they will hardly tell *me* anything—informed me that one of the workmen had seen him riding toward Morningdale Manor in the company of a Miss Wrothton. So behold me here in search of my son—although your nephew's wife informs me he is not here?" She ended her speech with a question and a delicate raising of one eyebrow, and Jane, realizing that some explanation was indeed in order, furnished the Duchess with the briefest account she could muster of the previous day's events. She ended by apologizing for her daughter involving the Duke in the family madness, but her apology was waved aside by the twinkling-eyed Duchess.

"My dear, nothing could be better!" Her Grace exclaimed. "I counseled my son to run off with your daughter, and it is she who has run off with my son! By all that's wonderful—if he can't manage this business now, he is not his father's son. Or mine either," she ended reflectively.

Jane blinked at her in some surprise but did not question her further as the Duchess chose that moment to rise, saying, "I see you are in the midst of preparations for what I would guess is going to be a very large ball, and I have already taken up a great deal too much of your time. Let me assure you that I am certain your daughter will come to no harm while she is with my son, and I expect we shall see them returning to us shortly. I hope they will have much delightful news to tell us."

On that rather mysterious note she took her leave after graciously accepting the invitation Jane extended to her to attend the evening's ball. "I know it's short notice," Jane told her, "but perhaps if the children don't return, their absence won't be so noted if I have another special guest to honor through the evening."

"What a tactful woman you are, Jane," Her Grace laughed before taking the lady's hand impetuously in her own. "But you and I know better than to despair. They'll return. I'm sure of it."

Jane was happy to hear her say so, and after her guest had been escorted back to her carriage, she found herself making her rounds with a lighter heart. She dealt with a crisis in the kitchen and a trying half-hour with Hester before slipping away to her chamber where she fell into an exhausted sleep. Worn out by the day's work and the previous night's worry, she did not hear the arrival of the second coach which drew up to the Morningdale steps, and it was Hester who was left to greet the new visitors who nervously paced about the morning-room rug.

Hester was aware of who awaited her when she entered the room, for Baxley had thought it best to drop a word in her ear before she faced the Hovingtons. Knowing it was them, she walked through the door with a frown on her face and an acidic, "And to what do we owe this pleasure, George?" dripping off her tongue.

Hovington was inclined to be testy and was heard to mutter that it would not seem to be too much to invite family to a ball the family might care to attend, but before he could dwell on his insult at not being invited, his wife called him to order by cutting him across his speech to dramatically inform Hester that they had come, not for a ball, but for their son.

Hester's chin dropped. "Your son?" she repeated. "Well I daresay you're welcome to him, but why you've come here for that moaning muckworm is beyond me."

"Not here?" Lavinia's voice rose as she sank dramatically into a chair. *"Not here?"* She turned to clutch her husband's hand as he took a hasty step to her side, saying, "We're too late, George, they've gone. Oh Percival, Percival, Percival. Mama didn't mean it."

Hester watched that performance with a good deal of interest, but that interest changed to amazement as Lavinia then flew toward her, shouting, "And it's all your fault, Hester, you scheming, interfering—how could you sacrifice my son on the altar of your spinster niece's desire?"

"What?" The word seemed to explode from her as she stared at the hysterical Lavinia. "Sacrifice your son—on the altar of my niece's—Good Lord, Lavinia, are you talking about *Matty*?" Then she considerably incensed her relations by bursting into laughter, gasping as she shook, "Matty—and Percy—sacrificial lambs—oh. Oh, oh, oh!"

"Well!" Lavinia snapped. "Of all the indelicate, inhuman, insufferable women—how can you laugh when my son has flown with a woman who can bring him naught but despair?"

Hester informed her with brutal honesty that it was quite simple before going on to say that if he had flown with Matty, she would be much more likely to bring him home than to bring him despair. At the look of amazement on the respective Hovington faces she added, as a clincher, "Besides, Matty can't have run away with Percy. She's already eloped with Crandon Pettigrew." She cursed herself silently for letting that slip but soon forgave herself the error at the bemused expressions assumed by Lavinia and George.

"But I thought Drucilla and Pettigrew—" Lavinia began uncertainly, but her husband told her angrily to keep quiet.

"I don't believe it," he said suspiciously, glaring at Hester. "It's my opinion you're throwing dust in our eyes while that scheming wench hies off with our Percy to tie the knot."

Hester stared at him. "What a fool you are, George," she marveled. "For your information, if Matty—who is, I admit, eccentric, but certainly not dim-witted—had, as you put it, 'hied off' with your ridiculous son, I would have been the first to 'hie' after her. I would never permit my niece to marry so far beneath her."

Noting with glee that that shaft had gone home in two seething breasts, she suggested that they look for their misplaced son elsewhere, "for we are quite busy with plans for tonight's ball, and I have no time for matters of such little consequence."

"Little consequence—," George sputtered. "Little consequence— Oh! Well! You shall rue this day, Hester. You'll rue it, I say. From this moment forward neither my wife nor I shall set foot in Morningdale Manor until you have tendered us a formal apology."

Hester smiled. "Promises, George," she sighed gently. "Always promises." She watched in satisfaction as the two made an angry departure and listened happily to the slamming of the door behind them.

"If only one could believe him," she sighed to the empty room. "If only one could."

Chapter XXVI

No one was in the manor hall when Drucilla and Matty returned to Morningdale that evening.

A harried Lady Jane had herded her sniffling niece-in-law and the mournful Hester to their rooms to dress for the ball and then retired to her own chamber to do likewise. Casting a distracted eye at the clock on her dressing table, Jane wondered aloud what she had done to deserve such tribulation. Her looking glass returned no answer, so with a shrug she gave herself up to the skilled ministrations of her long-faced dresser.

Baxley, whom the young ladies had expected to meet on their return, was away from his post when they came in the door and so missed their arrival. The worthy butler had been called to quell a minor uprising in the kitchen, and the various footmen and maids who might have been moving through the area and who might have seen the cousins enter were all interested spectators at the kitchen event. Two of the younger servants became so interested that they forgot themselves so far as to bet on whether Baxley or Cook would emerge victorious from the verbal exchange. Such behavior so scandalized the elderly butler that he immediately broke off his debate with Cook to scold them severely.

Finding his most worthy opponent's attention drawn elsewhere, Cook gave a gallic shrug and went back to muttering darkly over his sauces. The other servants, disappointed to find that what had promised to be a royal donneybrook was to end so tamely, all drifted away to attend to the last-minute duties necessary to ready a house for a large ball. Uttering one final word on the folly of young footmen, Baxley returned to his post to assume his anxious watch for the missing cousins.

His return was too late, for Matty and Dru, accompanied by Caesar and Cecil, had wasted no time in the hall, hurrying off to their rooms to make themselves ready for the ball.

Caesar might have made their presence known had not Matty thoughtfully provided him with a ham bone which made woofing inconvenient. Cecil, too, might have raised the house had he not been preserving what he called a dignified silence. That his irrepressible sister called his silence the sulks did nothing to improve his mood, and since all the things he longed to say were comments his code told him a gentleman should never say to a lady, he chose to retire at once to his chamber where he could be sure of the sympathetic—and adoring—attention of his wife. Feeling he had endured much the past two days, Cecil was heartily sick of his sister and cousin, and he wanted nothing more than a hot bath, a clean suit, and a large glass of port. Maybe two glasses. He considered the port question as he followed the ladies up the stairs and ignored them completely when they wished him good evening. Neither of the cousins seemed crushed by his neglect, Matty even going so far as to giggle.

"I'd hate to be Amabel," Drucilla whispered to Matty as they watched Cecil enter his chambers.

"Don't worry," Matty whispered back. "She'll fall on his neck and be so happy to see him that between the two of them they'll soon have him believing he's a hero who saved us from ourselves." She snorted. "What a peagoose my sister-in-law is!"

Dru laughed, pressed her cousin's hand, and slipped into her room, where she was able to handle her dresser's remonstrations with gentle dignity. Matty was not so lucky, for her redoubtable Polly was never easily quieted and did not give a snap for Miss Matty's dignity. Indeed, she was heard to wonder aloud if Miss Matty had any, for as she informed her mistress, Polly had "half a mind to leave you to your just desserts. This is by far the queerest of your queer starts, running off with a man to do Lord knows what—"

At that Matty grinned and raised her left hand where a wide gold band held a large sapphire and several diamonds. "This is what I've been doing, Polly my dear," she replied saucily.

The maid gasped. "Lord love you, you're married!" She rushed forward to fold the shorter lady in an all-encompassing embrace. Soon a second thought occurred to her and she bent back to regard Matty from her superior height. "You ARE married, aren't you?"

Matty's grin grew. "My dear Polly, how many times have I told you that I am not the marrying kind?"

The scandalized maid fell back a pace, pursing her lips and placing her hands on her hips. "Well I never—," she began, but Matty was not to know what she never, for the twinkle in the lady's eye made Polly pause.

"Miss Matty," she said severely, "you're roasting me."

"Up brown," the unrepentant lady agreed.

"Well!"

A look at the chagrined face before her made Matty move forward quickly to hug her friend. "It is well, Polly," she said happily. "It is very, very well." Another hug followed, and so they stood for several moments until Polly's eyes fell on the ball gown she had laid our earlier in the day in the hope Matty would return by evening. Recalled to her surroundings, she gave a gasp and began to scold her mistress out of the clothes she was wearing. "You've not much time if you're to be ready by supper," she said, "—and Lord, I'd like to be there to see your Aunt Hester's face—and look at your hair! Well that will need to be done again—"

In that vein she hurried on as Matty followed her orders with a grimace. Contenting herself with a good wash when she longed for a long, soaking bath, Matty filled her maid in on the events of the last twenty-four hours, dwelling on those things which had made their return so much later than they had intended.

"We meant to be back by midafternoon, Polly," she said, "for we knew you must all be worried, but that Cecil—" She ground her teeth at the thought of her brother, and Polly listened with interest as Matty recalled the unfortunate circumstances which had led to their late return.

"It was all Cecil's fault," she told her servant, her eyes darkening at the thought. "But then, it so often is."

"But I would have thought Mr. Cecil would be in a hurry to get back to the manor, seeing as how his ladywife has been crying her eyes out ever since he left," Polly put in as her deft fingers went to work on Matty's hair.

"He was in a hurry," Matty agreed, watching with interest the cascade of curls being arranged on her head. "He was so much in a hurry that he ordered his coachmen to take a shortcut. A country-lane shortcut."

Polly paused in her duties as her eyes met Matty's in the mirror. "A country lane? In this weather?"

Her mistress nodded. "Precisely. There we all were, bundled in Cecil's carriage—"

"You were all in Mr. Cecil's carriage?"

Matty nodded. "We were. And that's all Cecil's fault—" She paused to consider. "Well, no, maybe it's not," she conceded. "But he's so blamable."

"But what were you all doing in one carriage? And Mr. Cecil's carriage at that?" Polly asked again, so Matty had to explain how Dru and the Duke had arrived in Dru's phaeton and couldn't return that way in the rain; how she and Pettigrew would have taken them up in their carriage, only they had dismissed their hired vehicle in the belief they'd be returned in Miss Agatha's carriage; how Agatha had assured them they were welcome to her coach but "that young jackanapes"—Percy—had driven off in her carriage the previous day and hadn't yet returned it.

"And then Cecil walked in," Matty remembered, "and of course he had his carriage, so he offered—unwillingly, but he offered—to take us all up with him." She stood as Polly finished with her hair and moved to adjust her ballgown.

"Then what must he do but order his coachman to take a shortcut which landed us wheel-deep in mud. We *told* him to stick to the main roads, with the rain, but Cecil is stubborn as a pig and once he decided on the shortcut there was no turning back. If he hadn't fallen in the mud while trying to get the coach out, I don't think I would ever have forgiven him."

"He fell in the mud—," Polly gasped, and as her eyes met Matty's, the two burst into laughter.

"You should have seen him," Matty gurgled. "He fell and he couldn't get up, and when one of the farmers who was helping get the coach out tried to help Cecil up, he pulled the poor fellow in. It was terrible. And so funny—" She gasped at the thought.

"Poor Mr. Cecil," Polly said.

"Yes, poor Cecil," Matty agreed. Then she went off into whoops again.

*   *   *

Lady Jane was the first Morningdale Manor inhabitant to come down the stairs that night. Her anxious inquiry brought a negative nod from Baxley, and with a sigh she turned as the sound of rustling silk was heard at the top of the stairs. There stood Hester, the picture of tragedy, one hand held to her head as she proclaimed them undone.

"They are not here, Jane," she said sorrowfully, the preposterous arrangement of ostrich feathers which she wore in her hair nodding in sympathy. "Drucilla and Matty have not returned, and what are we to say to our guests?"

"Good evening is always a nice thing to say to guests—," a mild voice remarked, and with a shriek Hester turned to the young woman behind her.

"Drucilla!" she gasped. "And Matty! But how—when—oh, never mind! We're saved!"

Matty's eyes twinkled. "Saved?" she repeated. "Were you lost, dear Aunt?"

Her "dear aunt" replied with asperity that it was her nieces, not herself, who were lost—"lost to all propriety, and while I might expect it of you, why dear Drucilla?"

She interrupted her diatribe to stare at the two new figures just arrived on the scene.

"Cecil!" she gasped as that gentleman came down the stairs with a now radiant Amabel on his arm.

"When did you—" she began, but her question was interrupted by a loud knocking on the door. All eyes turned toward the sound as the dignified Baxley moved to admit a bubbling Dowager Duchess of Ratchford, her son, and Mr. Pettigrew, those two gentlemen having been left at their respective residences to change for the ball.

"My dear, dear soon-to-be daughter!" the Dowager Duchess cried, moving forward to fold Drucilla in a hearty embrace. "My very dear girl!"

Hester, bemused that the Duchess had not even stopped to remove her cloak before acting in this extraordinary way, gasped "daughter" and tottered to the nearest chair, from which she beseeched her sister-in-law to tell her if her ears had deceived her or if the Duchess had actually called Drucilla her soon-to-be daughter.

"I believe she did," Jane replied cautiously, "but surely there is some mistake—"

"Oh no, Mama!" a blushing Drucilla emerged from her soon-to-be mother-in-law's arms. "Indeed it is not a mistake, and I hope you won't mind—well, I'm sure you won't mind—but Sebastian and I are going to be married just as soon as arrangements can be made. And Matty was married last night at Grantham!"

"MARRIED!" The shriek was Hester's.

Seeming to have trouble closing her mouth, she gazed at those assembled before her. "Married!" she repeated so stridently that one of her ostrich plumes slipped to cover her left eye. "Drucilla to be a duchess! And Matty—" At that she sat bolt upright and gazed at her shorter niece in amazement. "Matty! Married!"

"Surprise, surprise!" that lady murmured as she moved into Mr. Pettigrew's arms. "Miracles really do happen."

"Indeed they do!" Hester nodded vigorously, to the amusement of most of those assembled. "By all that's famous—Matty. Married. Well, well."

Smiles and congratulations followed, but the happy everyone-talking-at-once mood was cut short by the loud rapping at the manor door which signaled the first of the evening's guests. The cousins, congratulated at first on their charming appearance, soon found themselves as well the recipients of many wishes for wedded bliss as Hester shared with her nearest and dearest the exciting news of her one niece's nuptials, and her other niece's soon-to-come marriage.

Midway through the festive evening, the Hovingtons arrived with their son and a very plain girl with a squint and no conversation in tow. It didn't take Matty long to ascertain that Percy had decided it might be more comfortable to marry for money instead of for love and that he had taken himself off posthaste the previous evening to ask the wealthy Miss Brown to do him the honor of being his wife. Miss Brown having accepted, he spent the night telling all who would listen about the "really grand" home he and Miss Brown would build—"a very good sort of place, not shabby like

227

that occupied by some of my relations." It was ill luck which made him make that remark within Hester's hearing, for she fired up to inform him that the only shabby thing she had ever seen at Morningdale was he.

Before that promising spark could be fanned to full flame, Dru diverted a scene by presenting General Peckingham to her aunt as a most desirable dancing partner. Before Hester could close her mouth, the bandy-legged little man had swept her off onto the ballroom floor. As they danced, the general confided that if it had not been for Drucilla he would never have known in what high regard Hester held him. That information caused the lady's mouth to drop open again, and she cast a fulminating eye toward the corner where her two nieces were regarding her with obvious amusement. That amusement grew through successive dances as, immune to the indignant lady's hints, the general remained by her side, dropping broad suggestions that he found Hester a fine figure of a woman and that he believed it might be time for him to be getting leg-shackled again.

Except for that, the evening passed smoothly, if one discounts the fact that Caesar escaped the confines of Matty's room and wandered downstairs to devour six of Cook's prize pastries before he could be stopped, and if one did not mind that just as Hester was shouting to the general that she had no wish to marry him (he was rather deaf and couldn't hear above the hub-bub of the ball), the music stopped and in the following silence she announced it to the world.

Dru and the Duke and Matty and Mr. Pettigrew didn't mind. As the gentlemen whirled their ladies around the room, they were hardly aware anyone else was in the world.

Lady Jane and the Dowager Duchess, lost in the dream of one day seeing their grandchildren dancing just so before them, didn't mind. What were pastries and shouting compared to the future?

The general told Hester he didn't mind, tucking her hand in the crook of his arm as he said, "I like a woman who needs some convincing. We old army men enjoy a good fight."

And Caesar—well, Caesar did mind, for there was a seventh pastry he'd had his eye on. But being a philosophical dog, he chose to settle himself in front of the fire and dream of the goodies consumed, heaving just one sad sigh for the one that got away.

27 million Americans can't read a bedtime story to a child.

It's because 27 million adults in this country simply can't read.

Functional illiteracy has reached one out of five Americans. It robs them of even the simplest of human pleasures, like reading a fairy tale to a child.

You can change all this by joining the fight against illiteracy.

Call the Coalition for Literacy at toll-free **1-800-228-8813** and volunteer.

Volunteer Against Illiteracy. The only degree you need is a degree of caring.

Ad Council Coalition for Literacy

Warner Books is proud to be an active supporter of the Coalition for Literacy.